PRAISE FOR KELLY HASHWAY'S
THE MONSTER WITHIN

"Hashway does a great job creating characters that stir your emotions and a mystery you want to unravel."

–Cherie Colyer, author of *The Embrace* and *Hold Tight*

"Witches, lies, black magic, murder…and the ultimate act of selfless love. Kelly Hashway has a spellbinding hit with *The Monster Within*."
–Michelle Pickett, bestselling author of *PODs*

"Resurrection has a dark price. *The Monster Within* is a fast paced and twisted read that will keep you guessing to the end."

–Heather Reid, author of *Pretty Dark Nothing*

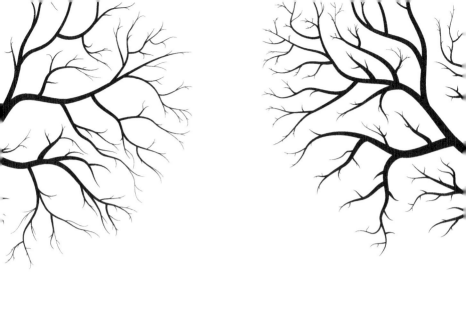

THE DARKNESS WITHIN

Kelly Hashway

SPENCER
HILL
PRESS

Spencer Hill Press

Contact: Spencer Hill Press
27 West 20th Street, Suite 1102
New York, NY 10011

Please visit our website at www.spencerhillpress.com

First Edition: June 2015.
Kelly Hashway
The Darkness Within/by Kelly Hashway–1st ed.
p. cm.
Summary:
Description: A new witch must figure out how to save
her boyfriend from dark magic.

Trademarks: Band-Aid, BMW, Coke, *Dark Shadows*, Gummy
Bears, *Harry Potter*, Mack, Mazda 6, *Sleeping Beauty*, *Star Trek*, *Star
Wars*, *Transformers*

Cover design by Lisa Amowitz
Interior layout by Errick A. Nunnally

978-1-63392-021-7 (paperback)
978-1-63392-022-4 (e-book)

Printed in the United States of America

Also by Kelly Hashway

The Monster Within (Spencer Hill Press)

Touch of Death (Spencer Hill Press)

Stalked by Death (Spencer Hill Press)

Face of Death (Spencer Hill Press)

The Darkness Within (Spencer Hill Press, 6/15)

To Ayla with love.

1

MY eyes closed as the magic filled me. I could feel it swirling in the air around the group, gold energy pumping life throughout my body. After dying of cancer and coming back as a monster, being this full of life was incredible. I wasn't exactly normal, but I wasn't a monster anymore either. And the witchy powers were definitely a plus. I had a family now. Dylan and Shannon were like a brother and sister to me. And Ethan... Ah, my Ethan, he was my world. Finally, the crap was out of my life. I'd survived, and I'd come back stronger than ever.

A jolt of something hot and electrifying surged through me. My stomach lurched, and I opened my eyes to see if anyone else felt it. Shannon was choking and grasping a greenish energy wrapped around her neck. I broke free from Ethan and Dylan's hands and rushed for Shannon. Her eyes widened, panic written all over her face. Dylan fell to the ground, landing at Shannon's feet. I stepped over him and pried the energy from Shannon's neck. It snaked around my hands, trapping me in magical handcuffs.

"Ethan!" He was the only one not affected by the strange green energy. The only one still standing with his eyes closed, oblivious to what was happening—to what was trying to kill us. "Ethan!"

Slowly, his eyes opened. He blinked several times before his vision focused on me. "Sam!" He lunged forward, reaching for the magic trapping my hands. The second he came in contact with it, the green energy vanished. Just disintegrated. Ethan stared at his hands. "What happened?"

"You tell me." Dylan sat up and rubbed his head. "Something knocked me out." It was an exaggeration, considering he'd already recovered, but I let it slide.

"And strangled Shannon." I motioned to Shannon, still rubbing her neck. She'd been affected the most by…whatever that thing was.

Ethan held me by my shoulders and stared into my eyes. "Are you hurt?"

"No. You stopped it before it had a chance to hurt me."

"Good." He sighed and ran a hand through his hair.

Dylan stood up and brushed the leaves from his pants. "What the hell happened to you, man? You just stood there while the rest of us were attacked."

"Yeah." Shannon's voice was weak, but her accusatory tone still came through, no problem. "Why weren't *you* affected by it?"

We all stared at Ethan. He looked as confused as we were. I reached for his hand, lacing my fingers through his. "It's okay. Whatever happened wasn't your fault. You're just lucky it didn't attack you."

"Yeah, lucky." Dylan shook his head, not willing to dismiss the issue that easily.

I glared at him. Maybe he was more used to being a witch than Ethan and I were, but I was still more powerful than he was. Thanks to the evil Nora making me her personal witch hunter, I'd drained the life and magic out of two witches, Rebecca and Ben. I didn't ever bring it up, especially since Ben had been Dylan's brother. Dylan said he'd forgiven me, since I'd been as much a victim to Nora as Ben had been, but still…I'd killed him. And now I had the power of two witches swirling around—or whatever magic did—inside me. Dylan called the shots as the coven leader, but we all knew I was the one with the most power.

Dylan backed off with a sigh so loud he could have been trying to blow out the campfire to the left of us.

"I didn't even know…" Ethan's voice trailed off.

I gently touched his cheek. "Seriously, don't worry about it.

Ignore Dylan. He'll get over it." I turned to Shannon. "You okay? That thing had you pretty good."

"It's going to take a hell of a lot of magic to get these wretched strangle marks off my neck." She huffed, but then her eyes fell on Ethan's face. "But whatever, I'll be fine."

"I'll help you get rid of the marks." I let go of Ethan and extended my hands to Shannon. She took them with a look of gratitude that was rare for her. Sure, she was my family now, part of my coven, but she still thought she was the Queen Bee, even after we'd done away with the popularity spell she'd placed on the entire school.

I focused my thoughts on the reddish lines circling Shannon's neck. The magic within me welled up, tingling my insides. I let go of one of Shannon's hands and waved in front of her neck. The red marks slowly faded until Shannon's neck looked like it had never been touched by that snakelike green mist. I lowered my hand and stepped back. "Better?"

She twisted her head from side to side, testing out her neck. "Good as new."

A sizzling sound filled the air as Dylan put out the fire. "I think we're done for the night."

Shannon put her hands on her hips. "What about my spell? You promised you'd help me fix things at school."

Dylan stood up and brushed his hands against his jeans. "If you hadn't tried to mess with people's memories, there wouldn't be a problem to fix."

Ethan shook his head and threw his hands out. "Enough!"

Dylan and Shannon were thrown backward. I stared at Ethan, or more accurately his hands. "You threw them." Ethan, my sweet Ethan who wouldn't hurt a fly, had attacked Dylan and Shannon. It didn't make sense.

Ethan looked down at his hands. "I-I didn't mean to."

Something was going on. Something was wrong with Ethan's magic.

He looked up, his eyes pleading with me. "I don't know why I got so angry."

"Damn it, Ethan!" Shannon stood up and twisted her body to see the big streak of dirt across her backside. "Look at this! Look at my pants!"

Dylan stifled a laugh as he got to his feet. "Looks like you shit yourself."

"Stop!" We had enough to worry about with Ethan's magic going all wonky. I didn't need Dylan and Shannon going at it, too. "Shannon, we have bigger problems right now. And, Dylan, lay off. You've been tormenting Shannon enough since she did that spell. Let it go. She knows she was wrong. Everyone makes mistakes." I turned to Ethan as I said that last part. Why was he making mistakes like this? And had what happened to Shannon in the circle been his fault?

"We'll fix your spell tomorrow, Shannon." Dylan walked toward his car without another word. Apparently, our meeting was over.

"Whatever." Shannon walked away too, smacking the dirt from the back of her jeans. If I hadn't been so worried about Ethan and what was wrong with him, I would've laughed at Shannon smacking her own ass.

Ethan stared at the remains of our campfire. He was lost in his own little world. He hadn't asked to become a witch. Then again, neither had I. This wasn't even something that was handed to us. We were forced into it. Kill a witch and absorb the magic, or die. It wasn't much of a choice. We'd both already died once. Neither of us wanted to do it again. So we'd done what we'd had to, to survive. We'd become witches. I was adjusting to it better than Ethan, though. He usually did pretty well when he was part of a group spell, but his individual spells definitely needed work. So what had gone wrong tonight?

Ethan's back was to me. I stepped closer to him, wrapping my arms around his waist and resting my chin on his shoulder. "Hey, where are you right now?"

"You shouldn't get too close. I don't want to accidentally—"

I slipped around him so we were face-to-face. "I'm not afraid of you, Ethan. I could never be afraid of you." I cupped his cheek in my hand and gently pressed my lips to his, but he barely responded to my touch.

"Are you sure that spell didn't hurt you? The one that strangled Shannon?"

"I'm fine. I felt something strange, like electricity running through me, but it didn't really hurt. It felt weird more than anything else." I paused, realizing he felt responsible for whatever it was that had happened. "Why? Do you think you're the one who created that snake thing?"

He shrugged. "I don't know. I guess so, since it didn't come after me."

"That doesn't mean anything. For all we know, you would've been next."

"Yeah." He didn't sound the least bit convinced.

"Hey." I took his face in both my hands this time. "I think I know a little something about dark magic and hurting people." I still had nightmares about the monster Nora had turned me into.

Ethan's hands were on my waist now, gently pulling me toward him. "No. That wasn't your fault at all. That was all Nora's doing. No one blames you, Sam."

That didn't make all the horrible things I'd done any easier to live with. I'd killed people. "It's not as simple as that."

"You don't think you—?" He stopped, looking embarrassed for even bringing it up.

"It's okay. You can say it." It's not like the thought hadn't crossed my mind. It was totally possible that the electricity I felt during the spell was *me* creating that thing. *Me* hurting Dylan and Shannon. If any one of us fit the profile for a killer, it was me.

Ethan's lips were on mine. His body pressed up against me so forcefully. He was trying to make me forget. Make me get lost in him. It almost always worked. Almost.

"Sam." My name was like a sigh on his lips. I melted into him. My eyes shut, and my lips parted, inviting him in. I wrapped my arms around his neck, and he lifted me off the ground. Kissing Ethan gave new meaning to being swept off my feet. It was heaven. Ethan was *my* heaven. And even with all that was going on in my head, I knew if we were together, we'd both be fine.

We stayed in the clearing in the woods for two hours, completely lost in each other, a tangle of limbs. I didn't want to leave. Sure, we lived alone in a cottage with no parental supervision, but this was somehow better. I didn't even care that we were lying in dirt. Ethan's arms were around me, and that was enough.

He kissed the top of my head and hugged me closer—although there wasn't any space between us as it was. "It's getting late."

"Ten more minutes." I traced my fingers along his stomach.

"We have school in the morning."

"My pretend mom will be happy to write me a note." The good thing about having a fake identity was that it made it easy to forge parent signatures.

"Do you ever miss your mom?"

I sat up a little, leaning on one elbow, and looked into Ethan's eyes. "You know I do. I miss everyone. Mom, Dad, Jacob."

"Me, too." Ethan had run away for me. He'd brought me back from the grave and given up everything to create this life for us. I'd lost my family to the cancer that slowly ate away at my body. For me, it hadn't been a choice to leave them. For Ethan, it had. He'd chosen me. That was a lot to live up to every day. But now that I was better—wasn't a monster anymore—it was easier to make Ethan happy. To give him some sort of a normal life.

"Do you want to go back?" The words were almost too hard to say.

Ethan sat up, reaching one hand into my long, dark hair and cupping the back of my head. "Not even for a second. My life is here with you now, Sam. There's nowhere I'd rather be. You have to know that. I love you."

"I love you, too."

His face changed, shuddered. For a moment, I thought I'd imagined it, but then his eyes went cold. "Don't say things like that anymore. Understand?" His voice was harsh, not at all normal.

"I didn't mean to upset you. I know you love me. I don't doubt that for a second."

He looked frozen in anger. I didn't know what to do or say to snap him out of it.

"Ethan?" I pushed a strand of his dark, messy hair out of his face. "I love you." Still nothing. I leaned forward, pressing my lips to his. This time he reacted. He pulled me close, kissing me hungrily. It felt…

off. But I kissed him anyway, hoping he'd ease up. Finally, he let go of me, and I leaned back so I could look into his eyes.

"Ready to go?" he asked, looking and sounding like himself again.

I nodded and let him help me to my feet. We held hands on the way to the car and the entire way back to the cottage. Ethan smiled at me as if nothing had happened. I smiled back, but I couldn't help wondering if Ethan had a monster of his own lurking inside him.

2

"GOOD morning." Ethan's smiling face was the first thing I saw when I opened my eyes. We'd been living on our own for a month now, but I still loved waking up in Ethan's arms. I felt safe here. Now that I didn't have to worry about my body giving out on me or needing to feed off another person's life energy, things were just about perfect. I could focus on Ethan without worrying about hurting him in my sleep.

"Morning." I returned his smile and nuzzled against his chest.

"You have bed head."

I jerked my head up and reached for my hair.

"No, don't. It looks sexy."

"Bed head? Really? You think that's sexy?" Sexy was Ethan coming out of the shower wearing nothing but a towel. Sexy was the way his smile was just slightly crooked. Sexy was just plain Ethan.

"Well, it's sexy on you."

I tilted my head back and found his lips with mine. As I pulled away, I noticed the redness in his eyes. "Did you not sleep well?"

He shrugged. "I woke up a few times. No big deal."

"What woke you?" I said a silent prayer that it wasn't my snoring.

"I don't know. Weird dreams or something like that. I can't really remember."

"You want to sleep in? We could skip first period."

"And make you miss Mr. Ryan's class? No way."

Mr. Ryan was easily my favorite teacher, even though he had made me read *The Strange Case of Dr. Jekyll and Mr. Hyde* during my dark period. He was the most popular teacher in school, and not just because he was young and kind of hot—for a teacher. He actually made class fun, and he had a voice that didn't put everyone to sleep.

"You're right." I flung the blankets off me. "If I'm not there, Shannon will drool all over him and make her social status go even further down the tubes."

"Why'd she do that stupid spell anyway?" Ethan got out of bed and rifled through the dresser.

"Because taking the popularity spell off the student population left her virtually friendless." I grabbed my outfit from the closet and draped it over my arm. Even though we were living together, I still wasn't comfortable changing in front of Ethan. It seemed a little too grown-up. I mean, it wasn't like we were married.

"Yeah, but I don't understand why she couldn't be happy being friends with the coven. Why did she have to go and mess with people's memories to try to make them think they'd been friends with her for years?"

I paused in the doorway, staring at the jeans and sweater in my arms. "Not everyone makes friends as easily as you, Ethan." When we came here, it took him all of two seconds to find a crowd to hang out with. That was just how it was with Ethan. People loved him. "Some of us have to try a little harder."

He stepped toward me, brushing his fingers along my cheek. "Hey, you have plenty of friends. The gang in art and at lunch love you."

"No, they love *you*. They talk to me because I'm with you."

"That's not true."

"Ethan, I love you, but you're not going to win this one. You're going to have to accept that you are Mr. Popular. I'm fine with it, so there's no reason for you not to be."

"But—"

I put my finger up to his lips and smiled. "I'll be in the shower."

As I turned to go, he said, "Is that an invitation?"

I started singing a really cheesy but totally catchy song from some overplayed commercial and pretended I hadn't heard him. The thing about living together—the one thing I didn't like—was that sometimes I felt like we were already married. I loved Ethan. I'd do anything for him. But in some ways, I missed the mystery that came with not always being together. I needed time to miss him, to crave his touch. That, and our stand-up shower barely fit one person.

We were in danger of being late, so I rushed through my shower and pulled my hair up into a messy bun. Even though I was moving as fast as humanly possible, Ethan had already dressed, eaten breakfast, and cooked me an egg sandwich by the time I was ready.

"Here you go. You'll have to eat it in the car."

I took the hot sandwich and grabbed my school bag. "Thank you." I leaned in to kiss Ethan's cheek, but he turned my face and pressed his lips to mine. The kiss was soft, yet full of so much emotion I felt a little dizzy when he pulled away. "And thank you for that, too."

He took my bag, flinging it over his shoulder along with his own book bag, and held my hand as we walked to the car. More than anything, I wanted to forget what had happened last night. I wanted to live in this moment where Ethan was as perfect as I'd always known him to be. But something was nagging me, making me question everything. It all felt a little too familiar. I knew what it was like to have a monster inside you, crawling to the surface. I had been powerless against the killer Nora had made me become. What if somehow Ethan was going through the same thing? What if he became what I had been, even though we'd broken the spell Nora had placed on us both? What if I lost him forever?

"You're quiet this morning." Ethan opened the car door for me and gently pulled our laced fingers to his mouth, kissing each of my fingertips. My heart leaped in my chest. The fact that after all this time together Ethan could still make me feel the flutter of first love was simply amazing. *He* was amazing.

"I was just thinking how much I'd rather stay here with you than go to school and learn a bunch of stuff I'll never actually use in real life."

He smiled and cocked his head to the side. "What would Mr. Ryan say if he heard you right now?"

I sighed. "That he's disappointed I can't see the value of a good education."

"Not bad. That sounds exactly like something he'd say." Ethan closed the door and walked around to the driver's side. I'd gotten to know Mr. Ryan pretty well over the past month. While he was cool—for a teacher—he still gave the occasional "a mind is a terrible thing to waste" speech.

"So, Jackson told me he's going to teach me how to make his famous omelet after school today."

Ethan and I were still working at the diner to pay our bills. That was another thing about living on our own. We couldn't lounge around or join sports teams after school like the rest of the student body. We had to work. At least Gloria and Jackson were awesome bosses. They treated us like we were their grandchildren—children, if you asked them. They didn't like to admit their ages. They were the closest thing Ethan and I had to family here—other than the coven.

Ethan pulled into his parking spot and immediately rushed over to open my door. We didn't even get to the front door of the school before Shannon and Dylan were at our sides.

"Morning," Shannon said. She looked better, no signs of the attack last night.

"Everything okay today?" Dylan skeptically eyed Ethan, making my claws come out a little.

"It's fine." Ethan squeezed my hand, and I realized my nails were practically digging into his skin.

"Oh, sorry." I loosened my grip.

He gave me a sympathetic smile and kissed the side of my head. Great. He was the one going through this…whatever it was…and he was more worried about me than himself.

"I wonder what Mr. Ryan will be wearing today." Shannon sighed, her eyes glazed over in a dreamy stare.

Dylan scoffed. "You do realize he's like thirty."

"Whatever. I didn't say I wanted to date him. He's just nice to look at." Shannon elbowed me, looking for confirmation.

I laughed. No way was I admitting to that in front of Ethan. Besides, I was still getting used to Shannon and me being friends. When we'd first met, she hated me. She even attacked me in the hallway at school. If we weren't tied by the spell making us a coven, we probably wouldn't say two words to each other. At least not two *nice* words.

Dylan said good-bye and headed to his locker. I was expecting Shannon to do the same, but she followed Ethan and me to my locker instead. I widened my eyes at her, not wanting her to hover while Ethan and I said good-bye.

"Whatever. The hallway is filled with people." Shannon turned around and faced the other way. "Happy now? Go ahead and slobber all over each other."

Ethan ran his finger down the side of my face. "See you in sculpture."

"What, no kiss?" I tugged on the front of his shirt. "Shannon turned around and everything," I teased.

He leaned down, pressing his lips to mine. I expected the kiss to be quick—we were in the middle of a crowded hallway—but Ethan didn't pull away. He deepened the kiss. I didn't know what to do. I felt self-conscious, and the cheers from the guys around us only made it worse. But Ethan wasn't backing off. "Ethan," I managed to say, pushing lightly against his chest. Still, he wouldn't let up. Finally, I turned my head slightly to the side. When he couldn't find my mouth, he pulled away.

I stared at him and the dazed look in his eyes. "Are you okay?"

"What? Oh, yeah, I'm fine. I'll see you next period." He turned and walked away without another word, leaving me there with a clueless expression on my face.

Shannon raised an eyebrow. Of course she'd peeked, most likely because of all the commotion the kiss had caused. "That was… interesting."

Tell me about it. I fiddled with my ruby ring, the one Ethan had given me for my last birthday. Something was going on with him, making him different, more aggressive even. I didn't like it, but school wasn't the place to address the issue.

"You're worried, aren't you?" Shannon leaned closer to me. "Maybe you should start wearing your necklace again. The one Dylan gave you."

Dylan had given me the necklace to ward off unfriendly spells. As it turned out, those spells had been Nora's doing. "Why do you think I need protection from harmful spells?"

Shannon shrugged, but I could tell she definitely had a reason. She just wasn't willing to say it. "Never mind. The warning bell rang. We're going to be late."

I followed her into class and took a seat in front. I used to sit in the back by Shannon's twin brother, Tristan, but since I'd joined the coven, I sat right next to Shannon. She didn't like me talking to Tristan, which kind of sucked because he was really nice. He even shared my old opinion that Shannon was a bitch. Come to think of it, maybe that was why Shannon didn't like me talking to him. She told me Tristan had no idea she was a witch, and she wanted to keep it that way. Her choice, I guess.

"Ladies." Mr. Ryan sat on the edge of his desk, which happened to be directly in front of us, and crossed one leg over the other. "Don't you think you're cutting it a little close this morning?"

"Sorry, Mr. Ryan." Shannon's voice was sweet as could be, making me want to gag up my egg sandwich. "We were caught up in a discussion about last night's reading assignment. We totally lost track of time."

Damn it! We had a reading assignment?

Mr. Ryan picked up his copy of Mary Shelley's *Frankenstein*. Great, another book about monsters. How appropriate. "Well then, maybe you two would like to start off our discussion today."

I hadn't read a single word. I only vaguely remembered getting the book in class yesterday. "Shannon, you had such great insights. I think you should start." I smiled at her, hoping she'd get the message.

Luckily, she nodded and took off on some symbolism in chapter one. I leaned back in my seat, relieved to have dodged that humiliating experience. My cell phone vibrated in my back pocket. Texting was not easy from the front of the room, only inches from Mr. Ryan. I kept my head turned toward Shannon and nodded, pretending to be interested in what she was saying, while really I wasn't processing a word of it. I slowly reached back and slipped the phone into the palm of my hand. I paused while the conversation shifted to Mr. Ryan. He went to the computer at the back of the class and projected an image up on the screen in front. Now was my chance. I moved the cell under my desk and opened the message.

Meet me in the girls' bathroom in the English wing

The girls' bathroom had become a favorite meeting spot for Ethan and me. I wasn't surprised he asked me to meet him there. After that kiss, I knew the boy had only one thing on his mind this morning. Of course, the kiss had left me with a very different thing on my mind—finding out what was messing with Ethan.

Going now. I put my phone back in my pocket and raised my hand.

Mr. Ryan beamed. "Yes, Miss Smith, I'd love to hear your take on the issue."

Oh no. I'd apparently volunteered to answer something the rest of the class had no clue about. Wonderful. "Um, actually, I was hoping I could be excused to use the bathroom."

Tristan laughed in his seat next to Mr. Ryan and the computer. "Hey, when nature calls."

"Very funny, Mr. Tilby." Shannon cringed when Mr. Ryan said Tristan's last name. She'd told everyone they were cousins, and it seemed like everyone had believed her. But that was before the spell mishap. Now she worried people would find out the truth, and that wouldn't help her popularity any. Tristan, while funny and spot-on about Shannon's ability to be a royal bitch when she wanted to be, was about as low on the popularity chain as a person could get. Mr. Ryan sighed. "Is it an emergency, Samantha?"

"Kind of." I could claim female issues, but I didn't really want to deal with all the disgusted looks from the guys in the class.

"Kind of?" Mr. Ryan pressed.

A stinging ran across my right pointer finger.

"She cut her finger." Shannon held up my hand and sure enough, blood was dripping down it. She'd used a spell to cut me! I glared at her, but she mouthed, "You're welcome."

"Oh," Mr. Ryan said. "Maybe you should see the nurse."

"No, really, it's just a paper cut. Nothing major. I'll rinse it off and put a Band-Aid on it." I shrugged to show him it was no big deal.

Mr. Ryan nodded. "Go right ahead."

I cupped my finger in my other hand and continued to glare at Shannon as I left the room. As soon as I turned the corner and was out of sight, I focused my magic on healing the cut. It didn't take long. Shannon had only given me a bad paper cut. I thought about how I'd get back at her while I walked to the bathroom.

No one was at the sinks, so I checked the stalls for feet. The only pair was at the very end. Black boots. "Dylan?"

The stall door swung open, and Dylan stepped out. "Good. I thought maybe you couldn't get out of class."

"Shannon handled that for me." I shook my head. "What are you doing here? I'm supposed to be meeting Ethan."

"No. *I* texted you."

"From Ethan's phone?"

"Not exactly." He looked away, totally guilty. There was a spell at work here.

"You put a spell on the message so it would look like it had come from Ethan's phone?"

He shrugged. "I had to get you to meet me. Without Ethan."

"Why?" I stepped toward him, hoping to intimidate a confession, and maybe even an apology, out of him. I had plenty of magic to make him talk.

"Do you know what's happening to Ethan?"

My mind raced. "Something happened to him?" I turned for the door, ready to run to Ethan's honors history class and save him from whatever was hurting him…maybe save him from himself.

"I'm not talking about what's happening to him at this moment."

I stopped and faced Dylan. "You mean last night. With the spell."

"Of course." He narrowed his eyes. "Wait, did something else happen?"

"No." It slipped out. The question was, was it a lie? Ethan had lost his temper with me before we had gone home last night, and then there was the kiss in the hall this morning. But I wanted to talk to Ethan before I told Dylan anything.

"Are you sure?" Dylan stepped toward me. His face was full of concern, and I had a feeling it was more for me than Ethan.

"Yes." I couldn't tell him, but I was interested in finding out what Dylan thought was wrong with Ethan. "Why are you asking? What do you think is going on with Ethan? You must think it's something if you tricked me into meeting you here."

Dylan reached for my hand, but stopped. I took a step back, not knowing what to make of the gesture. Was it concern? Or something more?

"You're freaking me out right now."

"Yeah, well, this is pretty freaky stuff." He took a deep breath. "I think your boyfriend is messing with dark magic."

3

I DIDN'T know if I should laugh or slap Dylan across the face. Ethan using dark magic? It was crazy. I couldn't figure out why Dylan would even suggest such a thing. Sure, he and Ethan had gotten off to an even rockier start than Shannon and I had. They'd beaten each other up. But to accuse Ethan of using dark magic was going too far.

I gritted my teeth and shook my head to keep from screaming at him. "I don't know if you think this is some sort of game or what, but this isn't funny. Ethan would *never* use dark magic. Never. I get that you two aren't the best of friends, but seriously, if Shannon and I can put the past behind us, you two need to do the same. Get over it."

"This isn't about a grudge, Sam." Dylan grabbed my hand—not forcefully, more like the way Ethan would. My eyes fell to our hands. What the hell? Did he have feelings for me? Was that what this was about?

"Wow!"

My head jerked to the side, and I tore my hand from Dylan's. Beth was standing in the doorway, staring at us.

"This is interesting. I heard you and Ethan liked to meet here. A little risky taking another guy to the place you sneak kisses with your boyfriend, don't you think, Sam?"

This couldn't be worse. First Dylan might have feelings for me, and now Beth catches me holding Dylan's hand? I wanted to scream at her to keep her nosy self out of my business, but I didn't want to make the situation worse.

"It's not like that, Beth. We were talking about Ethan. Planning his birthday party."

She wrinkled her forehead. "And you needed to hold hands to plan the party?"

"I had a cut on my hand. Dylan was looking at it for me." Hopefully, she wouldn't ask to see it, since I'd already healed myself.

She nodded, but didn't look the least bit convinced. "Isn't Ethan's birthday like a month away?"

Damn her for knowing so much!

"It's going to be a hell of a party," Dylan said. "We need to start planning now in order to put down a deposit to reserve the location."

Beth smiled. "I'll be expecting my invite soon then." She gave a little wave before entering one of the stalls.

I nodded toward the door. We couldn't talk anymore now that we had an audience—a loud, blabbermouth audience. Besides, I didn't have anything else to say to Dylan. I needed to get away from him.

The bell rang, and Dylan ran off before anyone else could see he'd been in the girls' bathroom. I pushed my way against the flow of traffic and back to Mr. Ryan's class. Shannon had my bag for me and was ushering me back out the door.

"Everything okay, Miss Smith?" Mr. Ryan called, following us out of the room.

"Yeah. Sorry I was gone for so long. I had trouble finding a Band-Aid. I'll be sure to get the notes from Shannon."

"Yeah, I'll make sure she's all caught up for tomorrow, Mr. R." Shannon draped her arm over my shoulder and practically shoved me down the hall. As soon as we got to the stairwell, she turned to me with a big grin on her face. "So, how was the meeting with Lover Boy?"

"The message wasn't from Ethan. It was from Dylan. He used a spell to make it look like it was from Ethan."

"Oh, he can go and mess with your head like that, but he gets all over my case for—"

"Shannon, focus please."

"Right. Sorry. Go on."

We exited the stairwell and paused. Our classes were in opposite directions. I lowered my voice. "Dylan thinks something's up with Ethan."

"Well, yeah. The guy can't get a hold on his magic." She shrugged. "He just needs more practice. Dylan is such a worrier. Don't let him get to you."

Maybe she was right. Maybe that was why Ethan was acting so strange. He was just having trouble adjusting to the magic inside him. "There's more." I swallowed hard. "I think Dylan may have feelings for me."

Shannon's eyes nearly popped out of her head. "What?" She grabbed my arm and pulled me into the bathroom. I was spending a lot of my morning in bathrooms. "What did he do? What did he say? Tell me everything."

"It's not a big deal. We were talking about Ethan, and Dylan reached for my hand. I think he's worried about me, too. Like he thinks whatever is going on with Ethan is going to hurt me."

"Whoa. I haven't seen him show interest in anyone in a long time. And considering," she paused and lowered her voice, "what you did to Ben, I'm surprised he'd feel that way about you."

"You and me both." I lowered my head, staring at my sneakers. "He should hate me." Killing his brother gave him every right to.

"Sam, it wasn't totally your fault. Nora made you into a monster."

I put my hand up to stop her. "Don't. I don't want to talk about it. We should get to class."

"What about Dylan? How are you going to handle him?"

"I'm not. I'm with Ethan. He knows that. Whatever he's feeling for me, it'll pass." I hoped.

I left Shannon to check her makeup. Ethan was already in sculpture and talking to Beth. I was afraid she'd told him about the bathroom incident, but Ethan smiled the second he saw me. He wasn't upset, which meant Beth hadn't said a word. Yet.

"How was English?" Ethan kissed the side of my head and moved closer to me at the table.

"Fine."

Beth stared at me, waiting for me to say something. Like I'd talk to Ethan about Dylan while she was listening in. I twisted in my seat so my profile was to her and I was completely focusing on Ethan.

"Want to spin some clay together?" Ethan wagged his eyebrows. I would've laughed, but the truth was, having our hands intertwined while shaping the clay was beyond romantic.

"Definitely."

Ms. Matthews turned on some music. It was her new thing. She said we should let the music wash over us and allow us to be more creative. She was seriously the coolest teacher here—next to Mr. Ryan. Ethan and I left Beth sitting alone at the table and walked over to the clay station.

"Joint project?" Ms. Matthews asked, raising a brow. "Trying to see what your chemistry will come up with?"

Ethan smiled. "That's what the music is telling us to do." Ms. Matthews ate up anything Ethan said. He had a way of making every teacher in the building fall in love with him, though it was definitely easier for him to work the magic of his baby blues on the female teachers.

"Well then, I can't wait to see what you come up with." She smiled and walked over to a group by the kiln.

I bumped Ethan's shoulder with mine. "You do realize you flirt with every female teacher here."

"Only when it gets me more time with you." He wrapped one arm around my waist, hooking his thumb through my belt loop. If we hadn't been in a classroom, I would've lost it right there. The boy could seriously make me melt. "Ladies first." He motioned for me to sit in front of the wheel. As soon as I did, he slid in behind me, wrapping his arms around me and resting his chin on my shoulder. I breathed him in, filling my senses with his scent. His spearmint gum sent chills down my spine as his lips grazed my ear.

"Are you trying to start something?" I turned and flashed him a smile. "Because two can play this game, and I know your willpower is no match for mine." Although mine was seriously depleting right now.

"Ooh, challenge accepted." He leaned down, placing soft kisses on my neck. Oh, crap. I was a goner. "Are those goose bumps on your arms?"

"Funny, but I'm wearing long sleeves."

"Are you denying the goose bumps?" He reached for my sleeve and tugged it up. I pulled my arm away before he could confirm his suspicion.

I summoned the magic inside and touched my finger to his cheek. Electricity gently sparked between us. "Check *your* arms."

"Using magic is cheating," he whispered in my ear.

Maybe, but everything Ethan did was like magic to me. I was only leveling the playing field.

"Um, are we still deciding what to make?" Ms. Matthews's voice shattered our competition.

"Kind of." I shrugged a shoulder.

"Well, maybe you should let someone else have a turn on the wheel while you two decide." She turned to walk away but stopped. "It might also help if you two put this game on hold for a more suitable time and place."

Ethan's face turned all different shades of red, and I was sure mine was no better. "Yes, Ms. Matthews."

"I just thought of what we can make," I blurted out, not wanting to give up our spot at the wheel or return to the table with Beth and her oversensitive ears.

"Then do get to work," Ms. Matthews said, eying us one last time before moving on.

"Do you really have an idea?" Ethan asked.

"Yeah. I think we should make a bowl."

"A bowl?"

I looked around, making sure no one—mainly Beth—was eavesdropping. "For when we need herbs to do spells. Dylan and Shannon were nice enough to take us in after everything…" My voice trailed off as images of Rebecca, Ben, and even Nora floated through my mind. Ethan opened his mouth, but before he could try to console me, I added, "It would be nice to make something the whole coven could use."

Ethan nodded. He knew me well enough to know I didn't want to talk about what had happened last month. It wasn't a topic he particularly liked, either. I mean, he'd died, come back a monster, and killed a witch, too. He'd been through the same things I had, just on a smaller scale.

I grabbed a lump of clay and turned on the wheel. We weaved our fingers together and manipulated the clay. Sure, we could magically make a bowl in a matter of seconds, but this way was much better, more intimate. Ethan's fingers lightly tickled mine. It was subtle at first, and for a moment I thought it was the clay making the tingling sensation on my hands. But then I saw the slight smile on Ethan's face. He was using magic.

The clay formed a perfect bowl, round and large enough to hold several herbs and the occasional fire needed for our joint spells. Even though our fingers were still intertwined and should have made ripples along the outside of the bowl, the clay was as smooth as could be. Being a witch, I could see the faint gold glow of the magic swirling around the clay.

"You're getting really good." I leaned back so Ethan's chest was pressed firmly against my back.

He didn't answer, so I assumed he was busy concentrating on the spell. He was taking longer to adjust to the magic than I had. But then again, I'd had to get a crash course in magic while we were battling Nora at the diner. Learn quickly or die. That had been enough motivation for me.

The tingling in my hands increased, and Ethan's fingers gripped mine. Was he losing control of the spell? Struggling to keep it up?

"That's enough, Ethan. Let it go. You did great."

His grip tightened, and his arms shook.

"Ethan." My voice was a loud whisper. I didn't want to draw attention to us. Who knew what this would look like to other people—non-witches.

The gold swirl of magic changed to a greenish color, a lot like the magic that had attacked us last night. It rippled around the clay, and bits of the bowl flew off in all directions. Several splattered my face and clothes.

"Ethan," I tried once more. Still nothing. I summoned my magic, planning to use it to put an end to his spell. Before I could do a spell of my own, the spinning wheel rattled. The clay shook like something was trying to burst out of it. The next thing I knew, the bowl exploded, sending clay flying everywhere.

4

"WHAT happened?" Ms. Matthews rushed over to us, her eyes and mouth wide with confusion.

Clay stuck to my hair, clothes, and skin. I must have looked like a monster from some old science-fiction movie. Jacob would've been so proud of me for even thinking that—if I was still living back home, that is.

"I don't know what happened." Ethan stood up, staring at his hands like they were deadly weapons. Maybe they were.

"The clay exploded." I whipped my head around at the sound of Beth's voice. She was only about three feet away, and judging by the clay on her shirt, she had been pretty close when Ethan's spell went volcanic. Had Beth seen anything strange? Anything that might've made her suspicious?

"Beth, you may be excused to go get cleaned up." Ms. Matthews pointed toward the door, a no-nonsense look on her face.

"But—" Beth's gaze shifted to Ethan and then me. Yeah, she was definitely suspicious. Crap.

Ms. Matthews jabbed her finger toward the door, and Beth walked out, sighing loudly enough for the whole class to hear. Everyone was staring at us now. "Back to work, all of you! If I see a single person not engrossed in their project, I'm docking ten points from your grade." Even though Ms. Matthews was usually laid-back, everyone listened to her. And now that she was being assertive, everyone jumped to obey her. She might be able to teach Principal Snyder a few things about commanding attention.

The second her eyes fell on me, I jumped to Ethan's defense. "Ms. Matthews, we're really sorry. The clay just sort of got out of control. I think maybe I had my hands—"

Ms. Matthews held her hand up. "That's enough, Sam." She looked back and forth between Ethan and me. "Both of you, get this cleaned up. Then head to the locker rooms and shower. I trust you have gym clothes to change into."

We nodded.

"Good. Then I'll tell your next period teachers about this accident."

"We have lunch next." My voice was small, guilty. Maybe it hadn't been *my* spell that made the clay explode, but I *was* responsible for Ethan becoming a witch. It all traced back to me in the end.

"Even better. I'll let the teachers on lunch duty know you'll be late." She motioned to the splattered clay and turned to help a group at a nearby table.

Ethan reached for my clay-covered hand. "Sam, I don't know what to say."

"Don't worry about it. It's no big deal. An accident." I shrugged a shoulder, trying to pretend I was fine with it, but inside all I could think was that Ethan was losing control. Or maybe he had never really had control. Either way, someone was going to get seriously hurt if we didn't figure this out.

We cleaned up the clay and headed to the locker rooms. Ethan hadn't said a word, so maybe he'd bought my lie. Maybe he thought I wasn't worried.

"Meet you back here in ten minutes?" He squeezed my hand once before letting go.

"Yeah." I turned toward the girls' locker room, but Ethan grabbed my arm.

"Are you mad at me?"

"No. Not at all." I stared into his beautiful blue eyes. How could I be mad at him? None of this was his fault. I ran my hand along the side of his face. We were both a mess, but I didn't care. I reached up and kissed his lips.

"Much better." He smiled at me, and I realized that was why he thought I was angry with him. I was going to leave without kissing him good-bye. We always kissed each other good-bye.

"Sorry, I guess the clay is clouding my brain."

"All it takes is a little clay to make you forget about me?" He was teasing, but I sensed some hurt buried in his comment.

"Not even all the clay in the world could make me forget about you."

"What about all the bad magic in the world?" He lowered his head and sighed. After staring at his feet like they were the most exciting things ever, he ran a hand through his hair and looked at me again. "Why can't I control it? You're doing fine with your power—better than fine, really. So, why am I having such a hard time?"

I stepped into him, wrapping my arms around his waist and leaning my head against his chest. "We'll figure it out together. Maybe you're trying too much. You need to ease into it."

"It's not like I haven't done spells. They were going right at first, but then…I don't know. Something changed."

I pulled my head back so I could see his face. "Changed how?"

"I'm not really sure. I feel different when I tap into the magic. It feels like it's not really mine—if that makes any sense."

"It *is* yours. You just need to focus and believe in your abilities."

"You're starting to sound like a teacher. Should I be worried you're spending too much time with Mr. Ryan?"

"Very funny, but Shannon's the one who has a thing for Mr. Ryan. I've got my eyes on someone else."

"Anyone I know?" Ethan flashed me his sexy smile.

"I don't think so, but he's gorgeous and has the most incredible blue eyes. Oh, and his body—"

He pressed his lips against mine softly at first, but within seconds they were crushing my mouth. He was scared. I felt his fear. I felt his uncertainty. Everything had changed. Because of me. I had to help him through this.

I finally managed to pull away from him before the bell rang and the hallway flooded with students. I gave him a quick good-bye kiss and headed for the showers. Luckily, the previous class was just finishing in the locker room. Everyone was dressed and waiting for the bell. I opened my locker and took out my gym clothes. Even though it was October, I'd be spending the rest of the day in shorts and a T-shirt.

I didn't have a towel, so I turned my clay-covered shirt inside out and used that to dry off after my steaming-hot shower. I was happy the steam shielded me from view of the changing area. No one really used the showers, except for in dire emergencies. They were wide open, and everyone in the locker room could see everything. I felt a little protected by the layer of steam blurring my body. Still, I rushed through the shower, quickly ran the dry shirt over myself, and pulled on my gym clothes.

I thought about using a spell to dry my hair and look somewhat presentable, but I wouldn't have any non-magical way to explain how my long hair had dried so quickly. So I squeezed as much water out of it as I could. I didn't have a comb, only a brush, and no way was I about to run a brush through my wet hair. I looked around the locker room, making sure no one was nearby. Then I summoned my magic and focused on my hair. I felt it ripple, like wind was blowing through it. It fell perfectly straight and knot-free down my back. No one would know I didn't have a comb. I grabbed my dirty clothes and practically ran from the shower area.

"Whoa!" Beth held her hands out and grabbed me before I ran into her.

"What are you doing here? You're supposed to be in lunch." God, was she following me around? She kept turning up everywhere.

"I wanted to make sure you were okay. I have extra clothes, so I thought I'd see if you needed anything."

I relaxed a little. Maybe Beth was just being nice. It was possible I was being overly jumpy around her because she was always so good at reading people. She'd never actually done anything even remotely mean to me. But the way she knew everything that went on in this school—well, *almost* everything—really put me on edge.

"I'm fine, Beth. Thanks. I just really want to get to lunch now."

"I'll walk with you."

"Oh, um, okay. I'm meeting Ethan first, though."

"Yeah, I saw him outside the locker room. I told him to go on ahead."

Of course she did. I plastered a fake smile on my face. "Great. Then, let's go." It's not like I didn't like Beth. She was nice enough. But I really wished she didn't take such an interest in me and Ethan. It wasn't easy having a secret with Beth lurking around.

"Ms. Matthews said the pottery wheel is broken."

"Oh no! Does she think Ethan and I broke it?" I had no idea how much one cost, but Ethan and I weren't exactly rolling in money these days.

"No. She said she found a part that was loose. She wrote up a report and everything. She said the school is lucky you and Ethan didn't get hurt or they'd have a lawsuit on their hands."

"Really?"

Beth shrugged. "That's what she said."

Was it possible the explosion *hadn't* been Ethan's fault? That the spinning wheel was broken? But if that was true, then did I imagine the green, swirling magic? Maybe my paranoia was messing with my eyes, making me imagine something that wasn't really there. I never thought I'd wish I was going crazy, but for Ethan's sake, I was kind of hoping just that.

We stepped into the cafeteria, which was already buzzing, no doubt with stories of the explosive clay. A few people clapped and pointed to me as I walked to my table. "Well, thanks, Beth. I guess I'll see you later." I sat down next to Ethan and gave Beth a small wave.

"Would it be okay if I sat here today?" She looked hopefully at the empty seat next to me.

"Hey, isn't that Mark Wilson?" Shannon asked, motioning behind Beth. "You two are dating, right?"

Beth turned around, already smiling. "Yeah."

"Oh, well I guess you probably want to sit with him." Shannon waved her fingers discreetly, passing it off as untangling her hair. Mark looked up and motioned for Beth to join him. "Have fun!"

If I wasn't so desperate to get rid of Beth, I would've been upset with Shannon for using magic on Beth and Mark like that. But my shoulders relaxed, and I leaned into Ethan. "You left me with her."

"Sorry. I didn't know how to get rid of her."

"No worries." Shannon wiggled her fingers and smiled. "I took care of that."

"Are you ever going to learn?" Dylan scoffed.

"Whatever. I didn't see you doing anything to help poor Sam." Shannon reached across the table and patted my hand. "Don't worry, sister. I've got your back."

"Thanks, I think."

Ethan slid his tray of fries over so they were in front of us both. "Peace offering?"

I took one and smiled at him. "If you had a vanilla shake to go with these, we'd be good."

"I can handle that, too." Shannon raised her hand over Ethan's bottle of water.

"Are you crazy?" Dylan snatched the water bottle away. "Why don't you just stand on the table and announce that you're a witch?"

"Sorry, *Dad*." Shannon's voice was laced with annoyance. I'd never seen her and Dylan fight like this. I couldn't help wondering if our joining the coven had been a bad idea after all.

I leaned forward, eyeing Dylan and Shannon. "Look, things have been kind of tense lately. Can we please lay off each other?"

Ethan nodded. "Sam's right. We're supposed to be helping each other. We've got enough to worry about right now."

"Like your little stunt in sculpture?" Dylan asked.

Yeah, of course he'd heard about that. I squeezed Ethan's hand, which only made Dylan's eyes narrow more. Damn it. I was definitely right about him having feelings for me. I wasn't sure when it had happened, when Dylan stopped looking at me as anything other than the witch who'd killed his brother, but I was in major trouble.

5

WE barely talked for the rest of the day. With the exception of Ethan and me, we all sort of went our separate ways, not meeting between classes—something we hadn't done since forming our coven. It felt odd, like part of me was missing. I guessed the spell we used to bind our powers was the cause of that emptiness in the pit of my stomach.

Ethan kissed my forehead as we stood outside my last-period science class. "I'm sorry I dragged you into this."

I squeezed his hands. "What are you talking about? You didn't do anything wrong."

"You don't have to defend me, Sam. I know I'm messing up lately. I just wish I knew why." He shook his head and sighed. "But Dylan better lay off. I don't like that he's taking this out on you, too. It's my problem."

"It's all our problem." I leaned closer, wrapping my arms around his neck. To everyone else, it looked like I was leaning in for a kiss before class—which I was definitely planning on doing—but I also had to make sure no one overheard me. "We're a coven. When something is wrong with one of us, we all have to come together to fix it. That's how it works."

"When did you become the expert on coven behavior? You're as new at this as I am."

"Just trust me, okay? I know what I'm talking about." I kissed him, my lips lingering on his.

"Okay, you two. Enough of that." Mrs. Stevens glared at us with her arms crossed.

I let go of Ethan and gave him a small wave before stepping past Mrs. Stevens and into class. She had an experiment all set up for us. We did more experiments than the honors class, which really struck me as odd since the name of the class was Chemistry for the Non-Science Major. Thank God the real Samantha Smith wasn't good at science. It was never my best subject, and since I was pretending to be Samantha Smith, it worked out well.

Instead of going to her desk, Mrs. Stevens followed me to mine. "Miss Smith, you know the school's policy on public displays of affection in the halls. I'd hate to have to write you up, but I won't allow a repeat of the little stunt you pulled in the hallway last month."

The little stunt she was referring to was the kiss I gave Ethan that got the attention of the entire school, teachers included. But who could've blamed me? I'd just found out Ethan was dying. Every moment I had with him had been precious. Not that I could even begin to explain that to Mrs. Stevens. She might be married, but the woman definitely didn't understand what love was. I wouldn't have been surprised to find out her marriage had been arranged.

I nodded without saying a word and took my seat. Mrs. Stevens explained the experiment we were conducting today, but not much registered. My mind was still on Ethan. He'd admitted he was messing up. That was a start. If he was willing to admit he needed help, the coven should be able to fix the problem. That is, if I could get the coven to work together again.

My cell vibrated in my pocket. I looked around, making sure Mrs. Stevens was too busy to notice me texting in class. She was helping Ricky Molson, whose beaker of chemicals was bubbling over. Knowing that would keep her busy for a few minutes, I slid my phone out.

We need to finish our talk. Dylan. I should've expected it. After lunch and the way we'd left things, of course Dylan would want to talk. He didn't trust Ethan to begin with, and after the exploding clay in sculpture, Dylan was going to want to put a stop to Ethan's spells. I didn't doubt Dylan had every intention of binding Ethan's magic. And not the kind of binding that made us a coven. The kind that made it so Ethan couldn't do magic when he wasn't with the rest of us.

I wasn't ready to have this talk, but if I didn't do something before Dylan brought up the subject to Ethan, things were going to get really out of control.

I checked on Mrs. Stevens again before typing, *When and where?*

Dylan must have been right on top of his phone waiting for my reply because almost instantly my cell shook with his response. *Diner. 4:30.*

Fine. I shut the phone and put it back in my pocket. It was good I was getting this conversation out of the way. I needed to do this for Ethan. For the coven, too.

"You can take two substances that are completely calm on their own, but when you combine them, the effects can be explosive," Mrs. Stevens said, addressing the entire class. When had she started lecturing? "When Ricky added the wrong chemical to his beaker solution, nothing appeared to happen at first. But after a while, the chemicals began reacting to one another."

"Yeah, and my experiment blew up all over my cell phone." Ricky held up his phone, which was covered in some green goo. "My dad's going to kill me. I just got this last week."

Mrs. Stevens nodded. "This is why cell phones aren't allowed in class, Mr. Molson."

As I stared at Ricky's phone, I couldn't help thinking about what Mrs. Steven had said. The chemical in the solution—it was calm at first. But then something happened, and the mixture exploded. Was this what was happening with Ethan? The magic in him was calm at first, and now it was bubbling up inside him, threatening to explode?

As soon as the final bell rang, I jumped up and ran to my locker. I couldn't pretend to care about school for one second longer, not that I thought I'd done a convincing job of pretending in the first place. Ethan was already leaning against my locker with a smile on his face.

"I missed you." His voice was airy, like a sigh. His hands found my waist and pulled me to him.

"Didn't we get in trouble for this once already today?" I playfully smacked his hands away, but I couldn't resist lightly pecking him on the mouth. "Excuse me. I need to swap some books before we head to the diner."

Ethan reluctantly stepped aside. "Think we have time for a quick drive before work?"

I shoved my books inside my locker and shut it. "Why? Do you have somewhere you need to go?"

He stepped into me again. "Yes. Somewhere we can have a little alone time."

We lived alone. What other high-school couple could say that? "What's gotten into you today?" I laced my fingers through his and tugged him down the hall before he did anything to land us in detention. We couldn't afford to be late for work.

Ethan shrugged. "Can't I just want to be with you?"

"Of course." There was more to it, but I could tell he wasn't up for talking. I squeezed his hand, and we walked to the car without another word. I felt like I was spending so much time in silence lately, afraid to say the wrong thing around the wrong person. Here I was, a witch with incredible powers, and I couldn't even say two words without worrying about who I'd offend or hurt. It didn't seem fair.

Ethan held my hand the whole way to the diner. I loved that he drove with one hand on the wheel and one on me. He'd always been this way, even before the cancer and the witch thing. It was just how Ethan was. He loved to be touching me, and I loved it just as much.

The diner was pretty empty when we pulled up. The after-school crowd wouldn't show up for about another fifteen minutes. Ethan cut the engine and turned in his seat, making no move to get out of the car.

"What's on your mind?" I asked, mimicking his pose.

"This is going to sound crazy, but I have to ask." He paused, and I knew I wasn't going to like what he was about to say.

"Go on." The silence was killing me.

"It's about Dylan."

Had Dylan said something to Ethan already? He was supposed to meet me here and talk it through with me first.

"Does he have a thing for you?" Ethan swallowed hard, like the words were painful to say.

"Why do you think that?" My voice shook, giving me away. I didn't want to answer that, but I didn't want to lie to Ethan, either. Still, if I told him I thought Dylan might have feelings for me, it would destroy our coven. Ethan would freak out, and he and Dylan would never be friends.

"I'll take that as a yes." Ethan slammed his palm against the steering wheel. "I knew it. Right from the start, I knew it. The way he followed you around, left notes for you. I'm seriously going to kill that guy."

I reached for Ethan's arm. "No, you're not. It's a stupid crush. He'll get over it. Besides, I'm sure it's really nothing. I mean, how can he like me? He should hate me after what I did to Ben."

Ethan's eyes narrowed. "I forgot Ben was his brother."

"Yeah. So you see, there's no way this will last. All I have to do is mention Ben's name and Dylan will go back to tolerating me for the sake of the coven. That will be the end of it."

Ethan shook his head. "I'm not so sure, Sam. He knows that was Nora's fault. He doesn't blame you. At least, not anymore. Just promise me you won't wear that necklace he gave you ever again. Something like that would give him the wrong impression, you know?"

The impression that I liked him back. Yeah, I couldn't wear it, even if Shannon thought it was a good idea. "Come on. Gloria and Jackson are expecting us."

Ethan didn't move. He wasn't letting this go so easily.

I moved forward and kissed him. Not a small peck. I kissed him the way I knew he wanted to kiss me at my locker. Ethan's hands were in my hair one minute and then wrapped around my waist the next, pulling me into his seat with him.

"Ethan," I managed to say between kisses.

He pulled back, breathing heavily. "Sorry." He looked kind of dazed, like his mind was somewhere else.

"Are you okay?"

"I wish everyone would stop asking me that." His face contorted, and his mouth tightened.

I took his face in my hands and made him look at me. "Don't ask me not to worry about you. I love you. You'd do the same for me."

His eyes softened. "I know. It's just been a rough day. I'll be fine."

I was afraid to ask what had made it a rough day. Sure, there was the incident in sculpture and the argument with the coven at lunch, but I had a bad feeling there was more to it. I kissed him softly on the lips. "How about right after work we drive to our favorite lookout spot on the mountain? We'll stay there until your day gets better."

"Sounds perfect." He tucked my hair behind my ear and leaned forward to whisper, "There's nothing I wouldn't do for you, Sam."

I had no idea what made him say that right now, but I knew he meant it. I wrapped my arms around him, pulling him to me. "Maybe we can be a few minutes late," I whispered back to him.

He gently pulled me back, just far enough to find my lips.

We entered the diner fifteen minutes later with a rush of "Sorry!" directed at Gloria's glaring eyes. Ethan headed straight for the kitchen, while I practically ran behind the counter and put on my apron.

"You do know I can see your car through the windows," Gloria said. "That boy needs to learn to control his hands."

I stifled a laugh. Gloria had no idea Ethan and I lived together, and I didn't dare let her find out. She'd have me fitted for a chastity belt before my shift was over. "Sorry, Gloria. Ethan's just having a bad day."

"Yes, well, *that* isn't the answer to a bad day." She didn't need to glare at me again for me to get the meaning behind "that."

I nodded, afraid anything I'd say would only make things worse.

The after-school rush poured in, and I happily ran to fill orders. Even waiting on my classmates was better than being lectured by Gloria, especially when I sensed a sex talk brewing. Tristan walked in and immediately waved to me.

"Hey, sit wherever you'd like. I'll be right there." I finished delivering a tray of sodas to a corner table and walked over to the booth where Tristan was. A girl was sitting across from him, her back to me. So Tristan was on a date. Interesting. I'd never seen or heard about him dating anyone. "Hi!" I said, eager to meet the girl, but my face fell the second I locked eyes on her.

Beth. Tristan was on a date with nosy Beth? No, she was dating Mark. Had Beth and Tristan become friends? Either way, this could only mean bad news for the coven. Because while Tristan might be oblivious to his sister's extracurricular activities in the woods with Dylan, Ethan, and me, Beth noticed everything.

6

I STARED at Beth like an idiot, unable to form words or even move. This was serious trouble. We'd been working so hard on keeping our identities a secret, and now Beth was getting seriously close to ruining everything.

"Are you going to pick that up?" Beth motioned to the ground. I had to tear my eyes off her to see that my pad and pen were lying on the floor. I hadn't even realized I'd dropped them.

"Um, yeah." I bent down, nearly smacking my head on the edge of the table.

"Whoa, watch it." Tristan reached forward and covered the edge of the table with his hand. "I don't want to have to drive you to the emergency room in the middle of my date."

So it *was* officially a date. I'd been silently praying this was an innocent meeting. They'd run into each other in the parking lot, or Beth had already been seated when Tristan came in looking for a seat. But this had been planned. They were dating. Something must have happened between Mark and Beth after lunch. Who knew Beth was the type to move on so quickly? Mark had dodged a bullet getting rid of Beth, but now that bullet was aimed right for me.

"Sam." Beth stared at me squatting on the ground. I still hadn't picked up the pad or pen.

I snapped out of it. The worst thing I could do was act strange. It would only make Beth that much more suspicious, and then she'd watch me even closer. I snatched up the pad and pen and got to my feet, being careful not to hit my head on the table on the way up. "Sorry. I haven't eaten much today and my blood sugar's a little low. I have to remember to grab a glass of lemonade next time I'm at the counter."

"I didn't know you were hypoglycemic." Beth stared at me like she was trying to diagnose me on the spot.

"I've never been tested. I just feel kind of shaky sometimes when I need sugar." I turned away from her and locked my eyes on Tristan. "So, do you need menus or do you know what you want?"

"I'm craving a bacon cheeseburger and curly fries."

"Great. Anything to drink?"

"Coke is good. Oh, and do you have any bendy straws?" His eyes lit up like a three-year-old's.

Oh, Tristan. This would be why I'd never seen him date before. "I'll check." I reluctantly turned to Beth.

"Wow, you're not even writing this down. You must have a great memory. You're lucky. People say I have a good memory, too. It makes school so much easier, don't you think?" She smiled as she waited for my response.

"Yeah. Definitely. Did you need a menu?" I asked, trying to hurry this along.

"No. I'll have a Cobb salad."

"And to drink?"

"That lemonade you mentioned sounded great."

I nodded. "I'll be right back with your drinks."

"Don't forget to pour yourself a lemonade, too!" Beth said.

I forced a smile and walked away. Seriously, she was nice, but she tried way too hard. So hard I questioned if the whole thing was a big act. I didn't trust her at all. I wrote up their orders and placed the ticket in the window for Jackson, but Ethan met me instead.

"All I can think about is going to the mountaintop later." He smiled, and my stomach fluttered.

"I can't wait." Maybe time alone, away from Beth and the coven and school, was exactly what Ethan and I needed to feel somewhat normal again.

I spent as little time as possible at Tristan and Beth's table, although she managed to corner me on her way to the bathroom to let me know she was dating both Mark and Tristan. Who knew she had it in her to juggle two guys? Not wanting to hear any more, I ran back and forth, taking Gloria's tables, too. Anything to avoid Beth. Of course I apologized for being so busy and not checking on her and Tristan more.

"Wow, the owner sure works you hard." Beth's eyes fixed on mine. "She doesn't seem to handle many tables on her own. Is it always like that?"

Why was I not surprised she was still watching me like a hawk even though she was on a date with Tristan? "Yeah, well, Gloria's great, and since her feet hurt when she's on them too much, I like to help out as much as I can. Can I get you two your check?" Hopefully, I didn't sound as eager to be rid of them as I actually was.

Tristan nodded and rubbed his stomach. "I'm as stuffed as a roasted pig."

I laughed. Maybe Shannon did have some good reasons for not wanting people to know Tristan was her brother. He had no clue what was embarrassing. I already had the check prepared for them, so I placed it on the table and cleared their dishes.

As I was heading back to the coffee pot to start my round of refills, I noticed the clock on the wall. 4:34. Damn it! Dylan was out back waiting for me. "Gloria, is it okay if I take five? I could use some fresh air." It was still warm for October, so luckily she wouldn't question the request.

"Sure. You go. You've been handling every table for the last hour. I can cover the coffee refills." She took the pot, and I smiled before dashing out the back door.

Dylan was leaning against the driver's side of his car. He drove a beat-up sedan he'd found abandoned on the side of the highway. But to anyone who wasn't a witch, it looked like a BMW. Dylan told us it would make kids accept him more easily if he drove a nice car, and since he was a transfer like Ethan and me, we let the spell slide.

"You're late." He stood up straight, not looking happy at all. At least he wasn't all googly-eyed. Maybe the crush was already a thing of the past.

"Sorry. The after-school crowd can get kind of crazy. Well, that *and* we have a problem."

His head cocked to the side. "What kind of problem? Ethan?"

"No," I snapped. Why did he have to go right for Ethan? "Beth."

Dylan sighed. "What's Little Miss Nosy up to now?"

"She's dating Tristan."

"Shannon's brother?"

"Are there any other Tristans at school?" I had to lose the snippiness, but it was tough, considering how Dylan felt about Ethan and how he might have been feeling about me. "Sorry, I'm a little on edge. She's watching me like a hawk. And you know if Tristan starts talking about Shannon or us, she'll piece the puzzle together."

"Then it looks like we need to work a little magic." Shannon walked toward us, appearing out of nowhere.

"What was that?" I asked. "Did you—?"

"Simple camouflage spell. Nothing to it." She waved her hand, dismissing the topic.

Dylan crossed his arms, obviously not happy. "Why did you need a spell to sneak up on us?"

"I wanted to hear what you two were talking about. It had to be interesting if you met in private. Keeping secrets from Ethan, Sam?" She *tsk*ed.

"Okay, can we get this all out in the open?" I looked back and forth between them. "We're supposed to be like family, yet you two attacked Ethan at lunch. We need to help him, and now more than ever."

Shannon sighed. "Because my twin brother is dating the blabbermouth."

"Exactly," Dylan and I said together.

"Cute." Shannon made a face. "Seriously, does Ethan know about this?" She pointed back and forth between Dylan and me.

"There's nothing to know about. I love Ethan. End of story." I said it more for Dylan's benefit than Shannon's, but she nodded.

"Good. As long as that's out in the open, I guess we can move on. Unless there's something you'd like to say, Dylan?" Shannon eyed him, and the corner of her mouth tugged upward like she was holding back a grin. I made a mental note not to tell her any more secrets. She was baiting Dylan. Letting him know she suspected his feelings. And worse, she was letting him know I was aware of them, too.

Dylan lowered his eyes. "I do have something else to say."

Oh crap. Was he really going to talk about this with Shannon here?

He raised his eyes, focusing on me as if Shannon wasn't even here. "I asked you to meet me because I think we need to do something about Ethan. He can't be trusted to use his magic right now. He's slipping up too much, and it could be dangerous for all of us."

"I hate to agree," Shannon said, "but now that Tristan is dating Beth, we need to be extra-careful."

She was right. If Ethan slipped up in front of Beth, we were all in big trouble. It was bad enough he'd made the clay explode in the same class Beth was in. What if he did something around Tristan and Tristan told Beth?

Shannon smirked, which broke me out of my mental torment.

"How can you smile right now?" I couldn't keep the annoyance out of my voice.

"I was just thinking."

That couldn't be good.

"I could do a little spell on Beth. Get her to stay away from Tristan and, by extension, us."

"Would you lay off the spells on students?" Dylan was red with rage. "Damn it, Shannon. Ethan may be screwing up, but at least he's not doing it on purpose. You're being stupid and reckless."

So Dylan didn't totally blame Ethan for his spells gone wrong. That was good news.

"Stupid and reckless? I think you're confusing me with your dear dead brother!" Shannon's fists were clenched at her sides, and I was afraid she was going to throw a punch. But at the mention of Ben, Dylan opened his car door and got inside. His eyes lingered on mine before he slammed the door and peeled out of the parking lot.

"Did you really have to bring up Ben?" I was more than a little pissed at Shannon.

She shrugged. "You should be thanking me. I'm helping him get over his little crush on you. That's what you want, right? Or are you bored with Mr. Can't Control His Magic?"

"No! I could never be bored with Ethan. He's everything to me."

"Good. Then let's figure out how to control his magic and get Dylan to stop going all gaga over you." She put her arm around my shoulder. "I'm on your side, Sam. You're actually the last one I want to fight with right now."

"Why? Because I have the power of two witches inside me?" I couldn't resist. Shannon and I had started off as almost enemies. It was hard to just let go of that and be best friends, even if the coven was forcing us together.

"I'm not going to lie; that's great motivation to play nice with you. But magic aside, it's the two of us against the boys."

I turned to face her, making her arm drop from my shoulders. "Why are we *against* the boys? I don't want to be against Ethan in anything."

"Ugh, love has made you blind." She shook her head. "Dylan and Ethan are guys. They're going to get all dominant with us. You just watch. I'd rather we were ready for that, so we can put them in their places."

"Their places are right beside us. We're all equals."

Shannon rolled her eyes. "Tell that to Dylan. He thinks he's the leader now that Ben's gone."

My stomach clenched. "Can we please stop mentioning Ben?"

"You seriously need to get over that. I get that Nora put you through hell, but you have to stop torturing yourself. No one else is."

"I guess you missed the way Dylan glared at me right before he tore out of the parking lot."

She narrowed her eyes at me. "Is that why you're being so tolerant of his feelings for you? Because you feel bad about killing his brother?"

"I'm not being tolerant of his feelings. I just flat-out told him I love Ethan. What more can I do? I'm not going to be mean about it. I owe him at least that much."

"Look, I get that you think I'm a bitch—"

"Shannon, I don't think you're a bitch."

"Fine. Maybe not anymore, but you did think that before." She had me there. "I'm not telling you to act the way I do or even did. I'm just saying be careful around Dylan. He takes after Ben."

"What's that supposed to mean?"

"Ben was a hothead. He was fearless to the point of stupidity. Do you think it was coincidence that Nora had you drain him first? He caused her the most trouble. When he found out she'd gone all dark with her magic, he went after her. Big-time. And she made him pay for it." No, *I* had made him pay for it. "Dylan's not much different."

"What exactly do you think he'll do? It's only a crush, right?" I couldn't see Dylan waging war against me over this.

"Think about it, Sam. He has a thing for you, and Ethan's magic is all screwy. Who do you think Dylan's going to take his frustration out on?"

Ethan.

7

SHANNON thought Dylan was going to attack Ethan. My mind flashed back to the fight at the cottage. Ethan had attacked Dylan. He'd gone after him with a hammer. Dylan had bashed Ethan's head into the side of the cottage, but he'd said it was just to get the hammer away from Ethan. He could've taken it and used it to... But he hadn't. He'd only disarmed Ethan.

"No. Dylan wouldn't do that."

Shannon put her hand on her hip. "You think you know him so well? Ask him why he wasn't in school before we formed the coven. Ask him where he's been and where his family is. Ask him what his last name is—his real one."

Real last name? Dylan was using a fake last name like Ethan and me? "Shannon, what aren't you telling me?"

"He should be the one to tell you."

I threw my arms out to my sides. "Yeah, well, he's not here. You are. I'm tired of the games. I want a straight answer. No smart comments or magic. I want to pretend for two seconds that we're normal teenagers. Nothing strange about us."

Giggling stopped me mid-rant. Beth and Tristan were coming out the back door. Gloria usually never let people—other than employees—use this door.

"Hey." Tristan smiled at us. "We were on our way to a movie. You guys want to come along?"

"No." Shannon was the perfect ice queen.

Beth's head jerked back like she'd been punched. "Oh, okay." She turned to me. "Sam, we left your tip on the table. We tried to wait for you, but you were gone for so long."

Crap! How long had I been on break? "I have to get back to work." I gave Shannon a look that said "we're not done here" and headed back inside.

Gloria was at the counter making more coffee. The place was pretty empty, but I could practically see the steam coming from Gloria's ears. "Maybe you should wear a watch to work from now on." She wouldn't even look at me.

"I'm so sorry. I ran into some of my friends and—"

"Samantha, I get that you're in high school and you have a social life." She turned to meet my eyes. "I even understand that you give up a lot of your free time to work here while all your friends are out having fun. But I can't afford to pay you for work you don't do."

"I'm really sorry, Gloria." My insides twisted, and for a moment I felt like I was back in my old life, before the cancer. This was so eerily similar to the time Mom caught me lying to her about where I was going. I'd snuck out to meet Ethan. We'd just started dating, and Mom and Dad hadn't met and approved of him yet. Mom caught me sneaking back in through the den window. She'd looked so betrayed and disappointed in me. Gloria was giving me that same look now. "I don't know what else to say other than it won't happen again."

She nodded and finished setting up the coffee. I bussed a few tables and wiped them clean. I wasn't sure why Gloria was so upset about me taking too long of a break, but she seemed bent out of shape over it. We barely spoke for over an hour. I worked through my dinner break to make up for it, but around seven, Gloria grabbed my arm and pulled me into the kitchen.

Ethan was sitting at the sink holding two plates of Jackson's famous lasagna. He smiled at me, raising the plates slightly so I had a better view of the food. Gloria patted my arm. When I met her eyes, she smiled and nodded toward Ethan. All was forgiven. I leaned over and kissed her cheek. I'd never done that before, but she was family to me and I wanted her to know that. Her eyes glistened with the threat of tears as she left the kitchen.

Jackson winked at me as I passed him on my way to Ethan. "What's the occasion? It must be something special if I deserve Jackson's lasagna."

"Actually, *I* made it."

"You?" My voice squeaked in surprise.

Ethan laughed. "I told you I'm getting really good at cooking. Jackson said I could have a real future in it."

The lasagna looked and smelled exactly like Jackson's. "You're sure you made this? You're not trying to put one over on me?"

"I made it. I swear." He patted the stool next to him. "Come on. Sit. I'm dying for you to try this and tell me what you think."

I sat down, and Ethan handed me my plate. It wasn't easy to cut the lasagna while holding the plate at the same time, but I managed. I took my first bite and chewed slowly, teasing Ethan by not making a sound or a single expression to give away my true thoughts, which were that this was seriously good!

His eyes widened. "Well?"

I held my fork up, motioning for him to give me a second.

"Sam, you're killing me! Tell me what you think." God, he was cute when he was impatient.

I leaned forward and kissed him. He tasted like lasagna too, which made me wonder how much he'd eaten before I got here.

"Don't make me turn that hose on you two," Jackson yelled across the kitchen.

Ethan and I pulled apart. His shirt was covered in his lasagna.

"Sorry. I made you lean on your food."

"Tell me you like the lasagna and I'll forgive you." He reached for a towel on the edge of the sink and wiped his shirt.

"I love the lasagna, and I love you."

"I really wish our shift was over."

"But you haven't finished your lasagna," I teased.

"This is my third piece." I gave him a look, and he shrugged. "You didn't think I'd feed it to you unless I knew it was delicious, did you?"

"It took three pieces to decide it was good enough?" I ate another bite.

"No. It only took one bite, but the stuff is addictive." He stared at me with such love in his eyes. "Kind of like you."

"I'm addictive?"

He shrugged again. "I can't ever get enough of you, so yeah."

Now *I* wished our shift was over. All I wanted was to be alone with Ethan. The day might have sucked, but there wasn't anything a little time alone with Ethan couldn't fix.

"Don't even think about launching into another make-out session," Jackson said. "I *will* get that hose. You sit there and eat your dinners and then get back to work."

Ethan and I laughed, but we were both disappointed. Quitting time couldn't come soon enough. We finished dinner without any more kissing, thanks to Jackson. I helped Gloria with the last tables of the night and cleaned all the tables and the counter while she balanced the register drawer in her office. I was about to yell good night and go collect Ethan from the kitchen when Gloria came back.

"Samantha." She looked serious. Something was wrong. I hoped I hadn't screwed up the register.

"Did I do something wrong?"

"Sit down for a minute." She motioned to the stools at the counter.

My legs wobbled as my mind raced with things she might say. After the long break, if I screwed up something big like a bill… Would she really fire me?

"That girl you talked to earlier this evening, is she a friend of yours?"

Had Gloria seen me with Shannon and Dylan outside? "Um, yeah. We go to school together and have been hanging out a lot. Why do you ask?"

"When I went to my office just now, the door was unlocked."

She never forgot to lock the office. I joked around with her about it all the time. "You don't think someone went in there, do you? You're the only one with the key."

She thought about it for a moment and waved her hand. "Never mind. You're right. Besides, nothing was missing. I must have just forgotten to lock it, or maybe the lock is acting up. I'll have Jackson look at it."

Something was still bothering me. "Gloria, why did you ask about Shannon?"

"I don't let customers leave through the back door for a reason. I don't want them near the office. Today two customers left out that door. They met you in the back lot."

"You're talking about Tristan and Beth, not Shannon."

"How many people are you bringing by my office, Samantha?" Her tone was very accusatory. Just great. I'd thought we were past her disappointment in me.

"I didn't bring them there. I was as surprised to see Tristan and Beth as you were."

"And the other girl? Shannon?"

"I wasn't expecting her either, I swear. And she was only outside, not near your office at all." I fidgeted with my hands. I wanted to reach out to her, to show her I never meant for anyone to be near her office, but she looked so…upset with me. "I won't take breaks out back anymore. I won't go anywhere the customers aren't supposed to be. That way, no one will follow me."

She shook her head and waved her hand, dismissing my idea. "*You* work here. *You* are allowed in those places. It's other people I want to keep out. Just do me a favor and promise me you'll come to me immediately if you see anyone by my office again. Oh, and tell your friends that the back entrance is for employees only. Unless they're looking for jobs, which I can't give them right now anyway, they are not to be back there. Got it?"

"Got it. I'm sorry, Gloria."

"Samantha, you can stop apologizing. You are entitled to breaks, and as long as you were telling the truth about not inviting those kids back there with you, you didn't do anything wrong."

If I was telling the truth? Did she not believe me? "Gloria, I wouldn't lie to you. You're like…" If I said "a grandmother to me," she'd get insulted. Gloria might be old enough to be my grandmother, but I didn't dare say that to her face. "You're like family to me. I don't really have a lot of family. I'd hate to think you don't know that you can trust me."

Gloria sniffled and pulled me in for a hug. "Sugar, I do trust you. I know you're a good girl. And for what it's worth, you and Ethan are like family to Jackson and me, too. We don't really have any family left, so we're more than happy to have you two."

I squeezed her, wondering how long it had been since I'd hugged anyone other than Ethan. Too long. I really missed Mom. And Dad. And Jacob. The list went on.

"Hey, what are we missing?" Jackson asked, coming out of the kitchen with Ethan right behind him.

"Apparently it's hugging time." Ethan held his arms out to Jackson, who swatted them away. We all laughed. Jackson joined Gloria and me. Ethan faked a frown. "Well, now I just feel left out."

"I'm sure you'll be getting plenty of hugs from this one as soon as you two get out of here." Jackson palmed my head and ruffled my hair.

Gloria pulled out of the hug. "Not too much hugging. Samantha is a lady. You remember that, Ethan."

He stifled a smile and gave a small nod. "Yes, ma'am."

"Good. Now, you two get out of here. We'll see you tomorrow. And let's not have a repeat of the car incident again." Gloria eyed me, and I felt two feet tall. How was I going to get over the embarrassment of her catching Ethan and me making out in his car?

Ethan opened his mouth, and I knew he was going to ask Gloria what she meant. I reached for his hand and tugged him toward the door. "Good night." My voice was small, despite my attempt to act casual.

Jackson wrapped his arm around Gloria and waved to us as we headed to Ethan's car.

"What was that about?" Ethan asked, opening my door for me.

"Gloria saw us making out before work."

Ethan turned bright red. "Oh man, for some strange reason that's worse than your dad catching us." I laughed as he walked around the car and got in. He wasn't wrong, though. My dad was a puppy compared to Gloria.

"Gloria's very old-fashioned. She wants to make sure you're treating me like a lady."

"Don't I?" Ethan looked a little hurt.

I brushed my fingers against his cheek. "Always." Okay, that wasn't entirely true. When Ethan spaced out and got aggressive, he didn't treat me like a lady. I couldn't really blame him for that, though. He'd be fine once he learned how to handle the magic inside him.

He smiled and laced his fingers through mine. "Does this mean you don't want to go to the mountaintop anymore?"

"Are you kidding?" I wanted to go more than ever. "If Gloria and Jackson weren't staring at us through the window, I'd be in your seat with you right now."

Ethan laughed. "And Gloria's worried about *me*?"

We drove to the mountaintop and parked. Even at night, the view was incredible. The stars lit up the sky, and the river glistened below them. Ethan opened the moon roof. The night air was crisp, but I snuggled closer to Ethan to keep warm.

"Think I could move the stars?" he asked.

"What? Why would you want to do that?"

"I could write your name in them."

I wasn't sure that was possible, even for a witch, but with the way Ethan's magic had been lately, I didn't like him thinking about trying something so huge. "I don't need my name written in the stars. All I need is you."

"You have me. All of me." He traced soft kisses from my temple down to my neck. I was done for. Ethan was using his most powerful magic on me. His love. For a moment, I couldn't help wishing he wasn't a witch. That he was just my Ethan again. He didn't need magic. He'd already been perfect. Maybe binding his magic wasn't such a bad idea after all. But if I gave in to Dylan and went along with his plan, Ethan would think I didn't trust him. That I didn't want him to be part of the coven.

How could I put him through that? Even if it *was* true?

8

I WAS up early. After being with Ethan last night, I'd had a change of heart. I couldn't let Dylan kick him out of the coven. I'd find another way to fix whatever was wrong. I had to. Ethan deserved that. He'd given his life for me. He'd become a witch for me. I couldn't be selfish now. I couldn't let Dylan bind Ethan's magic just because it was the easy solution. Ethan liked being a witch, almost as much as I'd grown to like it. I wouldn't take that away from him.

Dylan and Shannon met us in the parking lot, as usual. I gave Dylan a look that hopefully let him know I wanted to talk. I wanted to get Shannon in on it, too, to avoid being alone with Dylan and his strange new feelings for me, but having us all talk about Ethan behind his back like that felt too much like us ganging up on him. If Ethan ever found out, he'd be really hurt. I had to suck it up and face Dylan on my own. For Ethan's sake.

Dylan narrowed his eyes at me, giving me a questioning look every time I tried to hint at a secret meeting. Finally, I gave up. I'd have to text him from class. Ethan walked me to my English Lit class after we parted ways with Dylan and Shannon.

"Have I told you how amazing you are yet today?" He twirled a section of my hair around his finger. His hand grazed my cheek, sending chills down my spine.

"Maybe once or twice, but feel free to tell me again." I smiled before leaning forward and kissing him good-bye.

"I don't want to leave you." He tugged on my hands, pulling me closer instead of letting me go.

"I think you have to." Yeah, especially since I had to meet Dylan. He pouted, which looked sexy as hell. "You're playing dirty."

He wrapped his arm around my waist and tugged me closer still. "Ditch with me."

"Ditch?" This wasn't like him at all. He was always the responsible one. "Who are you, and what have you done with my boyfriend?"

"Ahem," Mr. Ryan said, glaring disapprovingly in our direction.

Ethan let go and sighed. "Morning, Mr. Ryan."

"Mr. Jones." Mr. Ryan nodded. "I suggest you get to class before the late bell."

I smiled at Ethan and walked into the classroom before he did something to land us both in detention. I took a seat next to Shannon, who was eying me suspiciously.

"You seem to have Ethan on a short leash."

"What? No, it's not like that. Why do you think that?" I never thought of myself as the overbearing girlfriend.

"He's so into you. He'd probably permanently attach himself to you if he could. Which *of course* means you two are having sex."

I dropped my copy of *Frankenstein* on the floor. I'd never told anyone that Ethan and I had…well, that we'd slept together. It wasn't like we did it all the time. Living together complicated things. I mean, yes, we slept in the same bed each night, but that didn't mean we were all over each other. It was kind of the opposite. We didn't want our relationship to get old by moving too quickly. I couldn't imagine anything worse than turning into an old married couple at seventeen. No, thank you.

"Why do you look so surprised?" Shannon picked up my book for me and put it on my desk. "You two have been together for practically forever. I'm sure everyone knows you're sleeping together."

"Could you stop talking about it?" I looked around, paranoid that the entire class was tuned in to the conversation. "For your information—not that I think it's any of your business—we've only done it three times."

She shook her head. "No way. You two liv—"

I slapped my hand over her mouth before she could rat me out to the class. I could deal with people knowing Ethan and I had had sex. But letting people find out we were actually living together was a completely different story. We could get in serious trouble. We were lying about where we lived, having parents to look after us, and even our last names. Hell, we were assuming the identities of two strangers. It was all so totally illegal.

"Sorry," Shannon mumbled under my hand. I pulled away, noticing her red lip gloss had left a big smear on my palm. "Oh, great. Now I need to reapply." She whipped out a compact mirror and a tube of shimmering lip gloss. "Want some? I bet Ethan would like it. It tastes like raspberry."

Ethan didn't need any encouragement lately. His hormones seemed to be on overdrive. "No. I need to go wash this off." I raised my hand, getting Mr. Ryan's attention.

"Yes, Sam?" He walked over, carrying his copy of *Frankenstein*.

I showed him my hand. "Can I please go wash this off in the bathroom? I don't want to get it all over my books."

He nodded. "But try to be a little quicker than last time, okay? I don't want you to miss important information that will be on the test."

We'd just started the book and already he was thinking about the test. Typical teacher. "Will do." Shannon was applying her third or fourth coat of lip gloss as I left the room. As soon as I turned the corner, I grabbed my cell from my pocket and texted Dylan.

Bathroom. Now.

Two arms encircled me from behind, and Ethan's familiar scent hit me a second before his lips found my neck. "Texting me to meet you?"

Damn it! What was he doing here? "Um, I was just going to say I missed you. I promised Mr. Ryan I'd only be gone for a second. I just have to wash Shannon's lip gloss off my hand."

"Do I even want to know how it got there?" He flipped my hand over to see the smudge of red.

"She almost outed us to the class." We turned the corner. Dylan was approaching from the other direction.

"Hey, what are you doing here?" Ethan asked him.

Dylan's eyes flew to me. "Um…"

I prayed he wouldn't tell Ethan I'd asked him to meet me. "Did Shannon get her slimy lip gloss on you, too?" I asked, holding up my hand.

"No. I just needed to use the bathroom."

"It's down the other hall, man." Ethan laughed. "How long have you been going to this school? A month, and you still don't know where the guys' bathroom is?"

"Must have slipped my mind." Dylan's gaze lingered on me before he turned back down the hall.

I paused in the doorway, not letting Ethan follow me inside. "I really do have to get back to class right away."

He cocked his head to the side and gave me his puppy-dog eyes. He was so good at this look because of his killer eyelashes. I wished mine were as long as his. Combine that with his bluest-blue eyes, and it was hard to resist giving in to him.

"Not today." It broke my heart *and* his.

"Is it because of last night? Did I do something wrong? I thought you wanted to—"

"I did. It's not that. I promise. Everything's fine."

He still looked disappointed, but he nodded. "I'll wait for you and walk you back to class."

"No." I swallowed hard at how quickly I'd answered. "I just mean, if Mr. Ryan catches us together, he won't let me out of class anymore, and then we'll never get to sneak back to our stall again."

"I'm really starting to not like him, you know."

"He's not bad at all. Actually, he's one of my favorite teachers. Him and Ms. Matthews. And speaking of Ms. Matthews, I'll see you next period." I kissed him lightly on the lips. He groaned before reluctantly walking back to class.

I washed my hand, not expecting to have my meeting with Dylan after Ethan had almost caught us. But his reflection in the mirror made me jump. "You scared me." I whipped around.

"I wouldn't have if Ethan hadn't been with you. What was that about?" He stepped into the bathroom and motioned for me to follow him to the last stall. Ethan's and my stall. Too weird. I stayed outside, which prompted a suspicious look from Dylan. "What, you want me to get caught in here?"

"No, it's just that Ethan and I kind of meet in this stall."

Dylan rolled his eyes and moved one stall down. "Better?"

"Yes, thank you." I knew it was stupid, but since I was feeling weird around Dylan *and* I was going behind Ethan's back, I didn't want to add any more weirdness into the equation.

"So, why'd you text me to meet you if you were with him?"

"I wasn't with him at the time. He sort of snuck up on me. I couldn't text you and cancel. He would've asked who I was texting and when I said you, he'd want to know why."

"He still doesn't like me, does he?"

"He's over what happened before. He doesn't have a problem with you."

Dylan didn't look convinced, but he dropped it. "I'm guessing since you texted me, you know we need to stop him from doing magic. Make sure he can't tap into any dark magic again."

I still didn't believe it was dark magic causing the problem. How would Ethan even get access to dark magic? He had no reason to, and I doubted he had the first clue what it even was. But I didn't have time to explain all that to Dylan right now. Mr. Ryan was expecting me back in class. "Actually, I texted you because I wanted to let you know he's been fine. No problems at all. He hasn't done a single spell."

"Good. But that just proves my point. We need to bind his powers."

"I don't see how that will help. He's still learning. We have to teach him. Show him how to control the magic. Cutting him off from it isn't going to help. The magic is part of him. He won't feel right if he can't tap into it." I couldn't help but wonder if Ethan's efforts not to use his magic had anything to do with why he couldn't keep his hands off me. Maybe that pent-up energy was finding another outlet.

"So, this is about protecting his feelings? The only reason you don't want to do this is because he's your boyfriend and you don't want to upset him. What if it was Shannon? What if it was me? How would you feel then?"

"What if it *were* you? What if *your* magic was going haywire and the rest of us wanted to bind your powers? Would you still think this was the best solution?" My blood pressure was rising. If Dylan wasn't careful, he was going to get my fist in his face.

"I *was* in Ethan's position." He pushed past me and out of the stall.

"What?" I crossed my arms, waiting for him to explain.

"I did lose control of my magic once. Things got really bad. My parents wanted to bind my powers. I refused. I said the same thing you just said. I didn't want to be separated from the magic that was so much a part of me. My parents freaked—they turned their backs on me."

My mind raced to the conversation I'd had with Shannon. *Ask him why he wasn't in school before we formed the coven. Ask him where he's been and where his family is. Ask him what his last name is—his real one.* I was about to hurl those questions at Dylan, but he kept going on his own.

"Ben took me away. He looked after me. Helped me get control." Dylan sighed and met my eyes. He didn't look angry. He looked sad, like someone who had lost a lot. "I know you don't believe this, but I want to help Ethan. I want to fix what's wrong with his magic. But I'm not Ben, and since he's not around…" His stare turned icy, and it was all I could do not to turn away. "I'm doing the best I can."

He really didn't have a thing for me. I had it all wrong. Dylan had been looking out for Ethan. It wasn't about me at all. Well, except for the part where I took away the only family member who hadn't abandoned Dylan.

"You and Ben lived on your own?" I choked on Ben's name.

Dylan nodded.

"Where were you before you started school here? Did you and—?" I couldn't say his name again. "Did you just stay home and practice magic?"

"Ben said we had to stay under the radar. He hadn't exactly gotten my parents' permission to take me away. They tried to find us, and let me tell you, it's nearly impossible to stay hidden from a locator spell, especially when the people searching for you are blood relations. The connection is too strong."

"So, you were hiding from your parents?" That sounded all too familiar.

"Yeah, and believe me, you're lucky your parents don't know you're alive."

"Ethan's hiding from his family." I didn't know why I'd admitted that to Dylan.

"I figured as much. You two try to keep a lot of secrets, but it's hard to fool someone who's been in the same situation."

I finally uncrossed my arms. "Believe me, it's not the same situation."

"Oh no?" Dylan stepped toward me, and now that I wasn't afraid he liked me anymore, I stood my ground. "You mean you aren't in hiding because of magic?"

Okay, so we were. "Is that why you changed your last name? So your parents couldn't track you by it?"

"That wasn't because of my parents. I told you they could find me through a locator spell. The name change was for everyone else's sake. I couldn't have them trace me back to my real family. Not that anyone gave a damn about me or Ben. We were invisible. And after a while, our parents stopped looking for us. Disowned us, I guess."

But why? There had to be more to this. People didn't disown their kids for no reason. "What did you do? How did your magic go wrong?" Dylan obviously didn't want to talk about it. He would've explained more if he'd wanted to, but I needed some indication of what might happen to Ethan, how bad things might get.

"You sure you want to know?" He leaned back against the sink, trying to act casual, but the tension in his face said otherwise. "Because we're linked now. If I tell you what happened and you end up hating me, you're still going to have to be in the same coven with me. Can you handle that?"

I wasn't sure. He was seriously scaring me now, but if I didn't find out after all this, I'd never trust him again. I'd always wonder what horrible thing he'd done, and my mind would probably think up things that were ten times worse than the truth. "I want to know."

He stood up straight and looked down his nose at me. "I killed Ben's girlfriend." He walked out without another word, leaving me with weak knees and my stomach doing flips.

9

I LUNGED for the toilet and threw up my breakfast. I'd killed people. Multiple people. And that had only been a month ago. But somehow hearing Dylan say he was responsible for the death of his brother's girlfriend sent my cereal hurtling into the toilet. Dylan had been using magic his whole life. He should've had it under control. He had never returned from his grave a monster and the pawn in a witch's game of dark magic and revenge. I didn't know the details, but I could tell that Dylan blamed himself for the girl's death. And not in an it-was-just-a-tragic-accident sort of way.

My mind raced back to the way he'd reached for my hand in this very bathroom. Maybe he did have feelings for me. Maybe those feelings were pushing him to the edge and thoughts of Ben and his dead girlfriend were surfacing, confusing him. Maybe it all felt a little too familiar to Dylan.

No, he wouldn't hurt me. We were in the same coven. We were linked by magic. But Ben was his blood, his brother, and Dylan had killed his girlfriend. Had he fallen for her, too? Was it a jealousy thing? I had to find out more. I had to know if I was in danger around Dylan. But how would I find out? I couldn't exactly ask Dylan. Did Shannon know? She was the one who had told me to ask Dylan those questions. She might have been trying to warn me. I had to talk to her.

I splashed water on my face and rinsed my mouth. Luckily, I had gum in my pocket. I popped a piece in my mouth and headed back to class. Mr. Ryan shook his head at me as I entered the room. I went to his desk and whispered, "I'm sorry, but I got sick. It came on suddenly."

His expression softened. "Are you all right now? Do you need to see Nurse Wentworth?"

"No. I think it was just my breakfast not sitting right with me. I'm okay now."

"All right, but if you start to feel sick again, you have my permission to just leave."

"Thank you." Just leave. I could take Shannon with me as an escort. Then I'd be able to talk to her about Dylan.

I sat down and pretended to follow along for a few minutes. I texted Shannon under my desk. *Going to fake sick. U R taking me to nurse.*

She read the text and nodded her head slightly. Two seconds later, I was covering my mouth and rushing out of the room with Shannon following behind, carrying my stuff for me. I waited until we were around the corner before I took my shoulder bag from Shannon.

"So, where are we going?" she asked.

"The nurse. I'm sure Mr. Ryan will check up on me, so I have to at least show up at the nurse's office and pretend to be sick."

"I thought you wanted to talk to me. That's what it seemed like, anyway."

"I do. We'll have to use a bubble spell so Nurse Wentworth doesn't overhear us." The bubble spell was one of my favorites. You could talk and no one could hear you. They couldn't really see you, either. If they focused on you, they could see you, but they couldn't stay focused on you for long.

Shannon slowed her pace and grabbed my forearm. "Did something happen with Ethan?"

"No. With Dylan."

She let go as we went down the stairs. "Did he do something? Hit on you? Try to kiss you? What? The suspense is killing me."

"Nothing like that. Worse. I think." I was definitely relieved he didn't have a crush on me. It would've been disastrous for the coven, but this wasn't any better. If Dylan was a killer…

I knocked on Nurse Wentworth's door. I couldn't hear anything on the other side of it, so hopefully that meant the office was empty. More people around would mean we'd need to cast a stronger spell so we could talk. My nerves were distracting me, which wasn't going to help me focus on the spell in the first place.

The door opened, and Nurse Wentworth reached her hand out. "Passes, ladies?"

I shook my head. "Um, we don't have any. I was sort of sick in class, and Mr. Ryan said if I felt like I was going to be sick again, I should just come here. He didn't write me out a pass."

"And what about you?" She turned to Shannon.

"Mr. Ryan thought I should escort her. She's thrown up so much we were afraid she'd pass out on the stairs or something. I think she should lie down."

"Very well. You may go back to class. I'll handle this from here."

"No!" Shannon couldn't leave. I thought quickly. Mind-control spells weren't easy, and I hated the idea of putting one on Mrs. Wentworth, but I had to find out more about Dylan. If he was dangerous or not.

Mrs. Wentworth felt my head. "I think you may be running a fever."

"Can I please stay with her for a few minutes? Mr. Ryan won't mind at all. And that way I can update him on how Sam's doing when I go back to class." Shannon was good, and I was relieved she hadn't gone straight to the mind-control spell. What did it say about me that it had been my first thought?

Mrs. Wentworth sighed. "Fine. A few minutes. That's all."

"Thank you." Shannon smiled and took my arm, leading me to the cot in the back of the office. Seeing it and the ugly green curtain reminded me of Nora putting a spell on Mrs. Wentworth and making her fall asleep on that very cot so she and I could talk. God, I was no better than her.

"Lie down. I'll get the thermometer." Mrs. Wentworth walked to the cabinet on the opposite wall. Shannon pulled the curtain closed and started mumbling the bubble spell. I joined in. We had to work quickly. It wouldn't take Mrs. Wentworth long to locate a thermometer. I felt the barrier go up as Mrs. Wentworth started walking back toward us. She veered off to her right and sat down at her desk. We watched her filling out paperwork, forgetting we were even there.

"We're good," Shannon said. "Now, tell me what's going on."

"I talked to Dylan. I asked him the things you told me to ask him."

She lowered her head and played with a tear in the sheet on the cot. "Oh."

What, she was going to get all quiet on me now? She was the one who'd put me up to this. "Shannon, he told me about his magic going wrong, like Ethan's. He said his parents disowned him, and Ben took him away. He told me about Ben's girlfriend."

"Ben was a good guy. A bit of a hothead at times, but so is Dylan." By the soft tone of her voice, I could tell Shannon had had a thing for Ben.

"I'm sorry if this is hard to talk about."

She shook her head. "No. It's fine. I liked him. There. I said it. But everyone liked Ben. He was amazing, and wickedly powerful."

"What about his girlfriend? What was she like?"

"Not a witch, if that's what you're asking."

Not a witch? That was shocking. "How did he date her, then? Wasn't that risky?"

"Extremely. When he came here, she followed him. They were in love." She rolled her eyes. "Rebecca and I recognized the magic in Ben and Dylan right away. And Nora recognized the magic in Dylan, too. She saw the darkness in him. She was attracted to it."

"Don't tell me they dated." That would just be too weird.

"No. Nothing like that. She was only after his magic—well, more like finding out how he'd tapped into dark magic. Once she got what she wanted, by totally tricking him, she backed off. Lost interest. Dylan was a little hurt at first, but then…"

"What?" She couldn't get the words out quickly enough for me. I wanted all the information, like, yesterday.

"He started talking about Mindy a lot."

"Mindy? Was that Ben's girlfriend?"

"Yup. She was a redhead with long legs and boobs I would've killed for."

I gave her a look. This wasn't the time for jealousy. Besides, the girl was dead.

"Dylan obviously had a thing for her, but Ben never caught on. He was oblivious. I had my suspicions that Dylan used a spell on Ben to make sure he didn't notice. I never proved it, though, so I can't be sure. Still, everyone seemed to know. And Mindy led Dylan on. She liked his attention. Ben was running the coven. It had been his idea to form it in the first place. He was busy a lot, and that left plenty of time for Dylan and Mindy to get close."

"How close?" I wasn't sure I wanted to hear this, but if it helped me understand what Dylan had done and why, then I had to force myself to listen.

"I'm pretty sure they were sleeping together."

Oh, yuck! Dylan had sex with the same girl his brother was sleeping with? "That's so messed up!"

"I know. I wanted to tell Ben, mostly so he'd dump Mindy and pay more attention to me." That was Shannon, totally not shy about her intentions, even when they were completely selfish.

"But you didn't?"

"No." She looked away again. "I should've. Maybe it would've stopped Dylan. But knowing him, it probably would've made things worse. And it might have been me he came after instead."

"Came after? What are you talking about? Did he kill Mindy on purpose?" My stomach lurched again.

Shannon shrugged. "I can't say for sure, but I do know Mindy told Dylan she wasn't breaking up with Ben. She said the thing between her and Dylan was just for fun, nothing more. He pretended to be okay with it at first, but he was falling for her pretty hard. Finally, he told her to choose between them. So she did."

"And he killed her for it?"

"I don't know. I guess that's what happened."

"What do you mean, you *guess*? I thought you knew this story!" Had she really put me through this without knowing what had happened?

"I know the next day Ben found Mindy's body. She was in her apartment, in the bathtub."

"How did she die?"

"Her heart stopped, or something stopped her heart."

"Was it magic? Was it Dylan? He told me he killed her, but maybe she had heart problems. Maybe she had a heart attack. We can't be sure."

"I can." The curtain opened. Dylan stared down at us. My eyes immediately flew to Nurse Wentworth. She was oblivious to Dylan, too. He'd put a bubble spell on himself. The only reason why we could see and hear him was because we were witches, too.

"Did you do a locator spell to find us?" Shannon looked pissed.

"Oh what, you're the only one who can use spells to sneak up on people and spy on their conversations?"

He had a point there. I couldn't believe our happy little coven had been reduced to this. Lies, secrets, and snooping. What happened to the group spells and the good times?

"I knew you'd run right to Shannon." Dylan glared at me. "I shouldn't have run out on you like that. I should've explained things myself, but you were getting under my skin with all your questions and the way you stuck up for Ethan."

"Of course she's going to stick up for Ethan." Shannon stood up, getting in Dylan's face. "She loves him, so get over it. This crush you have on her is ridiculous. She doesn't feel the same way, and hell if I'm going to let you hurt her like you hurt Mindy."

Seeing Shannon stick up for me was surreal. She really *had* become my friend over the past month. But did she actually think Dylan would hurt me? That I'd end up like Mindy?

"Stop! Both of you. This isn't helping." I turned to Shannon. "Dylan doesn't like me. It was a misunderstanding."

Dylan cocked his head to the side and took a sharp breath. "You think I—"

"No." I waved my hands in front of me. "I was wrong. When we were talking in the bathroom yesterday, I thought maybe you had feelings for me. It was stupid, but when you reached for my hand…I don't know. I guess I jumped to the wrong conclusion. But I don't think that anymore. You're still mad at me about Ben. I get that, and I appreciate that you're being nice to Ethan and me after everything we've been through."

"I'm not mad at you about Ben." He lowered his eyes. "Do you want to know the truth about Ben and me?"

I thought I'd just found out the truth. About how Ben took Dylan away and helped him find his way back from the dark magic.

"I hated Ben." Dylan met my eyes again. "He took away the one thing I ever loved."

"Mindy." Her name came off my lips as a whisper.

"He didn't love her. She was a plaything to him. Someone to have a little fun with and buy him stuff. *I* loved her, but she was blindly in love with Ben. She could've had me. Just me. But she wouldn't give him up." Dylan's fists clenched. "I tried to tell Ben I'd fallen for Mindy. He told me it was only a crush, that I only wanted her because I envied what he had with her. He wouldn't listen. So I went to Mindy. She didn't listen, either."

"Dylan, I'm so sorry." I reached for him, but he pulled back.

"I did the only thing I could think of. I tapped into the dark magic I'd stopped using at Ben's insistence. I tried to change her heart. Make her love me and forget about Ben."

"But her heart stopped," I finished for him.

Dylan nodded. "I hated Ben from that moment on. I wished I'd killed *him* instead."

10

HE couldn't mean that. He couldn't be happy his brother was dead. Even if he did blame Ben for losing Mindy, it didn't add up.

"So," he smiled at me, "you did me a favor, really."

"Don't say that." I barely recognized this person. He wasn't the same Dylan I'd come to know. "You're not happy about Ben. I remember how you reacted when I told you what I'd done to him. You were beside yourself, Dylan. I don't know why you think you need to put on this act right now, but it's just Shannon and me. You don't have to pretend."

"I'm not pretending." His voice was loud. He ran his hands through his platinum-blond hair and turned around, avoiding my eyes. "Yes, I was upset. He was my brother. But he and I didn't exactly have the best relationship. We were dating the same girl."

"No, Ben was dating Mindy. You were just screwing around with her on the side." Typical Shannon, calling it as she saw it. I glared at her. She was so not helping. "What?" She shrugged like she couldn't figure out why I was upset with her.

"She's not wrong." Dylan turned toward us again. "I'd been using dark magic, and it changed me. I wasn't the same person I am now or was before it. Dark magic is dangerous, Sam. That's why I want to bind Ethan's powers. I don't want him to end up the way I did. I really did wish Ben dead after I killed Mindy. I almost killed him myself." He looked to Shannon.

Understanding hit me like a sucker punch. "No way. Shannon helped you?"

"Why is that so unbelievable?" She crossed her arms, looking offended.

"It's just that you two have been at each other's throats lately. I can't picture you getting through something that huge together."

"Well, we did," Dylan said. "Rebecca helped a lot, too." Why was I not surprised Nora wasn't among the helpful ones?

"Sam, I hate to say this, but maybe Dylan's right about Ethan. Binding his magic would buy us time to figure out what's wrong with him. Why he's tapping into dark magic all of a sudden."

No. There was another way. They'd just admitted it to me. "You didn't bind Dylan's powers. You helped him through it. We can do the same for Ethan."

Dylan glanced back at Nurse Wentworth. She was on her computer, which meant our spells were still holding up. "It's not that simple."

"Why?" I hated feeling like they didn't want to help Ethan. Like he was the newbie gone bad in their minds.

Dylan and Shannon shared a look. "We didn't do it alone," Dylan said.

"Who helped you?" A thought struck me. "You can't be talking about Nora. Please, tell me you're not." If Nora had been the only one strong enough to help Dylan stop using dark magic, Ethan was doomed.

"Yes and no," Dylan said, resting his hands on his hips.

Great. More riddles. "What does that mean?"

Shannon sat down next to me. "Nora told us about a witch she'd met once. She was wicked old and knew just about every spell there was."

"So this witch is the one who helped you."

Dylan nodded.

"Great. Then, let's get her. She can help Ethan." I jumped up, ready to rush out the door and hunt this witch down right now.

This time, when Dylan reached for my hand, he didn't pull away before making contact. His fingers felt strange in mine. We'd held hands before during spells, but this was different. Our eyes met. Oh crap. He'd lied. Or maybe he'd never denied his feelings. I couldn't remember. But they were there. I felt them in his touch.

"After she helped me, she told us never to contact her again." His voice was soft, sympathetic.

"Why?" I could barely speak. All I could think about was his hand on mine. Why was he still holding my hand, anyway? I wasn't running away anymore.

Shannon gave Dylan a suspicious look, and her eyes dropped to our joined hands. Finally, he let go. She knew it, too. It was out there.

"Dylan, why doesn't this witch want you to contact her?" I tried to bring the conversation back to helping Ethan and off Dylan's inappropriate feelings for me.

"When she drained the dark magic from me, it had to go somewhere. She tried to put it inside some crystals, but they shattered and…" He took a deep breath, like it was too difficult to continue. Instinctively, I reached for him, but I stopped. I couldn't do anything that would lead him on. I wouldn't be like Mindy. "The magic went into her."

I wasn't expecting that. "So, now she has dark magic in her. *Your* problem became *her* problem."

He nodded. "I felt terrible, but she left. She wouldn't let us try to help her. She said she never wanted to see us again."

My heart sank. Where did that leave Ethan? "There has to be someone else. Another witch who knows how to do this the right way. Who won't end up like…what was her name?" I didn't know why I wanted to know. I just did.

"Mirabella," Shannon said.

"Pretty name." Of course that might have been the only pretty thing left about her if Dylan's dark magic had consumed her. "Can we try to find another witch to help Ethan? Please?" My eyes stung at the thought of losing him, at him turning into what Dylan had once been.

"You aren't safe around him right now, Sam." Dylan stared at me with such intensity, like he was looking inside me. I felt naked. "You should start wearing the necklace I gave you. It will protect you from any spells Ethan might cast on you."

"He's not going to cast any spells on me!" That was absurd. "He loves me. He'd never hurt me."

Dylan sighed. "I loved Mindy, and look what happened."

"But you—"

"Were going through the same thing Ethan is."

My heart clenched in my chest. How could I be afraid of Ethan? How could I wear a necklace given to me by another guy to protect myself from the one I loved? "Ethan knows that necklace came from you. If I start wearing it again, he'll get suspicious."

"Tell him it matches the ring he gave you. You always wear that."

My ring! "Didn't you put a protection spell on the ring?"

"No." Dylan fidgeted. "I needed a personal belonging for the spell box. The ring was only in there because it belonged to you. It's not going to protect you from anything."

"And you can't put it back in the box because Ethan would notice that for sure," Shannon said.

Yes, he would. "And the box would only protect me at home anyway."

Dylan and Shannon stared at me, waiting for me to admit the inevitable. I had to wear the necklace. As much as I hated it, it was true. "Fine. I'll put it on as soon as I get home."

"Not good enough." Dylan stepped outside the curtain. "I'll go get it for you now. You should put it on as soon as possible."

I reached in my pocket for my house key, but Dylan put up his hand to stop me. "I've got it."

Right. There weren't many locks a witch couldn't get past. Dylan gave Shannon and me one last look before walking out of the nurse's office.

"You okay?" Shannon asked.

"Not really, but I'll deal. We should get this spell down. I want to get to sculpture. I should keep an eye on Ethan."

Shannon started removing the spell. The second it was lifted, Nurse Wentworth remembered we were there. She rushed over with the thermometer. "I'm so sorry. I guess I'm a little distracted this morning."

"No problem," I said. "I'm feeling a lot better. I think it was just my breakfast. It didn't agree with me."

"Best to take your temperature to make sure." She swiped the digital thermometer across my forehead and waited for the beep. "Well, you're perfectly normal."

"Great! I'll head back to class now. Thank you."

"Take it easy and eat a light lunch. I have crackers if you'd like some." I took them to appease her.

"Thanks again." I waved good-bye, and Shannon and I headed to second period. The bell was going to ring any minute, so there wasn't time to go back to Mr. Ryan's class.

"See you at lunch," she said. "Dylan should be back by then."

"Yeah, great, and Ethan will see him give me the necklace. How am I going to explain that?"

Shannon wrinkled her forehead as she thought. "Tell him Dylan took the necklace back because you broke the clasp. That way it will look like he fixed it and is returning it."

"And what's my reason for wanting it back? Ethan's not going to buy the 'it matches my ring' excuse."

She threw her head back. "Ugh! You're making this difficult."

"I'm trying to cover all the bases to avoid a blowup in lunch." She didn't quite get the history Ethan and Dylan had. I didn't want any of that to resurface.

"Fine." She huffed and shook her head, but then her eyes lit up. "All right, I've got it. Say the necklace is a reminder of your new life with Ethan. It signifies new beginnings and the magic you both share. Some mushy crap like that."

Yeah, except why would a necklace given to me by another guy remind me of Ethan? I was going to have to come up with something on my own. "Thanks. See you in lunch." I waved to her and walked to sculpture.

Ms. Matthews must not have had a first period class because she was sitting at her desk, finishing up an egg sandwich. I knocked on the open door. "Is it okay if I come in or do you want me to wait in the hall?"

She waved me in since her mouth was full.

"Thanks. I was in the nurse's office and didn't think there was time to go back to first period. I didn't want to be late for your class."

She threw the foil wrapper into the garbage and brushed off her hands. "No problem. I wanted to talk to you anyway."

Great. This had to be about Ethan's explosion in class yesterday. "About yesterday, I'm really sorry. I don't know—"

"Relax. It's fine. Over and done with. I don't blame you at all." The way she said it, emphasizing the word *you*, made me clutch the strap of my shoulder bag tighter.

"Oh. Is it my project, then? Because I know I'm a little behind. I've been having trouble focusing lately."

"It's not that, either. Although I do need your project by next Monday. I can't play favorites or the other students will get bent out of shape."

"Yeah, like Beth." It slipped out, and I stiffened immediately. "I'm sorry. I didn't mean to say that out loud." Why had I said that? I was usually so careful not to draw attention to the witch thing or my paranoia about Beth. I saved that stuff strictly for the coven.

Ms. Matthews leaned forward and folded her hands on the desk. "Has Beth been bothering you?"

"No, not really. She just keeps an annoyingly close eye on me. It's like she's waiting for me to do something. I'm not sure what—slip up somehow, I guess. And she's a total blabbermouth. She makes it her business to know everything about everyone, and then she tells the whole school. It's hard to have a secret around her." I clamped my mouth shut, willing myself to stop talking. I'd already admitted so much, and to a teacher of all people. The only thing worse would've been running up to Beth and yelling, "Guess what? I'm a witch!"

"Secrets can be difficult to keep, but over time, you get better at finding ways to cover them up. Even fool people." She picked up a saltshaker from her desk. I hadn't noticed it before. I backed up, trying not to look suspicious. I used to love salt, especially on egg sandwiches like the one Ms. Matthews had just eaten. But now that I was a witch, pure salt was strictly off-limits. I'd seen how it could burn a witch's skin on contact. I could only imagine what would happen if I ingested it.

Ms. Matthews held the saltshaker out to me. "Here."

I held one hand up, making sure not to touch the salt. "No thank you. I try to avoid salt. It makes me bloat." Quick thinking. Good.

"I don't think this will bother you." She pushed the saltshaker closer to me. "Go on. Try it."

11

WHERE was the bell? Why was time dragging on like this? Something had to be wrong. I would've killed for class to begin, for kids to rush in. Hell, I would've loved to see Beth right now. Anything to get Ms. Matthews to take the saltshaker away.

My eyes flew to the clock over the door. That couldn't be right. The clock had to be broken. No way could it still be the same time it was when I left Nurse Wentworth's office. I shook my head. Maybe I really was sick.

"Something wrong?" Ms. Matthews asked.

"Um, I forgot I was supposed to meet Ethan. He's probably wondering where I am. I should go. I don't want him to be late to class because he's looking for me." I rushed out of the room, and the second I stepped into the hall, the bell rang. Kids flooded the hallways. I stood there, trying not to get trampled. I took out my phone and texted Ethan.

Already at sculpture.

Twenty seconds later, I got a reply. *Everything ok?*

Yeah. I couldn't tell him about Ms. Matthews in a text. He'd freak out. And I definitely wasn't telling him about the plan Dylan, Shannon, and I had come up with. Although I was going to have to find a way to explain why I'd gotten sick first period and had to go see the nurse. Ethan was bound to find out about that, right? I thought about who was in that class. Tristan. Tristan would tell Beth.

Beth would question me, and with my luck, it would be in front of Ethan. Damn her!

My mind raced with excuses. Bad breakfast? No, I'd eaten cereal. Unless I said the cereal had tasted funny. It was our last box. We needed to go food shopping. I could say I hadn't wanted to waste the food, and since I'd just brushed my teeth, I hadn't really been sure if the funny taste was the cereal or the combination of cereal and toothpaste. God! I was back to lying to Ethan. This was supposed to have stopped after Nora's spell ended. I wasn't the monster anymore. So, why did I feel like one now?

"Man, I missed you." Ethan's arms wrapped around me from behind. I hadn't even seen him sneak up on me.

I turned to face him, feeling guilty for even concocting an elaborate lie. No more lies. I'd still avoid telling him what I thought he'd be better not knowing, but I wouldn't flat-out lie anymore, either.

"Where are you? Come back to me." He lightly kissed my lips. My stomach fluttered in the way only Ethan could make it feel.

I reached for his face, caressing his cheeks with my thumbs. "I missed you, too."

"Want to see if Ms. Matthews will let us try the pottery wheel again?" I must have looked horrified because he added, "I won't do anything. I promise. It will just be us making art." He leaned in, his lips tickling my ear. "No magic."

Impossible. There was always magic between us.

"Aw, look at the lovebirds." Beth was hugging her books to her chest and tilting her head at us. She really made it hard to like her. "The late bell is about to ring." She walked past us and into class.

Ethan laced his fingers through mine, raising my hand to his lips. "I guess that's our cue." He kissed my fingertips before leading me into the room. It was one of the last places I wanted to be right now. Ms. Matthews had totally freaked me out, and on top of that Beth was waiting for us at our table. "I feel like I'm practically dragging you. Is everything okay?"

I pulled Ethan back before we reached our table. "I need to tell you something, but not here. Not around Beth."

"Where? Bathroom?"

I glanced at Ms. Matthews. She wasn't like the other teachers.

She didn't have that clueless look to her. "No. She'd figure out we were sneaking off together."

"Then, what? A bubble spell?" His voice was barely a whisper.

"No. It's too risky. Beth sees things other people don't notice. What if she figures out something is up?"

"Ethan and Sam, please take your seats," Ms. Matthews said.

Ethan shrugged and led me to our table. Beth was all smiles. She reminded me of one of those scary clowns at the amusement park. I avoided her eyes, turning toward Ms. Matthews's desk. The salt-shaker was gone. At least that was one less thing to worry about.

Normally, Beth wouldn't shut up all period, so Ethan and I didn't get a chance to be alone. He could already tell something was up with me and Ms. Matthews, though. Not that it was hard to tell. I jumped every time she came near our table.

Beth laughed when I dropped the ceramic swan I'd worked on for two weeks. "What's gotten into you today? You almost busted up your project. Are you that worried about Ms. Matthews seeing it before it's finished?"

"No." What was I doing? She'd given me an excuse. "I mean, yes. I want it to be perfect. First impressions are important."

Beth shrugged. "Hey, how are you feeling? Any better?"

Ethan's head snapped in my direction. "Were you not feeling well?"

"I'm fine."

"That's not what I heard," Beth pressed as she continued painting her ceramic pot. She didn't make eye contact with me at all, which seemed to make her comments come out all that much more devious.

"Enlighten me." I couldn't help it. She was bringing out the bitch in me. That or I'd been hanging out with Shannon too much.

She glanced up, meeting my gaze. "Sorry. I just thought you'd be interested to know that practically the entire school is talking about you. I don't have to tell you about it, though. Forget I mentioned it." She lowered her head again.

Ethan narrowed his eyes at me and mouthed, "What's up?"

I shook my head. Not here. It would have to wait for lunch.

Class dragged on. Beth wouldn't talk to me, which was about the only good thing. Ms. Matthews kept glancing over at Ethan and me like she was waiting for us to make something else explode. She'd said she was over yesterday's incident, but clearly she wasn't. The second the bell rang, I grabbed Ethan's hand and tugged him from the room.

"Seriously, what's going on?" He pulled me into an empty classroom and shut the door behind us. I cringed as his hand waved and the lock clicked into place. Why had he used magic to do that? He could've turned the lock by hand.

"You don't have to use your magic for everything."

He tensed, stiffening up. "I don't. Why would you even say that? Have you been talking to Dylan or something?"

Yes. "This isn't about Dylan. I'm worried about you." I stepped toward him, running my hand down his arm and stopping when our fingers intertwined. "I don't want to see your magic get out of control."

"It's not. See?" He nodded toward the door. "Nothing bad happened."

I nodded. He was right. It wasn't like the door exploded or flew off its hinges. I was overreacting.

"So, what's got you so freaked? I hope all this isn't over the little clay mishap yesterday, because that was only a fluke."

I doubted that. "It's not that. I went to sculpture early, after I left the nurse's office."

"And why exactly were you in the nurse's office? Beth said she heard you were sick."

"I kind of threw up."

All the color drained from Ethan's face. "You're not... I mean, you couldn't be..."

Oh God, he thought I was pregnant! "No!" I pressed my palm to his chest, trying to calm him. His heart pounded with fear.

"You're sure?" His eyes darted back and forth between mine, and I could tell he was trying to calculate when I'd had my last period. This was too much. I had to tell him about Dylan.

"I threw up because I found out something really disturbing."

"More disturbing than getting pregnant at seventeen?" His voice shook. He wasn't getting over this.

"I promise I'm not pregnant. Please, relax and get that thought out of your head." I cupped his cheek, and he pressed his hand against mine.

"Okay. Go on. What did you find out?"

"Promise me you won't freak out."

His eyes widened. "Sam, I'm already freaked out. How much worse can it get?"

A lot. I took a deep breath. "Dylan told me something. Something bad."

"When? He's not in first period with you." Ethan's face twisted, anticipating news he wasn't going to like.

"We met in the bathroom."

"*Our* bathroom?" His voice was low and full of rage. He pulled away, making my hand drop from his face.

"I had to talk to him. It was important."

"What was so important that you needed to sneak off to the place you and I meet up during class? The place you and I…"

I knew it was our place, as strange as it was to call a bathroom "our place."

"Oh my God! You met him right after I left you. That's where you were going!" He grabbed his hair in his fists.

"Ethan, calm down. You're making more out of this than it really was." He was totally losing it. This wasn't like him at all. I reached for him, but he pushed me away. The shock on my face must have registered because he stepped toward me and wrapped his arms around my shoulders. My face was pressed against his cheek. I could sense the magic in him. I felt it swirling beneath his skin. "You have to get control over this. Dylan warned me."

Ethan pushed me back by my shoulders so we were looking each other in the eyes. "Dylan warned you about me?"

"Not like that. He's been in the same situation you're in now."

"I'm not in a situation, Sam."

"Yes, you are. Your magic is off. Did you notice the green energy swirling around the clay pot before the explosion?"

"Green energy?"

He hadn't seen it. "Yes, the same green energy that attacked Dylan and tried to strangle Shannon. I think you're creating it, Ethan."

"No." He let go of me and walked to the window, looking out over the quad. "I wouldn't do something like that. I wouldn't hurt Shannon or Dylan. Sometimes I'd like to punch Dylan in the face, but I wouldn't use magic on him."

"I don't think you're doing it on purpose." I wrapped my arms around him from behind. "I don't think you even know when you're doing it."

"So, Dylan warned you. Does he think I'd hurt you?" He turned to face me, his eyes filled with tears. "I'd never hurt you, Sam. You're everything to me."

My heart broke for him. "I know that." I pressed my lips to his. He needed me right now. He needed to see that things weren't changing between us just because his magic was acting strange. His kiss was hungry. His hands pulled me closer until our bodies were pressed as close as possible. I could barely breathe, but I didn't care. If this was what Ethan needed to do so that he could come to terms with what was happening to him and so that I could help him, then I was glad to do it.

He finally pulled away, completely breathless. He leaned his forehead on mine. "I love you."

"I love you, too. I promise we'll figure this out. Dylan is fine now. He got help from another witch, someone named Mirabella. She swore she wanted nothing to do with Dylan or the coven ever again, but I'll track her down and make her help you if I have to. I won't lose you to this. I won't let you end up like——" I'd said too much. My emotions were overwhelming me, and my mouth was running like a faucet.

"End up like what?" Ethan scrunched up his face. "You said Dylan is fine. He got help. What aren't you telling me? What don't you want me to end up like? What did Dylan say that made you throw up?"

My throat closed. How could I tell him this? I reached my hand up toward his face, but he grabbed it and lowered it to my side. I wasn't going to be able to distract him with another make-out session.

"Sam, you have to tell me. I'm not letting you leave this room until you do."

I opened my mouth, but only a sob escaped.

"My God, how bad is it?" Ethan rubbed my arms, both trying to calm me and steady me. I was shaking.

"Dylan said it's dark magic doing this to you. That's what it was for him, too. He was dating this girl, Ben's girlfriend actually."

"He dated his brother's girlfriend?" Ethan scoffed. "Wow, what a douchebag."

"Ethan." The seriousness of my tone stopped him from insulting Dylan any further. "He fell in love with her, but she refused to leave Ben. She said Dylan was a fling but she loved Ben. Dylan got upset. *Really* upset. And the magic inside him turned really dark."

I had Ethan's full attention now. "What did he do?" His hands shook on my arm. He was already guessing the answer.

"He tried to do a spell on her, to make her love him, choose him." I paused, gathering the strength to say the hardest part. "The dark magic took over. He stopped her heart."

"He killed her." Ethan's face was deadly white. "He loved her and he killed her." He let go of me and walked to the door.

"Where are you going?" I followed, but he put his hand up to stop me.

"Don't. You need to stay away from me, Sam. Dylan's right. If there's dark magic inside me… I won't let you end up like that girl. I won't be responsible for…" He shook his head and walked out.

"Ethan!" I ran to the door and peered out into the hallway. No sign of him. He was gone, and something told me he wasn't coming back.

12

I DROPPED to my knees, sobbing. The ache inside was overwhelming. I couldn't breathe. I couldn't move. It felt so much like when my body used to give out on me and I needed to feed. But this wasn't the monster killing me. This was a broken heart.

I heard footsteps coming down the hall and summoned all my strength to cast a bubble spell. I couldn't let anyone see me like this, and I didn't have the will to get myself up off the floor. I sobbed in my protective shield. Every time I closed my eyes, I saw the terrified look on Ethan's face. He wouldn't let himself put me in jeopardy. If he thought there was even the slightest chance he'd hurt me, he'd take off for good. I'd never see him again. I couldn't live without him. Not after everything we'd been through. He was my life now.

Two hands snaked under my arms and lifted me. Had I dropped my spell? I swatted at the hands. "Relax, it's me," Shannon said. I sank in her arms. "Easy. I don't want to have to use magic to hold you up. You feel like a lead weight right now." She half-dragged me into the classroom, the same one Ethan and I had been in. Ethan. He was gone. Possibly for good. My sobbing got louder and more out of control. "Sam!" Shannon yelled in my face and shook me by my shoulders. "Get a grip. I can't help you if you can't tell me what's wrong. Now get a hold of yourself before I smack you across the face to snap you out of this."

My bottom lip sucked into my mouth, and I bit down on it. I

needed a different pain to focus on. The one in my heart was killing me.

"Better now, or should I warm up my hand for that slap?" She wasn't really going to hit me—at least I didn't think so. She was trying to ease the tension, distract me until my sobbing got under control. "Good. Now that you're breathing semi-normally, tell me what happened."

"Ethan." My body shook at the mere mention of his name. Shannon raised her hand in warning. "I told him what Dylan said, what Dylan did to Mindy."

"What? Are you an idiot?" Shannon threw her hands in the air. "Let me guess—he took off?"

I nodded, tears streaming down my cheeks.

"Damn it! When are couples in love going to realize telling the truth all the time just gets people hurt? Screw open, honest relationships. Sometimes you need to lie to protect the person you love."

I knew all about that. I'd lied to Ethan for too long now. "I couldn't lie to him anymore. And I thought telling him about Dylan would make him see he needs to be careful with his magic."

"Yeah, because guys always listen to reason." Her sarcasm cut through the air between us. "Guys are idiots. You have to tell them how to act and feel."

"That's ridiculous, Shannon. You don't really believe that." Or maybe she did, and that explained why she got turned down by a lot of guys despite her appearance.

"Whatever. Believe what you want, but Ethan's gone. I think that proves my point."

"We have to get him back. You have to help me. If we go right now, we can catch up with him. He doesn't have that much of a lead on us." I tugged on her hand.

"Not going to work." She shook free. "I did a locator spell on both of you. That's how I found you in the hallway. Your bubble spell was pathetic, probably because you were too busy crying to maintain it. Ethan, on the other hand, has one kick-ass shield on himself right now."

"Are you telling me there's no way to locate him?"

"No. I'm saying it's going to take time and we'll need Dylan's help."

Dylan. He probably had my necklace by now. If we did find Ethan, he'd know exactly why I was wearing the necklace. It would prove to him that I didn't trust his magic around me. I wasn't going through with it. I couldn't. I'd lose him forever if I did. I had to find him and show him I believed in him. Believed in us. What we had was stronger than dark magic. It had to be.

Shannon took out her phone and texted Dylan. "He'll be here in a second."

Great, another person to yell at me for telling Ethan about Mindy. Dylan definitely wasn't going to be happy with me. That had been his secret to tell. Shannon and I stood there in silence, neither knowing what to say. We knew we had to find Ethan. After that, we didn't have a plan.

Dylan walked into the room, holding my necklace out in front of him. "Here. Put this on."

I shook my head. "No. I've decided I'm not going to wear it."

"What?" Dylan and Shannon said, sharing a look.

"Ethan's gone."

"He's gone?" Dylan looked around as if he expected Ethan to magically appear in the room. "What happened?"

Shannon crossed her arms. "She told him."

"Told him what?" Dylan practically growled at me.

"About Mindy." My voice was as small as I felt.

"Damn it, Sam!" Dylan balled his fists, and I stepped back. He looked at his hands and then me. "I'm not going to hit you! What, I tell you my secret and now you're not going to trust me?" Could he really blame me for being on edge around him? He'd admitted to murder. "*You* killed more than one person, and I'm still talking to you. Hell, I'm still trying to help you. Though right now I'm not sure why."

"Okay, lay off." Shannon stepped between us. "Sam made a mistake. She knows that. You two will be fine…eventually. We don't have time to worry about it now. Ethan took off. He's afraid he'll hurt Sam. We have to find him before the dark magic consumes him."

"Fine," Dylan said through tight lips. "We'll do a locator spell."

"Already tried. He's using a spell to shield himself."

"He's using magic?" Dylan's eyes bugged out. "Sam tells him his magic is dark and he decides to go ahead and use it? What a moron!"

"Stop it!" My body shook. I couldn't take this anymore. "He's confused. That's more reason why we need to find him as soon as possible."

Dylan exhaled loudly and gazed out the window. "We need to go somewhere else to do a spell of this size. I need a few things, too." He faced us again, his eyes not resting on mine for long. "Go to the clearing. I'll meet you there as soon as I get the supplies I need." He stormed out, leaving me feeling like the black sheep of the coven.

Shannon and I used a bubble spell to get out of the school undetected. We were able to walk right past the school cop and through the front doors. At least one thing had gone right. Shannon drove since Ethan had taken his car. I sat in the passenger seat, staring at the leaves falling from the trees. Usually fall was my favorite time of year. Now every leaf that fell made me think of the things I'd lost in my life. My family, my friends, my real name, and now possibly Ethan.

It took me a moment to realize the car had stopped moving. We were in the clearing. I got out and ran to our meeting place. Dylan couldn't get here quick enough for me. I wanted this spell over with so we could find Ethan and bring him back. I needed to be with him. He might have dark magic inside him, but I could help him. I knew I could.

Shannon jogged after me. "Hey, slow down. Dylan isn't even here yet. There's no point in running."

"You don't have to run with me," I snapped at her. She didn't get it. I had to do something. Standing around, waiting for Dylan or casually strolling through the woods, wasn't going to get anything accomplished. At least running burned some of this energy inside me before it consumed me.

"Sam, stop!"

Something tugged at my waist, gently at first, but as I tried to push past it, it pulled back with more force. "Knock it off, Shannon!" How dare she use magic on me!

"No." She was in front of me now, her long, auburn hair blowing wildly behind her. "I won't stop. I'm not the one out of control here. In fact, I'm the only sane one left in our coven."

I'd never wanted to spit in someone's face so badly before. She was holding me back, and even though Ethan wasn't in these woods, even though I couldn't run him down, I had to move. "Get this spell off me. Now! Don't make me show you what I'm capable of. I have twice the power you do."

She threw her hands out to her sides. "Go ahead, Sam. Become your boyfriend, and Dylan before him." She stepped closer, getting right in my face. "Are you an idiot? You've seen what abusing your magic can do. Your emotions are beyond reason right now. If you tap into your magic, you'll be no better off than Ethan is." She stared into my eyes, her anger turning to sympathy. "And who will save him then?"

I stopped fighting the magic wrapped around my waist. Instead, I let it hold me up, support the pain I was feeling inside. "This is my fault, Shannon. All of it. Ethan wouldn't be a witch if it weren't for me."

She rolled her eyes. "Yeah, it's your fault you died of cancer at seventeen. That makes a whole hell of a lot of sense."

"It was selfish of me to continue dating him after I was diagnosed. I knew I was going to die, and I let him stick around for it. I let him watch me wither away." Tears choked my words. "All Ethan ever did was love me, and now he's being punished for it."

"Stop." She grabbed my shoulders and shook me. "What the hell do I have to do to knock some sense into you? Ethan made his own choices. Do you really think he would've left your bedside even if you did break up with him?"

No. He would've forced his way in. He would've found a way to be with me until the end. Just like he'd found a way to bring me back from the dead. "He doesn't deserve this."

"I know. I want to help Ethan, too, but what you're doing right now isn't working. You have to get a hold of yourself. You said it yourself; you have more power than I do. You're the strongest member of the coven. This locator spell won't work without you." She made it sound like she wasn't even sure it would work *with* me, and that sent chills through me.

"Sam, if we lose you, too…" She shook her head. "Dylan can't come back from dark magic twice. It will kill him. Mirabella told us dark magic takes a toll on the person who uses it. It comes with a price. Dylan paid part of that price when he took Mindy's life." Her eyes watered. "If he turns to dark magic again, it will be *his* life on the line this time."

Something in her eyes gave away the slightest bit of heartbreak. She'd never talked about Dylan as anything other than a member of the coven. Did she feel more for him?

"I know what you're thinking, and the answer is no. I don't have a thing for him. He's like family to me."

"What about Tristan?" She had a brother already. Why would she view Dylan that way when she tried so hard to avoid her own flesh and blood?

"Yeah, well, in case you haven't noticed, Tristan and I have nothing in common. So much for the whole twin-bonding thing. I mean, he has no clue I'm a witch. How is that possible?"

I'd heard about studies where twins could practically read each other's minds and feel each other's pain. Tristan and Shannon weren't anything like that. "I'm sorry. I didn't think it bothered you. I kind of thought you were ashamed to be related to Tristan. That's what he thinks, anyway."

"I'm not ashamed of him." She turned away, but I could tell she was crossing her arms in front of her, giving herself a hug. I would've hugged her if I wasn't still being held up by her spell. "Do you know my parents think he's the popular one?"

"What? How?" Tristan didn't have many friends. He kind of kept to himself most of the time. Now he had Beth, but she was the first girl I'd seen him even talk to other than me, and I was pretty sure she was still dating Mark, too.

"Because I let them believe that." Her tone wasn't superior, like she was saying they only thought it because she allowed them to. This was her way of saying she'd done a little magic on her parents.

"You really need to stop messing with people's heads like that, Shannon. How is that not tapping into dark magic?"

"Because I give them the choice to believe me or not." She turned back to me. "I only put suggestions in people's heads. I don't command them or tell them they have to believe what I say. They have the free will to think what they want after I put the suggestion there."

"But why'd you do it? Why'd you suggest to your parents that Tristan is popular? What's the point?"

"He's kind of a loser." Her voice was small. "I love my brother, Sam. I hate that people talk about him behind his back and sometimes even to his face. Tristan looks for our parents' approval." She shrugged. "So, I did what I could to make sure he got it."

Wow. All this time I'd thought Shannon couldn't stand her brother, but she'd been protecting him in her own weird way. She mumbled under her breath, and the energy surrounding me disappeared. I was free. "You do know he'd have an easier time at school if you'd be nicer to him, talk to him a little."

"He's a nice guy. Hanging out with Shannon the Bitch wouldn't get him any popularity points."

Hearing her talk about herself that way made my stomach churn. "You're not a bitch. I wish you'd let people see the real you once in a while."

"She can't." Dylan walked up to us with a wooden box and some herbs. "She's a witch. People don't respond well to that sort of thing." He arranged the box and herbs in the middle of the campfire. "Stay back. This is going to flare up and fast." He reached into his pocket and pulled out a toothbrush.

"Is that Ethan's?"

"I needed a personal effect."

"So you broke into my house for the second time today. Just great."

"Do you want to argue or do you want to find your boyfriend?" He glared at me for a moment before turning back to the campfire. He said a spell while waving over the twigs. They burst into flames, igniting the box and the herbs inside. "Stand back." Dylan dangled the toothbrush over the fire, letting the flames lick at the bristles. He motioned for us to join him.

Shannon and I joined hands. We weren't a circle by any means. More like an awkward triangle. Dylan began the spell, and Shannon and I repeated each line after he said it. On the third time through, we were in unison with him. Dylan dropped the toothbrush into the flames and the fire erupted. It danced through our joined hands now that Dylan had completed the triangle. I knew the flames wouldn't hurt me, but it was still surreal to see my skin touching fire and not burning.

An image appeared in the flames. "Ethan." My voice was a whisper.

"Don't break the spell," Dylan warned. The image began to shimmer and fade.

I joined back in. We couldn't lose him now. Ethan was looking out at the river. The sun reflected off the tears on his cheeks. He was in our spot. The mountaintop. I should've known he'd go there. But then again, why would he? I would've thought he'd go somewhere I'd never look. That he'd stay hidden. Yet there he was, out in the open, like he was waiting to be found.

He stepped forward. Rocks and dirt at his feet tumbled over the side of the ledge. Realization hit me, doubling me over in pain. He hadn't gone to our spot to wait for me. He'd gone to die. He was going to jump.

13

"**E**THAN!" My scream shook the surrounding trees. Birds scattered, flying off. Leaves fluttered to the ground. Ethan's image disappeared.

"Sam." Shannon's wide eyes pleaded with me to stop, to get control.

My body trembled with magic. I was tapping into it without meaning to. It was responding to my fear. "How do we get to him?" My eyes darted back and forth between Dylan and Shannon. "How?" There had to be some magical way to teleport—something. "He can't die. Tell me how to get there!"

"You can't." Dylan's voice was stern but caring. "We can't fly or teleport or anything like that."

"But she can astral project," Shannon said.

I didn't know that was a real thing, but I'd heard of it. There wasn't time to debate or even think. "Tell me how."

Shannon rushed over to me and placed her hands on my shoulders. "You need to center yourself. Calm your breathing." Like that was possible right now. Ethan was about to end his life—and mine with it. "You have to picture yourself leaving your body, and then visualize yourself with Ethan." This seemed crazy, but I didn't have any other options. Dylan came to my side and placed one hand on my shoulder next to Shannon. They both started breathing deeply, and I could feel my lungs respond to them, mimicking them. My heart rate slowed. I closed my eyes and pictured my astral-self floating out of my body.

"Find him." The voice was in my mind, but I knew it was Shannon. As much as it pained me, I visualized the image of Ethan standing on that cliff. I heard the rocks slipping from the edge. I smelled the dirt beneath his feet.

"Sam?" Ethan said.

I opened my eyes. It had worked. I was on the edge of the mountain with Ethan. He looked shocked, like he had no idea how I was there with him. "Ethan, don't! You can't jump. You can't leave me. You brought me back. I shouldn't be here, and without you I don't want to be here. We're in this together. All of this. If you jump, I'll go with you. I'll get back to my body and follow you out here for real."

"No." He shook his head and waved me off. "Don't even talk like that. You're supposed to live. That's why I have to do this. I won't be responsible for hurting you, Sam. I won't let myself kill the one person I have left in this world." He reached for me, but I wasn't in my physical body. I was nothing more than a ghost.

"We've both lost everything. *Everything.* You're all I have left. If you do this, all we've been through will be for nothing."

"You'll get to live without having to worry about me ending up like Dylan." He stepped closer to the edge again and peered down. "This is the only way. I love you, Sam."

Out of my body, I couldn't access any magic. I was powerless in that sense. So, I used the only thing I could think of. "You selfish bastard!" He turned, looking more hurt than I'd ever seen him look. "This is what you brought me back for? What, is this payback? I made you watch me die of cancer, so now you're going to make me watch you kill yourself? If that's what this has come to, then I wish you would've left me to rot in my grave!"

I felt my hold on my astral-self slipping. My emotions must have been pulling my physical body out of its relaxed state. I hoped Dylan and Shannon could keep my breathing and heart rate steady, just for a little while longer.

"You think I'm doing this to hurt you?" Ethan stepped toward me again. "You know I'd do anything to keep you safe."

"Then come back to me. I'm at the clearing with Dylan and Shannon. We know how to help you. Let me save you the way you saved me. Please, Ethan. Please."

He stared at me, debating all of this. Weighing his options. "You'd really kill yourself if I jumped?"

"I wouldn't have to. My heart would stop the second you jumped. Sending my body over that ledge after you would just be a way to dispose of the remains."

His head lowered, and he looked lost. "I can't risk hurting you. I won't jump, but I have to get away from you. I have to leave, and you can't follow me. You have to promise you won't come after me." He raised his head to meet my eyes.

"There's something else we can do. A way to protect me so you can stay."

His eyes bored into mine. "Sam." He didn't believe me. He thought I was grasping at straws. Maybe I was, but I wasn't going to let him walk out of my life, especially when his own future was so up in the air.

"It's true, Ethan. Dylan wants me to wear the necklace he gave me. Remember how it protected me from Nora's magic?" I had no idea why I'd wanted it back after Nora had stolen it. Maybe my witchy magic had been able to predict something like this happening. Maybe deep down I knew I'd need that protection again some day.

"You think it will protect you from me?" I could tell the words pained him. He couldn't bear the thought of losing control, of using magic on me.

"Dylan thinks so."

Ethan's head jerked. He didn't like the uncertainty one bit.

"He *knows* it will. Nora wouldn't have stolen it if it wasn't effective. It'll work."

Ethan was quiet for a moment. This was a lot for him to process. He was going through something I couldn't even imagine. Well, maybe I could. I tried to be patient, but my nerves were making it harder and harder to stay in my astral body, to keep from returning to the clearing with Dylan and Shannon.

"Okay, but I'm not coming near you until you're wearing the necklace. And even then, I'm keeping some distance."

"What does that mean?" We lived together. How much distance could he get?

"I'll see if I can stay with Dylan."

"No! Ethan, this is crazy. The necklace will work. We can even test it if you need proof."

His eyes widened. "I'm not using magic on you to test whether or not the necklace will block it. You can't ask me to do that." He was breathing hard. Things were going in the opposite direction of how I wanted them to.

"Okay, we'll figure it out. Just come to the clearing. I'm there with Dylan and Shannon. Dylan has the necklace. I'll have it on long before you meet us there."

"I'm serious about the distance."

I couldn't argue with him, not when I needed him to get off this mountain and come to the clearing. "I know." I wasn't going to lie and say I agreed or was okay with his decision.

"I'll see you in the clearing." He didn't move, and neither did I. "What is it?"

I hated not trusting Ethan, but I had to see him get in his car and drive away. I had to make sure he wouldn't go back on our deal. "You first. It will only take me a second or two to get back."

"You think I'm lying? That I'm just waiting for you to leave and then I'm going to hurl myself over the edge?"

"I think the dark magic inside you is clouding your thoughts. Humor me. Please."

He sighed and walked to his car. His eyes never left mine. He was hurt. I'd never not trusted him before. I knew how this seemed to him, but I was only trying to protect him. He peeled out on the gravel and down the hill. I stepped forward, looking out over the edge of the mountain. I'd loved this view. This had been one of my favorite places to be with Ethan. Now, it would never be the same.

I closed my eyes and pictured my astral-self reuniting with my body in the clearing. Dylan's and Shannon's faces filled my mind. It must have been working, because they smiled as I sailed closer to my body. I opened my eyes, and I was standing in front of the fire. Ethan's image was still showing in the flames. He was in his car, and he was almost here.

"I need the necklace." I held out my hand to Dylan.

He reached into his jacket pocket. "That was the only way you were able to convince him to come back, wasn't it?" I nodded and grabbed the necklace from his hand. He kept hold of the chain. "Turn around." He wanted to help me put it on. I looked at Shannon for help. This was weird. With all the questions about Dylan's true feelings for me, I didn't want him helping me put on the necklace he'd given me. "You're not alone in this, Sam. Stop acting like you have to do everything on your own."

Maybe he was right. Maybe I was being stupid. I swept my hair to one side and turned around, letting Dylan fasten the necklace for me. His hand grazed my neck, and I felt the slightest electrical charge. I twisted my head to look at him, to see if he'd done it on purpose. His cheeks reddened. No. He hadn't done it on purpose, and that proved one thing. He did have feelings for me. I stepped toward Shannon, putting distance between Dylan and me. "Ethan will be here any minute. I want to meet him."

"He knows the way here," Dylan said. "Give him time. This can't be easy on him." Dylan would know. I had to trust him. I nodded, but I continued to watch the Ethan-cam going on in the fire. Guilt churned my stomach. Not being able to trust Ethan was killing me. I just wanted to see him, wrap my arms around him, and tell him I loved him. I wanted to make him better.

Shannon placed her hand on my shoulder. "Relax. He'll be here soon."

"It's taking forever." My voice shook. Damn it, I didn't want to cry.

"It only seems that way to you."

The sound of tires on gravel stopped our conversation. The image in the fire burned out. Ethan was here. I ran to the edge of the clearing, looking for signs of him. He'd walk the rest of the way from where we usually parked. My heart pounded so loud I couldn't hear anything else. His red shirt broke through the trees lining the edge of the woods. Instinctively, my hand reached for the necklace. "Please work." I started toward Ethan, but he raised his hand to stop me.

"Stay back, Sam. Please." He veered to my right, going toward Dylan. Dylan's eyes met mine, and he nodded. He was going to help Ethan any way he could. It was strange to see the two of them seeking each other out like this. They weren't friends. The coven had joined them, but that was all. Until now. The dark magic was giving them a common bond.

"Glad you came back, man." Dylan put his hand on Ethan's shoulder.

Ethan nodded. "I could use a place to crash until…this is over." I didn't like the way he'd said that. Like he thought this was going to end with his death.

I moved closer, and Ethan stepped behind Dylan. He was truly scared to be around me. "Dylan, tell him the necklace will keep me safe. He doesn't have to move out."

Shannon wrapped her arm around me. "Ethan, watch." Her eyes closed, and she mumbled a spell. When she opened her eyes again, she looked me up and down. "See? Nothing. If my spell had worked, she'd be covered in pig's blood."

I backed away from her. "What? Why would you try to do that to me?"

"Because the spell had to be unfriendly. The necklace protects you from spells meant to harm you in some way. If I would've done something lame like curled your hair, the necklace wouldn't have stopped the spell."

"How would pig's blood hurt her?" Dylan asked.

Shannon shrugged. "I may have added something about the pig's blood attracting a wild animal. A *hungry* wild animal."

I turned and smacked her hard on the shoulder.

"What? I was trying to help." She looked to Dylan and Ethan, but they didn't come to her defense. "It proves the necklace works and Ethan doesn't have to stay away from you. You should be thanking me." She was always doing stuff like this and then thinking I should be grateful. The girl's social skills were definitely lacking.

Ethan moved a few steps closer, his eyes going back and forth between Shannon and me. "You really tried to do that to her?"

"If you don't believe me, try a spell yourself." Shannon stepped aside, motioning I was all Ethan's.

I stared at him, knowing he wouldn't try anything. He was too afraid to.

"Seriously, man, if you don't at least try something, you're never going to relax around her." I knew Dylan was only trying to help, but asking Ethan to do this was too much.

Ethan took a few more steps. If I reached out, I'd be able to touch him. "Sam, what do you think?"

Was he asking for permission to try a spell out on me? "I think the necklace works."

He stood there staring at me. His hands rose, and my body stiffened. He was going to cast a spell. My Ethan was going to test the strength of the necklace. I winced as his hands moved closer. My eyes shut, and the next thing I knew, his arms wrapped around me. Tears spilled down my cheeks, and I squeezed him tightly. I was so happy to have him in my arms again, to breathe in his scent.

14

ETHAN insisted on sleeping on the couch. He said he felt a little more in control and able to believe in the necklace's protective spell when he was awake, but at night, when he wasn't fully aware of his surroundings, was a different story. I wanted to protest, but at least I'd gotten him to agree to come home. Baby steps. This was only temporary. Still, I stayed on the couch with him for hours. We called Gloria and Jackson, and for the first time ever, we called out sick from work. I felt guilty for lying, but the part about neither of us being in any shape to wait tables or cook food was true. We were both feeling off. Gloria understood and said she'd have Jackson make a big pot of chicken noodle soup for us. She told us to swing by in the morning before school and they'd have it ready for our lunches. I thanked her and hung up the phone.

"How are you feeling?" I asked, snuggling against Ethan's side.

"Like I might explode at any moment."

I lifted my head. "Why? Are you angry about something?"

"Yes. I'm angry that I'm in this situation. That I have dark magic inside me. That I'm a threat to you and the others."

I sat up, using his shirt to pull myself closer to him. "We'll fix this. You'll be back to your old self in no time. Dylan texted me to say he's going to try to track down Mirabella. And in the meantime, you have me to watch over you. I've got the power of two witches. I'll keep you safe."

"You know, when we first got our powers, I stupidly thought it was like a reward for all we'd been through. Everything with Nora was pure hell. The magic sort of made up for it. But now…I wish I wasn't a witch—or warlock or whatever you call it. I'd give the magic back in a heartbeat."

I didn't know how to respond to that. I got what he was saying. He wanted our lives to be normal again. This was supposed to be our second chance at happiness. But I loved being a witch. When I'd had cancer, I had no power over what was happening to me. Now, I had so much power. I could control things. I wasn't defenseless.

I reached for his face, tracing my finger along his jaw and gently pulling his chin toward mine. My lips brushed his.

He pulled away. "Sam, don't. I don't want to lose control. It's too risky. Every time we're close, I can't think straight."

"I'll stay in control for the both of us." He shook his head, but I cradled his face and pressed my lips to his. He resisted for a second, so I gently bit his lower lip, tempting him.

"Sam." I loved when he said my name like that. Like a sigh. His lips parted, and he gave in to me. I kissed him, deeply, passionately. I wanted him to feel loved. To know what we had was stronger than the dark magic inside him. We'd get through this together. I'd make sure of it. Somehow, I was in his lap. I tugged on his shirt, trying to get it over his head. He reached for mine, but stopped.

"What's wrong?" I trailed kisses down his neck.

"I can't do this." He picked me up and placed me on the couch next to him.

"Ethan, you won't lose control. We'll both be fine." I was breathing heavily.

"You have no idea what being that close to you does to me. I'm already losing it. I can feel the magic going crazy inside me." He stood up, running his fingers through his hair. He paced the length of our tiny living room. I wouldn't have doubted he could run a marathon with all the adrenaline he was holding in.

"Okay. I'm sorry. We can just sit here together."

He stopped and looked at me. "I think I need to be alone for a little while. Clear my head."

"I'll make us some dinner. You can relax and watch TV." I got up and headed to the kitchen. I knew there was nothing dinner-like to make. Our cabinets had cereal, protein bars, and pretzels. We ate all our major meals at school or at the diner. We never had a reason to cook anything here.

"Why don't you go see if Jackson made that soup yet?" Ethan leaned on the counter, watching me stare at the almost-empty cabinets. "You can even stay and work for a while if you want. I'll be fine here on my own."

He was testing me. Trying to see if I trusted him. "Tell you what. I'm not up to serving food right now, so I'll go pick up the soup and bring it back home. That should give you some time to yourself, and then we can watch a movie until we're ready to go to sleep."

He nodded and leaned forward to kiss my forehead. "Thanks for understanding."

I'd made him wait almost an eternity before I was ready to be with him that way. This was the one and only time he'd turned me down. I owed him a little understanding. "I'll be back soon." I grabbed the car keys off the counter, threw on my jacket, and headed outside.

I nearly dropped the keys when I saw Dylan leaning against the driver's-side door of the car. "What are you doing here?"

"Checking up on you guys." He stood up straight. "How's he doing?"

"Okay."

"You're a bad liar." He stepped aside so I could get in the car. "Sam." He held the door so I couldn't shut it. "You're the best and worst thing for Ethan right now. You have to be careful."

"Best *and* worst? What's that supposed to mean?" I was seriously sick of people talking in riddles.

"He needs your support, and he may even need your magic to calm him down at times." He raised his eyebrows at me. "But what he doesn't need is you throwing yourself at him and making him lose control."

I narrowed my eyes at him. "Were you spying on us?"

"Relax. I didn't see anything. It was only a listening-in kind of spell. I stayed right here by your car the whole time."

I reached for my necklace. "I wish this thing blocked eavesdroppers. Now would you let go of the door? I have to go get our dinner."

"I'll stay here and keep an eye on him until you get back." Dylan stepped back. It was hard to be mad at him when his intentions were good.

I nodded. I couldn't thank him for being nosy, even if I did sort of appreciate it. I closed the door and backed out of the driveway. Ethan's Mazda 6 had some speed, and I tested that out on the way to the diner. I didn't want to be gone too long. I parked in our usual spot and rushed inside. The place was slammed. Guilt washed over me. How was I going to run in and out with Gloria in over her head like this?

Her eyes lit up the second she saw me. "Oh, thank goodness, Samantha." It came out as one long sigh of relief.

"Gloria, I'm sorry. I really can't stay. Ethan's at home, and he's really sick. I was hoping Jackson had that soup ready so I could bring some to him."

Her face fell. "Of course. Go right on back and help yourself. Don't you worry about me. I'll be fine."

I doubted it. There was only one way I was going to get out of there without a guilty conscience. Magic. "Hang on." I grabbed my apron behind the counter and tied it on. The coffee pot was empty, six tables needed to be cleared, and through the kitchen window, I could see plates of food sitting under the heat lamps. I turned away from any watching eyes and mumbled a spell. A simple spell of speed. I couldn't overdo it or people would notice something was different about me—something supernatural. I felt a tingling run through my limbs, like adrenaline fueling every part of my body. Quicker than humanly possible, I brewed a fresh pot of coffee, cleared the dirty tables, wiped them clean for new customers, and brought the plates of food to the tables. Jackson didn't even have time to say hello before I was out of the kitchen.

"There," I said, out of breath. "That should do. I gave tables six and eight their checks. Tables four, seven, and nine have their orders placed. And it looks like the crowd is dying down. I'm going to grab that soup and head home to Ethan."

Gloria's mouth hung open. "Samantha, how on earth did you move that quickly?"

I shrugged. "I guess I'm feeling better." I squeezed her hand before disappearing in the kitchen. Jackson made me take enough soup and crackers to feed an army. Ethan and I would be able to eat for days. He even threw in a leftover piece of Ethan's lasagna. "Thanks, Jackson. See you tomorrow." I was out the door and in my car before Gloria could pour a cup of coffee.

I settled into the seat and said the words to end the spell. I felt the magic drift away, but my heart still fluttered. I started the car and backed out of the spot, but as I did, I saw Beth in the parking lot. She cocked her head to the side, staring at me like I had six arms or something. I waved, trying to act casually, and that prompted her to rush over and tap on my window. I plastered a fake smile on my face and lowered the window. "Hey, Beth. Can't talk. Ethan's sick, and I have to get this soup to him."

"Oh, is that why all four of you left school early?"

Of course she'd noticed Shannon and Dylan were gone, too. That was Beth. "We all came down with something. It must be food poisoning. We had dinner together last night."

"Really? That's odd. Weren't you here for dinner? I didn't see Dylan and Shannon eating with you."

Ugh! I was so tempted to use a blinding spell on her. "What I meant was we all ate the same thing. They came to pick up their food."

"Oh, right. I saw you all in the back lot."

"Yeah. So anyway, I have to go." I started to pull away before she could protest.

"Tell Ethan I hope he feels better," she yelled after me.

The Mazda got me home almost as fast as the speed spell would have. Such a great car! I grabbed the soup and ran to the front door. Dylan stepped around the side of the cottage, startling me. The soup flew out of my hands, but Dylan caught it.

"Sorry. Everything's fine. He just watched TV."

"Thanks. See you at school."

"About that. I'm transferring myself into all of Ethan's classes. I think it's best that way."

I sighed. "Don't you think that's going to rile him up?"

"He'll understand it's for the best. And it's an easy enough spell."

"And you said *I* was bad at lying." The spell would require the strength of the coven because we'd have to alter the minds of just about everyone at school to make them think Dylan had always shared the same schedule as Ethan.

"We've done it before. No sweat." He shoved his hands in his pockets and walked away.

"Hey, where's your car?"

"I felt like walking. It helps me clear my head." He waved without looking back.

I had to accept that I might never fully understand Dylan. There was still so much I didn't know about him, like where he lived. I pushed the thought away and went into the house. "Honey, I'm home." I smiled at Ethan, camped out on the couch. "I've always wanted to say that." I put the soup on the coffee table in front of him and headed to the kitchen for bowls and spoons. "Sorry it took me so long."

"Diner was slammed, huh?" He opened the bag and took out the large container of soup.

"Yeah. I couldn't leave Gloria hanging like that. I hope you don't mind."

"No, it's fine. I told you that you could've stayed and worked."

"I'd rather be here with you. Besides, I did a speed spell and got Gloria and Jackson caught up and then some." I sat down and started pouring soup into the bowls.

"You used a spell?"

"Yeah. I was careful, though. I didn't up my speed too much. I didn't want anyone to notice. It probably looked like I was on an adrenaline high, which I sort of was."

He grabbed my arm. "You're sure no one noticed."

"Gloria made a comment about how fast I was, but believe me, no one was complaining. Everyone was fed and happy."

He let go and dug into his soup.

"I did run into Beth on my way out, though."

Ethan let his spoon drop into his bowl. "Beth? Was she inside while you were using the spell?"

"No. She showed up after. Well, not totally. I undid the spell in the car, and that's when I saw her." My mind brought up her image and the way she'd stared at me. Had she noticed something? Had she seen me muttering the spell in the car?

Even if she had, there was nothing I could do about it tonight. So I ate my soup and watched Ethan devour two bowls before moving on to the lasagna. The boy could eat, and yet he looked like a perfectly sculpted statue with his washboard abs. I'd have killed for his metabolism.

We watched some old movie on TV, and finally I crawled into bed. Alone. Ethan still wouldn't come to bed with me. He slept on the couch. I cuddled his pillow, hoping the smell of him would comfort me. It didn't.

***

The sun filtered through the window, waking me up before my alarm. I stretched and reached for Ethan's pillow, which was somehow down at my feet. Apparently, I'd thrashed around a lot last night. All I could think about was seeing Ethan's face, so I kicked the covers off, stepped into my slippers, and walked into the living room.

The couch cushions were a mess. Some were tossed on the floor. Others were standing on their sides. Where was Ethan? I turned toward the bathroom, the only place I couldn't see from the living room of our tiny cottage. The door was closed, but the light wasn't on. I pushed it open. My heart rate quickened as I ran out the front door.

The driveway was empty.

Ethan was gone.

15

I RAN back into the house and to my bedroom. My cell was on the nightstand. I snatched it up and dialed Ethan, but the call was kicked right to voicemail. Damn it! I hung up and dialed Dylan's number. He picked up on the fourth ring.

"He's here."

Air rushed from my lungs. Ethan was with Dylan. He was okay. Wait, *was* he okay? "What happened? Is he all right? Is he hurt? Was it the magic?"

"Whoa, calm down, Sam. Here, you can talk to him yourself."

I heard a lot of fumbling on the other end of the line. "Hey." Ethan's voice brought wetness to my eyes.

"What happened? Why did you leave? I was so scared when I woke up and you weren't here."

"I'm sorry. I left you a note."

I looked all around. "Where?"

"On the bed."

The bed—it was a mess from my restless sleep. I tore the covers off and a piece of paper—a receipt from the gas station—fell to the floor. I picked up and read it. *Feeling strange. Called Dylan and he invited me to his place. Don't worry. I'll be fine. Call me in the morning.* "I found it."

"Sorry. I thought you'd see it first thing. I didn't mean to make you worry. I just didn't want to risk staying there when I wasn't feeling right. Dylan helped me through it. I'm fine now."

"Good." I didn't know what else to say. Ethan had felt something was off with his magic, and instead of coming to me he'd gone to Dylan. I knew he'd only been trying to protect me, but it still hurt.

"Get ready for school. Dylan and I will be by to pick you up in twenty minutes."

"Dylan's riding with us? Is something wrong with his car?" Was that why he'd walked last night?

"His car's fine. I asked him to come along with us." Wow, Ethan didn't trust himself at all.

"Did he tell you about his schedule change?" Maybe Ethan wouldn't be against the idea after all.

"Yeah. He wants to meet at the school a few minutes early to do the spell, so go get ready. Love you." He hung up before I could ask any more questions.

I should've been relieved. Ethan was fine. Dylan was helping him. But Ethan's lack of resistance only made me worry more. How bad did he have to be to let Dylan babysit him all the time?

I was ready before Ethan pulled into the driveway. He got out to open my door for me. At least he was still acting like himself. That was a plus. The ride to school was more than awkward. Dylan sat in the back seat like a chaperone. It was worse than being on a date with my dad supervising. Shannon was already at the school when we arrived. She tapped her watch. She never had been one for patience.

"Where are we going to do this?" I asked.

"Guidance office." Dylan said it like it was the most logical place.

"Are you crazy? I'm sure the staff is in the building already. How are we going to pull this off?"

"Already taken care of. We can walk right in." Shannon held the front door open for us.

I looked around, waiting for the school cop to stop us. He wasn't around. The lobby was full of teachers, though. "Just walk by them?" I kept my voice to a whisper.

"Yup. Like this." Shannon grabbed my hand and pulled me through the crowd. No one stopped us. No one even looked in our direction.

"How are you doing this?"

"I put a spell on the entire school to make myself popular. Compared to that, this was a breeze. We're invisible to them."

"Do you mean really invisible?" I looked at my arms. They seemed normal, not see-through at all.

"No. You haven't changed. I made it so no one inside the building can see or hear us."

I had to admit, the spell rocked. It was ten times better than the bubble spell. I smiled, and Shannon's grin lit up her face. We headed straight for the guidance office and walked in like we owned the place. "This, I could get used to."

"Pretty amazing, right?" Shannon smiled and led us all over to the computer on the secretary's desk. "Okay, I'm going to change the schedule in the computer system first. Once it's in place, we'll start the spell." Her fingers hovered over the keys, not moving.

I looked over her shoulder. The screen was locked. Of course. "I don't suppose you know the password."

"Give her a second," Dylan said.

Shannon mumbled under her breath while she stared at the screen. Seconds later, her fingers were pressing keys.

"Cool spell," I said.

"Yeah, but it's limited. I have no idea what I typed."

That was strange. Some of these spells really *did* take over your mind. I glanced at Ethan and managed a weak smile. He'd been so quiet, and he was still keeping his distance.

Shannon fiddled with Dylan's schedule, giving him fake grades and everything. "Congratulations, Dylan. You're now on the honor roll."

"Are you crazy? I don't want to have to use spells all year to fake my grades. Put my grades back to normal." Dylan scoffed and walked away. He'd never liked the way Shannon was so quick to use magic. Not that Dylan was a saint. He'd just been through a lot with dark magic taking him over, so he was more cautious. He wasn't watching where he was going, and Mrs. Melrose, the secretary, almost walked right into him.

"Whoa!" I grabbed his arm and jerked him out of the way. Mrs. Melrose was headed for her desk, which was currently occupied by Shannon. "Shannon, get out of there!"

She hit a few buttons on the keyboard, most likely closing the screen she had open, and literally toppled out of the chair and under the desk, crawling out the other side. "Go!"

"What about the spell?" We couldn't leave without finishing what we'd come here for.

"We have to find somewhere else to go. I'm getting a weird vibe from this lady. It's like she senses us or something." Shannon pushed us toward the door, careful not to bump into anything or anyone. We scrambled down the hall and to the janitor's closet. "Inside!"

We couldn't find a light switch and it was really cramped, but we huddled together. Shannon whispered something and a flame jumped from her pointer finger. She brought her other fingertips together with it, and they lit up in flames as well. It was freaky, but at least we could see.

"Let's get this over with before the morning bell rings and we have to explain why we're all coming out of the closet together." Shannon snickered. I glared at her. "You know what I mean."

"Relax, the invisibility spell is still protecting us." Dylan's breath tickled my neck, and I was suddenly aware of how close to me he was. Ethan was wedged between Dylan and Shannon. I met his eyes, feeling like he was miles away.

"How do we do this spell?" I wanted to get it over with. I'd feel better knowing Ethan was safe all day long, that Dylan would be keeping him safe. And somehow I thought doing this for Ethan was good for Dylan, too. He was making up for his past.

"I'll start chanting the words and you follow along." Shannon flicked her fingers, and the flames formed a ball of light in the middle of us. She reached for my hand and Ethan's. "Complete the circle. We need to be connected so the magic can circle through us."

My heart pounded. Why was I so nervous? Maybe it was because of the terrified look on Ethan's face. "Are you up to this?"

He nodded. "I'm fine." *Fine.* It was a code word for "not good at all."

My eyes flew to Dylan. Would he recognize signs that Ethan was in trouble? He took Ethan's hand, which was still so weird to see. "Strength in numbers." Ethan nodded again, but this time to Dylan. They had some secret understanding that I wasn't a part of. That realization tugged at my heart. I wasn't Ethan's everything anymore. I shook my head, trying to force the thought from my mind. I couldn't be selfish right now. If I wanted Ethan to get better, I had to accept that he'd need help from more than just me.

"Strength in numbers," I repeated. Ethan gave me a half-smile.

"All right, let's do this." Shannon exhaled loudly. "From the past, now do remember, identical schedules from September."

I almost couldn't keep from laughing. That was probably the worst-sounding spell I'd ever heard. She shot me a look and repeated the line. The rest of us joined in. We said it five times, and each time I felt the magic in me grow stronger. The gold energy swirled between us. As we finished the final word, the magic disappeared under the closet door.

Shannon let go of my hand. "It should settle over the school in a matter of minutes."

I exhaled, trying to calm my nerves. "So, by the time we make it to first period, everyone will think Dylan and Ethan have always had identical schedules?"

"You got it." Shannon blew out her finger lights, leaving the closet in complete darkness.

Fingers tickled my left palm. Dylan was still holding my hand. I gently tugged free from his grasp. Maybe he was trying to reassure me that the spell would work, that everything would be okay, but tingles ran down my spine because there was still the other "what if." The "what if he really does have feelings for me?" He was so difficult to read. One minute I was convinced he liked me, and the next I wasn't so sure.

"Come on, people. Move!" Shannon gently shoved me toward the door.

"Maybe you should've kept the fire burning until we got the door open," Dylan said. He fumbled, but finally managed to turn the knob.

The bright lights from the hallway hurt my eyes. I squinted. "I'm guessing sunglasses are against school policy."

"What isn't?" Shannon scoffed. "This school is like a prison."

"I have to go to my locker," Dylan said, looking back and forth between Ethan and me. "Will you be okay for a few minutes?"

Ethan adjusted his bag on his shoulder. "I have everything I need. I'll go with you."

What? He always came to my locker with me in the morning. "Ethan, come with me. Please."

Dylan nodded. "You'll be fine. I'll meet you in five." I wanted to thank him, but he turned and headed up the stairs before I could say a word—or more likely before Ethan could argue.

I slipped my hand into Ethan's. His fingers didn't curl around mine. They didn't respond to my touch at all. "You don't have to be afraid to touch me. I'm wearing the necklace, remember?"

"I want to take every precaution, Sam."

Shannon mouthed "good luck" and walked away.

"I wish you hadn't left last night." I started walking toward the stairs, and thankfully Ethan followed, although his hand was still stiff in mine.

"I had to. I need you to understand that."

"I do. I just missed you."

Finally, his fingers curled around mine. "Do you remember how you told me you ran away from the cottage when you were having an attack?"

Of course I remembered. That had been the worst time of my life. Worse than when the cancer had taken over my body. "That was different. I was dying, and I would've killed anyone near me. I couldn't be around you."

"That's how I feel." He stopped at the top of the stairwell. "I feel like I'm not me when the magic takes over. I sort of black out. I don't know what's happening around me, so I can't control my actions." He reached up and brushed my hair off my face.

"I had no idea." I tried to keep my voice steady. The last thing I wanted was for him to think I was in any way afraid of him. "Just remember I have the necklace to protect me. That, and I have a lot of magic inside me. Enough to protect myself."

He let go of me and ran his fingers through his hair. "I hate that you have to protect yourself from me. You don't know how much that kills me."

Yes, I did. It was killing me, too.

16

I BARELY paid attention as Mr. Ryan droned on about *Franken-stein*. It was just about the last thing I wanted to talk about, and not because, yet again, I hadn't done the required reading. I didn't want to hear about monsters anymore. Did this school ever assign normal books about normal people? Not that I'd be able to relate to them. But see, that was the problem with *The Strange Case of Dr. Jekyll and Mr. Hyde* and now *Frankenstein*—I could relate a little *too* well.

Shannon kicked my ankle. Hard. "Ouch!" I yelled. Laughter rang out in the classroom, bringing me back to reality. All eyes were on me.

"Subtle, Shannon," Tristan said. "Next time, don't kick her so hard."

"Ms. Smith, is my class boring you?" Mr. Ryan stood in front of me, his eyes burning into me.

"No." I sat up straight, using my left leg to rub my sore ankle. "I'm a little out of it today. Sorry."

"Cut her some slack, Mr. Ryan," Tristan said. "She wasn't feeling well yesterday. She and Ethan had food poisoning or something like that."

Beth strikes again!

"Oh." Mr. Ryan's face softened. "Well, if you are feeling sick, let me know. Otherwise, I'll pick on someone else with this question."

He smiled at me, and his look seemed to say "please, don't throw up on my shoes."

"Thanks."

He turned to Shannon. "Ms. Tilby, what do you think? Do you support the theory that Dr. Frankenstein's monster is really just an alter ego? Is this a case of Dr. Jekyll and Mr. Hyde all over again?"

So there was a reason why he'd planned these two books back-to-back. He thought they were a lot alike. Even though I hadn't even started reading *Frankenstein* yet, I could see his point. I mean, how likely was it that a monster made of spare body parts came to life and started killing people? Sure, I'd come back to life and killed people, but I wasn't normal. I couldn't help wondering if these authors had been witches, too. They seemed to know about strange things other people would pass off as fiction. Maybe these weren't made-up stories after all.

Shannon was pretending to be deep in thought, which really just gave her an excuse to stare into Mr. Ryan's hazel eyes. Unbelievable. I wished I had a hose to cool her off. Finally, she leaned forward, and I couldn't help noticing the way she rested her arms at her sides, so they were conveniently pressing against her boobs, making them appear larger. No morals at all! "Well, Mr. R., I think we all have a little monster in us, don't you?" She winked. Actually winked. At a teacher.

I had half a mind to freeze time—if I had any clue how—and slap some sense into the girl. Every time I thought she was making progress, she did something like this and set herself back to square one. I couldn't resist. I reached my leg across the aisle and kicked her ankle. Hard. Payback's a bitch.

"Ow!" She glared at me, but I simply shrugged my shoulders.

Mr. Ryan eyed me and Shannon. "I'm going to pretend I didn't see that."

The bell rang, and I couldn't have been happier about it. Shannon needed time to cool off, and I was dying to see Ethan. I practically ran to sculpture. I was about twenty feet from the classroom when I remembered my strange conversation with Ms. Matthews. I hadn't told anyone about it yet. I had to remember to bring it up at lunch. I didn't think she'd do anything weird like that in front of the class, so as long as there were other people around, I'd be okay. Probably.

I spotted Ethan as soon as I walked through the door. Dylan was sitting next to him. In *my* seat. I'd forgotten the new schedule change would put Dylan in sculpture with us. I tried to act casual about the seating arrangement. Beth wasn't there yet, so I took her seat across from Ethan.

"Hey," Dylan said.

"How's it going?" I was trying for casual, but my words sounded forced.

I must have been staring because Dylan started to stand. "Is this your seat? I didn't even think."

"It's fine." Ethan grabbed his arm. Dylan was stuck half-sitting, half-standing. He looked about as awkward as I felt. My own boyfriend didn't want to sit next to me. Was this how it was going to be until we straightened things out with his magic?

"Yeah, it's fine." I stressed the word *fine*, making sure Ethan knew it totally wasn't. His eyes lowered, and he continued doodling on his notebook.

"Hey, new seating arrangements," Beth said, sitting beside me.

Dylan's head jerked in my direction. He was worried, and I knew why. The spell we'd cast should've made Dylan's presence seem perfectly normal, commonplace. The fact that Beth noticed the change in her seat wasn't a good sign.

"Sorry, that was my fault." I forced a smile. "I wanted to be closer to Ethan." I reached across the table, placing my hand on top of his. "You know, now that we've been dating for a while, I thought we should sit by each other. You don't mind, do you?"

"No, not at all. I just figured you would've taken Dylan's seat next to Ethan, but if you want to sit across from him so you can stare at each other all period, that's fine, too." I could tell she meant it. As much as I hated having her around, I had to remind myself that she wasn't all bad. Too observant, yes. Evil, no. "So, Ethan, are you feeling better?"

He nodded. "Not a hundred percent, though." He slid his hand out from under mine, making my heart sink. He'd said that for my benefit, to explain why he didn't want to get too close.

"Well, these things can take time to bounce back from. That's why I was so surprised to see Sam running all around at the diner. I've never seen anyone move like that. She was amazing, almost a blur." She laughed, and I made myself laugh along.

"Yeah, fevers do weird things to me. First I crash, and then I'm a ball of energy." I wasn't sure where I was pulling these lies from. I was just glad they were coming to me.

"Well, I wish fevers affected me like that. You were, like, superhuman."

Another nervous laughed escaped my lips. "So, Beth, what are you making for your next project?" I didn't care in the least, but I wanted to talk about something else—anything else.

"Dylan, you look fine today, too," Beth said, as if I hadn't spoken at all. "Do you share Sam's strange reaction to fevers?"

Dylan met my eyes, looking for help.

"Oh, well, Dylan went home early yesterday more as a precaution than anything else. Shannon, too. They saw how sick Ethan and I got, and they assumed since it was food poisoning and we'd eaten the same thing that they'd be sick too. Luckily, they weren't affected by it. Gloria said that was the first and last time she ordered fish from that supplier." I hoped Beth wouldn't think my mini-recap of our conversation last night at the diner was weird. I had to get Dylan and Ethan up to speed.

"Oh, well that's good." Beth sat back in her seat. Apparently her line of questioning was finished.

"Yeah, Shannon and I got lucky," Dylan said. "Of course, we didn't pig out like these two did."

I got that he was trying to act normal, but I really wanted to get off the topic all together. Ms. Matthews introduced a new project and sent us all off to work. We were supposed to work in pairs. Not good. Ethan and Dylan were now attached at the hip. I looked around the room, searching for an acceptable partner.

"Hey, Sam." Beth's smiling face blocked my view. "I was thinking we could partner up. You know, since Ethan's working with Dylan."

"Oh, um…" Damn it. Why didn't I know anyone else in this class? Where was the guy who used to sit with us at lunch? What was his name? Elton? "I kind of promised Elton I'd work on the next project with him."

Beth's face scrunched up. "You did? I haven't seen you talk to Elton in weeks."

"Yeah, I knew I'd been neglecting him since Ethan and I started dating, so I promised him the next chance we had to work on a project together, we'd partner up."

"That explains why you aren't working with Ethan. I thought it was kind of weird you two weren't pairing up. You always do."

I snuck a glance at Ethan, knowing he'd heard Beth. "Yeah, I'll definitely miss working with Ethan, but a promise is a promise."

Beth stood up. "Time to find me a partner before all the good ones are taken." She practically skipped away.

"You better go talk to Elton," Dylan said. "I see someone else heading his way now."

Crap! I jumped up and called Elton's name across the room. The guy walking over to Elton paused, and I pounced on the opportunity. I slid into the seat next to Elton. "Hey, want to partner up?" Before he could answer, I said, "Great!" and gave him a big smile.

The other kid turned and walked to another table. Dylan met my eyes and nodded. Ethan was still looking away, and the thing that bothered me the most was that I wasn't surprised.

Elton turned out to be an awesome partner. He designed our entire project. All I had to do was keep saying, "Uh-huh. That sounds great." Elton liked being in charge, and since I sucked at art, I let him. My head wasn't in it anyway. I was too busy staring at Ethan, watching him look everywhere but at me.

As soon as the bell rang, I rushed over to Ethan and slipped my hand in his. Dylan was right there, so Ethan was just going to have to deal with the whole touching-me thing. One minute he was okay with it and the next he was avoiding me like the plague. I couldn't keep up, and I didn't want to. He was going to have to give in to me because I wasn't taking no for an answer. I squeezed his hand as we walked to lunch. He gave me a slight squeeze back, but it was halfhearted.

Shannon was already at our table, and I could tell she had a spell in the works. The faint golden glow only visible to us shimmered around our designated spot. I didn't let go of Ethan when we sat down, so he was forced to sit by me. Dylan nodded to him and took a seat across from us, next to Shannon.

"Well, you look like a fun bunch." Shannon rolled her eyes before mumbling the rest of her spell to enclose us all in the bubble.

I rolled my eyes, too. "I'm glad we can't be heard, because there's something I have to tell you guys." Ethan's fingers tensed, and I finally released his hand. "It's about Ms. Matthews." I could see relief wash through Ethan. Had he really thought he'd done something he didn't even know about? Was that possible? He'd said he sort of blacked out when the dark magic took over. Had that been happening lately? Was that the reason he'd left last night—why he'd run to Dylan's?

Shannon took a sip of soda. "Who's Ms. Matthews? I don't know her."

"The sculpture teacher," Dylan said, giving me a look that said "why haven't you mentioned this before?"

"Something happened yesterday before class. I meant to tell you guys, but then…"

Ethan turned his head, pretending to be interested in the sandwich he'd taken out of his bag. Had Dylan made them both lunch? This male bonding was really getting to me. Of course, I'd forgotten my own lunch in my rush to see Ethan this morning.

"Okay, so Ethan took off and you forgot to tell us." Shannon waved her hand at me. "Go on." She had no clue how to be subtle.

I placed my hand on Ethan's leg. He looked back at me, handing me half his sandwich. "You should eat something."

"Thanks." It sucked that something like sharing his sandwich—a totally normal thing to do—was such a big deal right then.

Shannon shook her head. "Earth to Sam, tell us the story."

"Okay, well, Ms. Matthews said she wanted to talk to me, and I assumed she meant about the clay incident." Ethan's head lowered again. "But it wasn't about that. She said something about not being able to play favorites because some of the other students might get mad. Like Beth."

"Beth?" Shannon nearly spit her soda at me. She covered her mouth and mumbled a sorry.

"Yeah, Beth. And the next thing I knew, I was rambling on about how Beth keeps an annoyingly close eye on me. I didn't mean to say anything. It sort of slipped out like I had no control over my own mouth."

"This is so not good, Sam," Shannon said.

"Yeah, well, it gets worse."

Dylan slammed his fist down on the table. I jumped, not sure if I was ready to continue my story. "What happened?"

"She was eating her breakfast. An egg sandwich, and she had this saltshaker on her desk. She started talking about secrets and how to hide them. I didn't know why. But then she kept trying to give me the saltshaker. It was weird and totally freaked me out."

"What did you do?" Ethan asked, taking my hand like he used to.

"I made up an excuse and ran out. I didn't know what else to do." I shrugged.

"So, Ms. Matthews might know you're a witch," Dylan said.

Hearing Dylan confirm what I'd only suspected—what I'd tried to convince myself wasn't true—was too much to handle. I couldn't answer him, so I nodded.

"Wonderful. Now in addition to avoiding Beth and fixing Ethan's magic, we have to watch out for Ms. Matthews." Dylan pounded the table again. This time I didn't jump. My stomach lurched as I realized all these problems came back to me.

17

SHANNON shoved Dylan's shoulder. "Lay off, Dylan. What the hell was she supposed to do?"

"I don't know what she should've done, okay? It's just crap that we keep running into more problems." He stood up and stormed off toward the food line.

Ethan squeezed my hand. "Don't worry about him. Eat your lunch. I'll get you a soft pretzel." He kissed my temple, and it was all I could do not to cry. I watched him walk after Dylan, catching up in seconds and placing his hand on his shoulder.

"Those two are certainly getting along well." Shannon picked at her salad. She always ate the croutons first. "That's got to be weird for you—the guy you're in love with and the guy who's got a thing for you."

"I think Dylan's feelings for me are definitely back in the negative column after the Ms. Matthews thing." He was furious with me. Maybe it was better that way. Our relationship had always been rocky, right from the start.

"Nah, that's just Dylan. He's kind of a hothead. More so when it has to do with something he really cares about." Shannon ate a cucumber drenched in ranch dressing.

"I don't know what to do. It's like bad stuff follows me everywhere, and now it's affecting Ethan."

"He doesn't blame you, if that's what you're worried about," she said with a mouth full of cucumber.

"Pretty." I shook my head.

"Please, inside this bubble I don't have to be perfect. No one's watching me. Well, except for you, but I don't care if you don't find me sexy." She winked.

I couldn't help laughing, and it felt good. "What do I do about all this?"

"You help Dylan and me track down Mirabella. There's a spell we can do. It's like a locator spell but with a twist."

"What kind of twist?" I finally took a bite of Ethan's sandwich.

"Well, you know how Ethan put up a spell to block us from finding him, but we did anyway?"

"Yeah." It hadn't been hard either with the three of us working the spell to find him.

"Well, multiply that times about ten."

"She's that powerful?"

"She's wickedly powerful." Shannon put her fork down and stared intently at me. "You have no idea what we're dealing with. And if we do find her, and she gets pissed about it…"

"But this is our only option, right? There's no other way to save Ethan."

"It takes a seriously powerful witch to remove dark magic. Even Mirabella screwed up the spell somehow. That's how she ended up taking the dark magic into her own body. That wasn't part of the plan."

"What if she's…not the same person because of that dark magic? What if she's evil?"

"Then we're seriously screwed."

Ethan and Dylan returned. Both looked more relaxed. Ethan had enough soft pretzels for all of us, but he only handed one to me, keeping the rest for himself. Shannon and I eyed him, but he shrugged. "What? Dylan said I have to keep my strength up if I'm going to keep control over my magic."

I snuggled into him. Seeing him eat like this reminded me of the old Ethan, pre-magic Ethan. "Thanks." I kissed his cheek and broke off a piece of pretzel. Of course it was unsalted.

The rest of lunch was pretty normal, which was heaven as far as I was concerned. Until Ms. Matthews came into the cafeteria. She looked around the room like she was trying to find someone. I knew we were protected by the bubble spell, but she seemed to look right at me. I shivered.

"Relax," Ethan said, wrapping his arm around me. God, it felt good to be in his arms. I would've given anything to stay that way.

"Keep an eye on her," Dylan said, his eyes like daggers on Ms. Matthews. "She's not all that different from Beth. Way too observant, and sees things she shouldn't be able to."

My mind flashed with images of made-for-TV movies. "You don't think they're, like, witch hunters or something, do you?"

"No." Dylan shook his head. "No one really hunts witches. I mean, a few have tried, sure, but they usually wind up dead."

"Unless they're Sam." Shannon leaned forward, focused on Ms. Matthews.

"Thanks a lot for that," I said. As much as I liked her, I still wanted to smack her about five times a day.

"What? It's sort of a compliment if you think about it. You're strong. Most people couldn't have done what you did and lived to talk about it."

The problem was, I didn't want to talk about it. I wanted to forget about that part of my life.

Ms. Matthews removed a glass jar from her pocket. "The salt-shaker!" I blurted out without even meaning to. "She carries it around?"

"Hmm." Shannon finished her soda, tipping it back to get the last drop. "Maybe you're wrong, Dylan. Maybe this school does have a witch hunter lurking in the halls." She said it like she wasn't really worried, like this was a game.

I glared at her. "How can you be so calm about this? Ethan's magic is out of control. Do you have any idea what this could mean for us? For all of us?" Ethan's arm slipped off my shoulder. Crap. I shut my eyes, feeling the sting of tears. "I didn't mean it like that." I looked at him, but he was facing Ms. Matthews.

"No, you're right. I'm a danger to all of us. I should probably drop her class. Stay away from her." He shrugged. "It's not like I'm into art anyway. No big deal."

I looped my arm through his. I needed to be close, to touch him. "It *is* a big deal. You shouldn't have to change your schedule."

"Why not?" He met my eyes. "Dylan changed his for me. If anyone is going to have to suffer because of the darkness inside me, it should be me."

"Good man," Shannon said.

I threw her a look that would've made any normal person cringe. But she wasn't normal. She was Shannon.

She widened her eyes at me. "I mean it. He's protecting the coven. That's good. It says a lot about him."

"I hate to agree with Shannon," Dylan said, "but the fact that Ethan would rather be the one making sacrifices shows he hasn't given in to the dark magic. That's a good sign."

Maybe, but my girlfriend claws were out. "If he changes classes, then you'll have to, too." Let Dylan argue with that. We'd already done the spell to change the minds of the entire staff and student body, and we'd almost gotten caught. I doubted Dylan or Shannon wanted to risk that again. Especially now that we thought Ms. Matthews might be a witch hunter.

"Let's not panic." It was odd for Shannon to be the voice of reason. "We don't know anything for sure yet. Besides, for whatever reason, it's not Ethan that Ms. Matthews is suspicious of. It's Sam. Sam will keep her distance from Ms. Matthews as much as possible."

"Ethan too," Dylan said, "just to be safe."

"Wait a minute." My mind swam with thoughts, trying to piece everything together. "Ms. Matthews thinks I did something to make that clay explode. She thinks it was me, not Ethan. And when I mentioned Beth watching me, that made her all the more suspicious. I could lure her away from Ethan. Protect him."

"No way." Ethan turned in his seat and took me by the shoulders. "Sam, I'm not letting you risk exposing yourself to keep Ms. Matthews off my trail. It's not happening. I'd rather go straight to her and confess."

"You can't do that!" we all yelled at him. Thank God for the privacy bubble.

"Then promise me you won't do anything to make Ms. Matthews suspect you any more than she already does."

I hated this, but I had to lie to him. The last time I tried to tell him the truth, he ran away. If keeping him here—safe with us—meant lying, then I had to do it. "Okay. I promise."

Shannon's eyes burned into the side of my face, but I refused to meet her gaze. It would give me away. I'd explain it to her later. Maybe she'd been right in assuming it would come down to us versus the guys in our coven. Ms. Matthews slipped the saltshaker back into her pocket. What had that been about anyway? I couldn't help wondering if the saltshaker was meant to draw me out of the crowd.

After lunch we split up again. Ethan and Dylan headed to Mr. Ryan's class. Shannon grabbed my arm before she headed to her class. "You need to fill me in on whatever plan you have in the works in that pretty little head of yours."

"I will. Later." Right now I had to get to trig and figure out what to tell Mr. Malinowsky. I went through the list of excuses in my head. I'd left my books in sculpture. I'd forgotten to turn in my test paper at the end of class. Yeah, I could pull that one off.

"We'll talk in chem." Shannon gave me a stern look and turned away.

More reason why I had to do this now. I had to figure out this Ms. Matthews thing before last period. Before anyone could stop me. It was stupid and dangerous, but I had to do it…for Ethan.

I grabbed my books out of my locker, along with an old art history test Ms. Matthews had given about a week ago. Then I mustered up some tears, which with all that had been going on was more than easy to do. I ran into the classroom and straight to Mr. Malinowsky's desk. "Mr. Mal." Only his top students called him that. I wasn't one of them, but I thought it might make him more receptive to me.

He looked up from his desk, and immediately his face fell. "Sam, is everything all right?"

"No. I really screwed up. Ms. Matthews gave us a test before lunch. It was really hard, and I studied so much, too. It took me all period and when the bell rang, I didn't realize that I accidentally put my test paper in my book and turned in my chem homework instead." The words flew out of my mouth. I figured the faster, the better. Let him think I was completely distraught. "I have to give her this test right now! If I wait any longer, she'll think I switched the papers on purpose so I could look up the answers in lunch. I swear I didn't." A tear streaked my cheek. Perfect timing.

Mr. Malinowsky wrinkled his brow and pointed to the test paper in my hands. "Are you sure that's the test? There are red marks on it like it's already been graded."

I'd been trying so hard to cover up the grade at the top, I'd forgotten about the red marks. "Yeah, I had a few questions during the test and she wrote on the paper so she didn't interrupt the other students with her explanations."

He nodded in understanding. "All right. Go see Ms. Matthews. But hurry back. We're starting a new unit today."

"Thank you, Mr. Mal." I ran from the room. Good. This was going well. Now all I had to do was figure out what I was going to say to Ms. Matthews. Was scaring her the best way to go? Or did I try to put a spell on her, tamper with her memory so she didn't remember anything that made me look like a witch? Scaring her would only confirm her suspicions. I had to do the spell. Even if I outed myself as a witch and cast the spell in front of her, she'd forget it once I finished.

As I approached her classroom, I wished I had Shannon with me. She was better at the mind-altering spells. She'd had more practice. And I hated doing something that felt so close to dark magic. But I had good intentions—saving Ethan—and that had to count for something.

I was surprised to see the classroom empty again. When did she teach other than second period? Of course, the empty room made this a little easier for me. I wouldn't have to worry about getting her alone.

"Ms. Matthews?" I said, entering the room.

"Ah, Sam." She smiled up at me from her desk. "I've been expecting you."

18

EXPECTING me? How? The only one who knew I was coming here was Mr. Malinowsky. Unless she really was a witch hunter and had been following me, anticipating my every move. I stepped toward her desk, my feet moving comically slow. "How did you know I'd come looking for you?"

Her smile widened. "After lunch, I knew you'd come looking for answers."

Answers? No, I was coming to erase her memory. Stop her from being so nosy. "I don't understand. What thing at lunch? What answers?"

She reached into her pocket and pulled out the saltshaker, placing it on her desk. I froze. If I backed away, this could all get worse. If I moved closer, this would *definitely* get worse. "Go ahead. See for yourself."

"I don't like salt." It was all I could think to say.

"What if I said it's not salt?" She raised a brow and pushed the saltshaker closer to me. "Do you think I'd lie to you, Sam?"

Maybe. If she thought I was a witch, she'd probably do just about anything to keep me from using magic on her.

She reached down on the ground next to her. Everything inside me was screaming "run!" But curiosity—and maybe fear—was keeping me grounded. She pulled a small cooler bag onto her desk. "I have this thing for egg sandwiches. I know it's not exactly healthy to eat so many of them, but lately I've had this craving I can't ignore." She removed the top bun and shook some salt onto the eggs. "Want some? There's more than enough to share."

"No, thank you." My voice didn't sound like my own. I sounded like a terrified puppy.

She closed the sandwich and held it up to me. "Are you sure?"

"You were kind of heavy on the salt, don't you think?"

"Was I?" She slid the saltshaker across the desk again. It stopped at the edge. My eyes locked on it.

"It's funny how people make assumptions, isn't it? They see something they think they know and their minds fill in the gaps."

"What are you talking about?"

"Are you sure you don't want at least a bite of the sandwich? It didn't look like you ate much at lunch."

"I don't want the sand—" My heart raced, and the old test I was clutching fell to the floor. "You saw me in the cafeteria?"

"Barely. Those pretzels aren't any better for you than these egg sandwiches are for me, you know."

"How? How did you...?" The spell, had it failed? Was that why she was looking at my table? Had Dylan and Ethan somehow messed up the boundaries of the spell when they got up for food?

Ms. Matthews stood up, grabbing the saltshaker in her hands. "I told you, Sam. People see what they want to see. Although seeing you and your friends wasn't easy with that spell you had up."

No doubt about it anymore. She knew. And more than that, she knew I wasn't the only witch. She knew about the others.

She held the saltshaker out to me. "Smell this. You don't have to touch it. Just smell it. I'll even hold it for you."

"So you can throw the salt in my face? I don't think so."

"Smell it. I could make you, but I'd really rather not." She held it out to me.

I could turn and run again, but where would I go now that she knew I was a witch? She could come after me or the others whenever she wanted. And she was a teacher, so no one would question her if she tried to take us out of class and corner us one at a time. I grabbed the saltshaker, careful not to spill any.

"Go on."

I slowly brought it to my nose. What would smelling it do to me? Would it burn my nose? Would the salt travel up to my brain and kill me? So many things could go wrong. Ethan's face flashed in my mind. I had to do this for him. I sniffed, barely getting a whiff of the salt at all. No wait…that wasn't salt. What was it? I smelled it again, breathing more deeply this time. Sugar. Ms. Matthews had sugar in her saltshaker. "You put sugar on your eggs?"

"I know it sounds a little weird, but if you think about it, French toast is bread, egg, sugar, and cinnamon, right? I'm only missing a few ingredients." She smiled. "Besides, it makes it look as though I'm like everyone else."

Like everyone else? Wasn't she? Oh God! "You're a witch?"

"Why do you look so surprised? Really, I thought I'd be the obvious guess."

Sure, Ms. Matthews was a little different. Not your typical teacher at all. But I didn't think any of my teachers would turn out to be witches. "Are there any others?"

"Yes." She kept eye contact with me, challenging me to figure this out on my own. Who did she hang out with? I'd never really paid much attention to the teachers before. They usually holed themselves up in the teachers lounge when they weren't in their classrooms. "Sam, if you're going to survive as a witch, you need to be able to recognize other witches around you. You've certainly spent enough time with one of these people. You should know he's—"

"He?" My mind raced. No way. She couldn't mean… "Mr. Ryan?" My voice cracked.

Ms. Matthews nodded. "Why else would that popularity spell Shannon cast not have worked on him?"

He'd been immune to Shannon's spell. Could it be that he recognized she was a witch and somehow blocked any spells she might try to use on him? "I think I'm getting a headache."

"Maybe you should sit down."

"No. I'm fine." Despite my words, my legs bent and I found myself sitting in the nearest chair.

"Trust me, I think it's better this way." Ms. Matthews smiled at me.

"Did you just…use a spell to make me sit?" It wasn't the first time she'd used magic on me, either. "The other day, when you got me to talk about Beth…that was a spell, too. You keep using magic on me."

"Is that what you really want to talk about? We're running out of time."

"What do you mean?" Did she know about Ethan? Did she know something was happening to him?

"Look, we need to join our covens if we're going to figure this out."

Join covens? Great, Dylan and Shannon were going to love the idea of bringing teachers into the group. Then it hit me. "Who else is in your coven? It can't only be you and Mr. Ryan. You need more witches, don't you?"

"Yes. There are five of us."

"Five?" My mind raced, trying to come up with three more teachers who might be witches in disguise.

"I don't think you'll guess these three. Well, maybe one. He did tell me you were on your way here."

"Mr. Malinowsky?" He knew I was lying about the test, and he'd told Ms. Matthews I was on my way.

"Jason thinks you don't apply yourself in his class, by the way."

"I don't care about trigonometry right now!" How could she mention grades at a time like this?

"Sorry, Sam. I *am* a teacher, after all. It's kind of my job to care about your academic achievement."

"Well, all I care about is figuring out what's going on with Ethan and how your coven can possibly help him."

Ms. Matthews laced her hands in front of her, and I saw the blue moons she'd painted on her black nails shimmer. Her nervous energy was creating magic in her fingertips. But why was she so nervous? What was she hiding?

"Is there something you're not telling me?" I motioned to her nails.

She laughed. "Thomas is always telling me I should stop painting designs on my nails. They give me away every time."

"Thomas?"

"Mr. Snyder."

"*Principal* Snyder? He's a witch?" Now I felt faint. We had a witch running the school. With all the spells my coven had cast, this was definitely not good news.

"Relax, Sam. Yes, he knows about your spells, as does the rest of the coven. But you aren't in any trouble."

I took a deep breath, wondering how much worse this could get. "Who's the fourth witch in your coven?"

"Eileen." I stared at her for a moment before she realized I didn't know any teachers by their first names. "Oh, sorry. I mean, Mrs. Melrose."

"The guidance secretary?" I shook my head. "Now I know you're messing with me. She's old enough to be my grandma, maybe even great-grandma."

"She's what we call a crone. She's very wise and very powerful."

Now that I thought about it, it really did make sense. When we were in the guidance office doing that spell, Shannon had said she picked up on a weird vibe from Mrs. Melrose. She said it felt like she sensed us somehow. The only way that would be possible was if she was overly perceptive like Beth, or she was a witch. "Does this mean she knows Ethan and I lied about—?" I caught myself. We hadn't told anyone we were using fake names. Not even Dylan and Shannon.

"We all know, Sam. You and Ethan have fake IDs and are using the school records of two very real students. All very illegal. But…" She stopped fidgeting with her hands. "We understand why you are doing all of this. I can't say I blame you after what happened. You were dealt an unfair hand with the cancer, and then with what Nora did to you on top of that."

"Wait. Does this mean you know about Trevor, too?" Trevor, Shannon's boyfriend, who I accidentally killed during one of my episodes?

Ms. Matthews nodded. "We know. We helped cover it up for you."

No way. I swallowed hard, feeling like my tongue was swelling up to the size of an anaconda. This couldn't be happening. I'd had a coven of witches covering my tracks for me. But they were adults, teachers. Why would they dismiss a dead teenager so easily? They should have busted me. Something wasn't right. "But then, why didn't you help me? Stop me? Stop Nora? I was a monster. I was—"

"Sam." Ms. Matthews sat down across from me and placed her hand on mine. "It wasn't that simple. Your actions left traces. It took us a little while to piece it all together. Witchcraft isn't an exact science. By the time we found out it was you—"

"But you said I needed to be able to recognize other witches. Why couldn't you recognize me? I had Ben's and Rebecca's magic inside me."

"That was after you killed Trevor. And even then, your magic came in a very different way. Most witches are born with it. It's part of who we are. Your magic is—for lack of a better word—stolen. It was harder to detect."

My stomach lurched. She was right. The magic inside me wasn't really mine at all. And neither was Ethan's. "Is that why Ethan's having such a difficult time controlling his magic? Because it's not really his?"

She nodded, and I could tell she was biting the inside of her lower lip. Something was bothering her. Something she'd assumed I'd figured out. What was I missing? Okay, Ethan's magic didn't really belong to him, so it was sort of acting out in a way, like a disobedient child that only wanted to listen to its mother.

Mother.

No. No, no, no! "Oh my God!"

"Sam, try to stay calm." Ms. Matthews reached for my hands, but I pushed the chair back from the table and stood up.

"Ethan can't control his magic because it's not his to control. It's Nora's! She's dead, but her magic is still messing with us, with Ethan. It's trying to make him into what she was. Evil."

19

MS. Matthews stood up and walked around the table to me. "I know this all seems really bad to you right now, and I'm not going to lie to you and tell you it isn't. But you need to stay calm and listen to me."

Calm? That wasn't an option. Nora's dark magic was crawling around inside Ethan. I had to get to him, to the coven. We had to do something now. Maybe these teachers had covered for me, but they hadn't tried to fix the monster inside me. Most likely because they didn't know how, which meant there was no way they could help Ethan now. Only one witch had the power to do that. Only one witch had done it before. Forget about trying to track down Mirabella and calling her. We had to go to her *right now*. We had to make her help Ethan. "I have to go." I ran from the room with Ms. Matthews calling after me. I knew she'd alert her coven immediately, which meant we needed to get out of the building as soon as possible or they'd try to stop us. I ducked into the boys' bathroom, thinking Ms. Matthews wouldn't look for me there—unless she was already doing a locator spell on me. I whipped my phone out and texted the others.

Get out of the school now! Meet at Ethan's car. I'll explain later. Go!

I checked the hallway. It looked clear, but I used a bubble spell anyway. I couldn't be too careful. I walked right out the front doors, undetected. So far so good. I hoped the others were as lucky. I ran to

Ethan's car. It was locked, but he kept a spare key inside the wheel well. I grabbed it and got in. Even with the bubble spell, I ducked down, keeping out of sight. Who knew how often the school cop patrolled the parking lot looking for ditchers?

I sensed the others before they got there. Their spells were making the air shimmer. Not good. If I could sense them, so could Ms. Matthews and her coven. I appreciated that they wanted to help. Really, I did. But I was done taking this slowly. If Nora's magic was the problem—the thing corrupting Ethan—I wasn't losing another second thinking about the best plan of action.

Ethan opened the driver's-side door, and I jumped over the middle console into the passenger seat. Dylan and Shannon hopped in the back. "What's going on?" Ethan asked, following my lead and clicking his seat belt.

"Drive. I'll explain on the way. We have to get away from this place."

Ethan pulled out of the parking lot and headed for the highway. I didn't know where we were going yet, but the highway seemed like a good starting point.

Dylan leaned forward, his head between my seat and Ethan's. "Sam, spill. What's this all about?"

They weren't going to be happy about me seeing Ms. Matthews on my own, but I didn't have time to worry about the backlash. "I found out why Ms. Matthews was acting weird."

Shannon shoved the back of my seat. "You were supposed to wait for me. We were going to handle her together."

"There's no time for apologies. Ms. Matthews is a witch."

Ethan swerved, most likely because he jerked his head toward me and wasn't watching the road. "She's a witch?"

"Yes, and she's not the only one." I told them about Mr. Ryan, Mr. Malinowsky, Mr. Snyder, and Mrs. Melrose. "They've all been covering for us—well, mostly for me. They figured out what happened to me a month ago. They tried to help, but apparently the magic inside me wasn't easy for them to trace. Ms. Matthews said that's because the magic I have isn't really mine."

"It's Ben's and Rebecca's," Dylan said, slumping back into his seat. Yeah, I didn't believe for a second that he was glad his brother was dead. They'd had their problems and were completely dysfunctional as far as family goes, but Dylan missed Ben.

"Whoa." Shannon leaned forward this time. "Does this mean…?"

I turned and nodded to her.

"Mean what?" Ethan nearly drove off the road again. "Someone get me up to speed here."

"How about you ease off the speed?" Dylan said. "Either that or pull over and I'll drive."

"I'm fine. I just need to know what Sam and Shannon aren't saying." His hands gripped the steering wheel. I stared at his right hand, the one that usually held mine while he drove. I reached for it. He resisted at first, but I wouldn't give in. I laced my fingers through his.

"Ethan, the reason your magic is fighting you is because it's not yours. It's Nora's."

His fingers tightened around mine. He was scared. "What does that mean for me? Will I become the way she was?"

"I won't let that happen." I met Dylan and Shannon's gazes, needing to confirm my suspicion. "Only a truly powerful witch can remove dark magic, right?"

"There's only one we know of," Shannon said. "No offense to Mr. Ryan or the others, but they're teachers. How badass can they really be? We need powerful witches who aren't afraid of dark magic."

"We need to find Mirabella," Dylan said. "We have to go to her and make her help Ethan."

"My thoughts exactly." It was good that we were all back on the same page, working together instead of fighting over everything.

"Locator spell. That's what we need." Shannon fumbled inside her shoulder bag. "I thought I had some herbs in here."

Dylan tapped Ethan on the shoulder. "Find a place to pull over. We can't do the spell in the car. We need everyone's magic for this to work. Mirabella isn't going to want to be found, especially by me and Shannon."

"What if she's…?" Ethan couldn't say the words, but we all knew what he meant. What if she was a dark witch now? Our problems would be multiplied by about a million and two.

I squeezed his hand tighter. "There are four of us and only one of her. We'll *make* her save you if we have to."

"And then what?" Ethan turned his head and met my eyes. He looked so lost, so helpless. I'd never seen him like this. He was my Ethan, my protector, my strength. At least, that was what he used to be. "Will we have to kill her to keep her from coming after us? Is that what this is going to come down to?"

Maybe. I didn't want to be responsible for killing anyone else, not even a crazy dark witch. But for Ethan…there was nothing I wouldn't do.

"Take that exit," Dylan said. "I know this place. There's an old playground. No one will be there now." No, everyone was in school. Everyone except delinquents like us. Ethan pulled off the highway and followed Dylan's directions to the playground. He parked and leaned his head back against his seat. I could see the weight of the situation on his shoulders. The worst part for me was that he blamed himself. He loved me so much he couldn't even see this was my fault.

"I never meant for any of this to happen. You know that, right?" He touched my cheek, lightly, like he was afraid he'd hurt me. "When I brought you back, I thought we'd get our second chance. I thought the universe owed us that much. Just in case this doesn't end well, I want you to know, I don't regret bringing you back. You'll be fine."

Tears burned my eyes and throat because I knew he meant I'd be fine without him. No, I wouldn't.

"Don't say that. I'm not losing you. I refuse. You're right. The universe owes me, and I'm cashing in." I leaned forward and pressed my lips to his. I didn't care that Dylan and Shannon were sitting in the back seat. I didn't care that Ethan was afraid to touch me. I needed to kiss him. I needed to feel close to him again.

Dylan tapped my shoulder. "Guys, we need to do this spell before Ms. Matthews and the coven of teachers find us. I doubt they'd approve of us seeking out a witch who might be consumed by dark magic."

Shannon smacked him. "You're such a tool. Can't you see they need a minute?"

"We don't have a minute to spare."

I pulled back, but my hand stayed on Ethan's face. "Dylan's right. We have a witch to find."

Ethan nodded. Until he'd said it, I hadn't thought about why he'd felt responsible for all this. I'd traced it back to my sickness—the one Nora had inflicted on me, the one that had made me a monster. But Ethan went back further than that, to bringing me back. He'd been the one to contact Nora and get her to help me. He'd made the deal to slowly end his life in order to save mine. I could see things through his eyes now, but I still didn't blame him. He'd acted out of love, and I could never hold that against him.

We got out and met on the merry-go-round. Shannon said the circular shape would help with the spell. It sort of made sense since we were a coven of four and made more of a square than a circle. Shannon created flames from her fingers again. After this was all over, I was going to have to ask her how she did that. Dylan was twisting herbs together, tying them in elaborate knots. None of it made sense to me, but I wasn't about to slow the spell down by asking them to explain.

"This may take a few tries," Shannon said.

Ethan looked like he'd been spinning on the merry-go-round for an hour—one step from losing his lunch. I ran my hand down his arm. "We'll find her. No matter how hard she's trying to hide, we'll find her."

Shannon and Dylan exchanged a look. They weren't as confident as I was choosing to be. That wasn't going to stop me. I knew my magic was strong. I'd figure out how to tap into all that power. It would be a crash course. I was fine with that. Shannon nodded to me, like she was reading my mind. I could always count on her not to be afraid of the big spells. Dylan held back sometimes, probably because of his dark-magic phase. Ethan would probably do the same, not wanting to risk tapping into Nora's dark magic inside him.

"Wait!" I couldn't believe I hadn't thought of it before. "Dylan, didn't you tell me that magic isn't evil? It's only magic? It's how the person uses it that makes it dark?" I knew he'd told me that. Before Ethan killed Nora, I worried about this exact thing happening. Dylan assured me it wouldn't. "Did you lie to me? Did you use Ethan because you wanted Nora dead?" I swallowed hard, looking at Dylan like he was no better than Nora had been.

"I didn't lie, Sam. I didn't think this would happen. When my magic turned dark, it was because I let it. I liked the power, and that dark magic left a trace inside me, corrupting the rest of my magic, which is why Mirabella had to take it."

"So you're saying Ethan used dark magic on his own and it tainted the rest of the magic inside him?" No way. I didn't believe that for a second.

"No. One of the reasons why I wanted to be the one to help Ethan is because I wanted to look for signs, ones I'd remember from my dark days. But there weren't any signs that he'd caused this."

"Then who?" Dylan turned away, so I looked at Shannon. She must have known. "Who?"

"Nora." The flame in Shannon's hand flickered. Her emotions were making her lose control of the spell. "When she knew she was going to die, she did one last spell. Dylan and I felt traces of it in the air, but we didn't know what it was until recently."

I should've expected Nora had gone down swinging. "What was it? What did she do?"

Dylan gripped the bars on the merry-go-round. "She focused on the traces of dark magic inside her, making it corrupt all of her magic. She cursed Ethan for taking it from her." He pushed off the bars, looking back and forth between Ethan and me. "I'm sorry. I was the one who told Ethan to kill Nora. I feel responsible."

There was a lot of that going around lately, people feeling guilty. Only the problem was that the one person who truly *was* responsible was dead. She didn't feel bad about any of this. She was probably smiling up at us from Hell. "This is Nora's doing. All of it. None of us brought this on. I'm done feeling sorry for something she did."

"Hear, hear!" Shannon's ball of flames grew again. She released it into the air, letting it hover between us. "Let's fix this now. To hell with Nora. We'll show her we're stronger than her pathetic attempt to curse Ethan."

I wasn't sure how pathetic it was. Ethan was in bad shape, but I appreciated Shannon's enthusiasm. "I'm ready."

Ethan and Dylan nodded, and we all joined hands. I had a feeling this spell was going to be intense. Shannon started it, saying words I knew weren't English. How were we supposed to chant along with her if we had no idea what she was saying?

"Focus your magic on Shannon, on mimicking her," Dylan said. "Your magic will let you repeat her words even if you don't know what you're saying."

I swallowed the lump in my throat and did what Dylan had said. I let my magic thread its way to Shannon. I felt her words fill me. They still made no sense, but I could at least repeat them.

We all chanted along. The magic swirled around us and the ball of flames grew bigger. Shannon's words changed. She must have been digging deeper, trying to find a stronger spell. Mirabella didn't want to be found. Shannon shook, and since she was holding on to Dylan and me, we shook, too. And then we started to spin—or the merry-go-round did. Faster and faster. My stomach lurched. The golden glow of magic whipped around us, picking up strength as the merry-go-round circled.

I thought I'd throw up, but suddenly we stopped. We were torn apart, landing hard on the grass. My back slammed into the ground, knocking the air out of me. I lay there for a moment, trying to fill my lungs. I choked, and so did the others. Raising my head, I saw a blast of green magic burst from the ball of flames in the center of the merry-go-round. It flew right at us, knocking us down. My head hit the ground, and everything went black.

20

MY eyes fluttered open. I felt like a Mack Truck had run me down. I moaned and propped myself up on my elbows. Ethan was about twenty feet away, lying in a crumpled heap. I rolled onto all fours, feeling the pain of every move, and pulled myself over to him. "Ethan." My voice was weak and hoarse. Someone groaned, but I didn't look back. I had to get to Ethan. I had to make sure he was okay.

"Sam?" Shannon called.

"Check Dylan." I grabbed Ethan's shoulder and gently shook him. "Ethan, can you hear me?" I brushed the grass and dirt off the side of his face. "Ethan." Panic gripped my heart and lungs. I didn't know what kind of magic it was that had hit us or what it had done to Ethan. I gently lifted his head, noticing the cut near his temple. "Shannon!"

She rushed to me. "What? Is he hurt?"

"He's bleeding. He must have hit his head on something."

"Like that." Shannon pointed to a sharp rock sticking out of the ground.

"Can you help me heal him?"

She bent down next to me. Healing took a lot of energy. She held her hand over the gash on Ethan's head. I placed my hand right on it, careful not to hurt him further. I wasn't scared of a little blood, especially not Ethan's. We both focused our magic on healing Ethan's head. I felt the cut closing under my fingers, and I knew the magic was extending deeper, healing any damage we couldn't see. Ethan stirred, and Shannon pulled away. I lowered my hand and touched his chest, holding him back so he didn't try to get up too quickly.

"What was that?" His voice was hoarse, but otherwise he seemed okay.

"I don't know, but take it easy, okay?" I looked back at Dylan. He was sitting up, but he looked a little dazed. "You all right?"

"Working on it." His eyes closed as he focused on healing his injuries. Finally, he stood. "Broken wrist. I'm okay now."

Even though I'd just helped heal Ethan and watched Dylan heal himself, I couldn't get over the extent of our powers. Forget modern medicine. Being a witch was a thousand times better.

I helped Ethan sit up. "We healed your head, but are you hurt anywhere else?"

"No. I'm okay. A little freaked by whatever that thing was that attacked us."

"Do you think it was Mirabella? Was she blocking us, fighting back?" My eyes traveled the coven, searching for theories.

Shannon shrugged. "Your guess is as good as mine."

Great, so we were basically clueless, and we hadn't located Mirabella. "What now? Do we try again?"

"No way." Ethan stood up. I kept my hand on him, making sure he was steady on his feet. "Sam, I'm not going to break. You can relax."

Shannon and Dylan turned away, pretending to check out the merry-go-round for clues about what that green burst of magic was and where it had come from, but I knew they were trying to avoid the awkwardness of the situation between Ethan and me.

I sighed. "Ethan, I don't mean to coddle you, but you've been pulling away from me so much and relying on Dylan like you need a babysitter."

"I don't want to hurt you or anyone else. Do you think I like having Dylan hovering over me all the time?"

"You seek him out, and you find excuses to avoid touching me."

He looked down at the ground. "Because I'm scared."

I rubbed his arms. "We're going to fix this. You'll be yourself again soon."

"That's not what I'm worried about." He met my eyes. "If I ever hurt you…"

"You can't. I'm wearing—" Oh, God! The necklace hadn't stopped that magic from reaching me. I was thrown with everyone else.

"What?" Worry lines creased Ethan's forehead.

"Guys!" I waved Shannon and Dylan back over. "The necklace. It must not work anymore."

Shannon held her hand out. "Let me see it." I took it off and handed it to her.

Ethan stepped back. "Sam, back away from me. I don't want you near me without that on."

"It didn't protect me. I was thrown off the merry-go-round just like you were."

"Damn her!" Dylan yelled.

"What is it?" Who was he talking about? Had Mirabella destroyed the necklace somehow—removed the spell on it?

"Nora." Dylan threw his hands in the air. "She removed the protective spell from the necklace. This wasn't protecting you at all."

My eyes went to Shannon. I half-expected her to look away in shame, but she met my gaze head-on. "You never tried to do a harmful spell on me."

"I only had to make Ethan think I did." She shrugged. "It worked, so you can't be mad at me for not really trying to cover you in blood and sic hungry animals on you."

Ethan looked horrified. I reached for him, but he pulled away. "Don't."

"Don't you see? You didn't hurt me. Even without the necklace protecting me, you didn't hurt me. Think about it, Ethan. In sculpture, in the clearing in the woods, you didn't hurt me either time."

"That's true," Shannon said. "Only Dylan and I felt the wrath of your dark magic. And by the way, thanks again for that."

I shot her a look before grabbing Ethan's hands. He tugged, but I persisted. "You won't hurt me. You could have several times already, but you didn't. Something inside you is stronger than this magic. I don't need the necklace because *you're* protecting me."

"Oh, gag me." Shannon rolled her eyes. "Don't break into a whole 'our love is stronger than any evil' speech because I'll throw up right here, and I promise to hit your shoes."

"Give the sarcasm a rest, Shannon," Dylan said. "This is serious."

Ethan was quiet for a minute. "Can you put the spell back on the necklace—or better yet, on her ring?"

Put a spell to protect me from Ethan on the very ring he'd given me? No! "I don't want a spell put on my ring. I love this ring, exactly how it is. And for the thousandth time, I trust you, Ethan."

"Well, I don't!" He pulled away from me and ran his fingers through his hair. "You're giving me too much credit. I'm not like you, Sam. I didn't battle cancer. I didn't fight back from a spell that made me kill or die all over again. You survived those things. All I did was watch helplessly from the sidelines."

"That's crap, Ethan, and you know it!" I stormed over to him, tired of this distance he kept trying to put between us for my safety. "You didn't sit back and watch. You pulled me through it all. I would've given up if you hadn't been there to give me a reason to live. You were strong enough for the both of us." I grabbed his face in my hands and pressed my lips to his. This time he didn't back away. He kissed me, like we hadn't kissed in ages, which was exactly how it felt.

I forgot about Dylan and Shannon. I forgot about Nora's dark magic lurking inside Ethan. I forgot we were standing in a playground and not in the privacy of the cottage. Time stood still for us. Nothing else mattered except for us being close, in each other's arms. I tightened my grip on him, breathing him in like air. Completely breathless, we tilted our foreheads together and came up for air.

"Sorry." The word was barely audible, but Ethan brushed his lips quickly across mine, silencing me, so I knew he'd heard it.

"I'm not. I needed that, and not just the incredible kiss. I needed to hear that. I'm not weak. I hate that this magic is making me feel like I am. It's not me. Maybe I'm not as strong as you, but I'm not going to cower in the corner, either."

"You *are* as strong as I am." I laced my fingers through his. "And we're in this together. It's not just your fight. Let me repay you for how much you've helped me be strong in the past. Together, Nora's spell is in for some major ass-kicking."

He smiled. "Together." It was how things were always supposed to be with us. We were Ethan and Sam. We went together. We made sense.

"If you two are done sucking each other's faces, you might want to come over here." Shannon waved us to the merry-go-round. "We think we found something."

Hand in hand, Ethan and I walked over to them. "What is it?" I asked. Had we located Mirabella after all?

"Whatever it was that attacked us," Dylan raised his hand like he was feeling the air, "it left a trail. I think together we can trace it back to the source." *Together.* There was that word again. I loved the sound of it.

"What if the place it leads isn't where we're trying to go?" Ethan asked. "We don't know who tried to attack us."

Shannon shook her head. "There's no *tried* about it. We were attacked. You were unconscious, and Dylan broke his wrist. That thing succeeded."

"Okay, fine, but Ethan's right." I had this nagging feeling. "Do you think the coven, Ms. Matthews's coven, is searching for us? That they're the ones who did that, to stop us from finding Mirabella?"

Ethan rubbed my arm. He knew I felt guilty for going to Ms. Matthews on my own. It had been a stupid, reckless idea, and now we were all on the run because of it. "Do *you* think they're after us? I mean, how did she seem after she told you she's a witch?"

I sighed. "I don't know. My mind feels like mush right now."

"Try to remember, Sam." Ethan squeezed my hand, giving me strength.

"She said we should combine covens. She said it was the only way to help you."

"Wait." Dylan held his hand up. "You told us about all the weird things Ms. Matthews has been doing. When did she offer to help Ethan? How does she even know about him?"

That was a good question. "I don't know how she knows about him. She didn't say. I'm not sure I trust her. She was so cryptic and strange. I ran away from her because I wasn't about to sit around and wait for her coven to make a decision. They're teachers. They wouldn't let us attempt something this dangerous, even if it is the only way to save Ethan." My voice broke. "They'd probably want to be in charge of us if we joined with them, and we can't waste time arguing about the best way to get rid of this dark magic inside Ethan."

They all nodded in understanding. We were a family now, and we had to do what was best for ourselves.

"So what do you think Ms. Matthews is really after?" Shannon crossed her arms, and for once it wasn't an expression of boredom or annoyance. She was nervous. She was hugging herself, comforting herself.

"I don't know, but you guys said the dark magic Mirabella took from Dylan went into her, right?"

Dylan and Shannon nodded.

"Well, what if Ms. Matthews—or one of her coven—wants that dark magic?"

Ethan shook his head. "Who would willingly take this? I feel out of control, like I could set the world on fire at any moment. I'm struggling every second of the day to suppress this darkness within me. I can't imagine someone wanting to feel this way."

"That's because you're not evil," Dylan said. "You're not a dark witch. You didn't bring this on yourself. It was done *to* you, without your knowledge."

Shannon shrugged, but she kept her arms crossed. "I don't see what the big deal is. We want the dark magic out of Ethan, so if Ms. Matthews wants it, let her have it. What do we care?"

Dylan scoffed. "You can be such an idiot sometimes."

"Don't start. Either of you." Why was I always having to play referee with them? "We aren't going to figure this out by arguing. I think what Dylan is trying to say," I paused to glare at Dylan, "is that letting a witch who wants that kind of dark magic take it would be a really bad thing."

"Try a hell of a lot worse than bad." Dylan rolled his eyes. "She'd be unstoppable. She could take us all out, easily."

"Then what do we do?" Shannon dropped her arms in defeat.

I looked at Ethan. He was staying quiet, letting us think through all this. I knew he didn't want to put us in any more danger, but I really wanted his opinion. "What do you think we should do?"

He took a deep breath and let his gaze fall on each of us. "I think we have to trace this magic and see who's trying to hurt us. If it leads to Ms. Matthews, at least we'll know where she is and how to avoid her. If it leads to Mirabella, then all the better."

Dylan stepped closer, making our more-square-than-circle group tighter. "You should know that if we trace this magic, whoever cast it can then trace our spell back to us. If it's Ms. Matthews and her coven, we'd be leading them right to us. We could run, but they wouldn't be far behind."

"That's a risk we're going to have to take," Ethan said.

The rest of us nodded in agreement. One way or another, we were about to track down an evil. One that could easily track us down in return.

21

THE merry-go-round looked almost menacing, like it was challenging me. I stepped up, taking the same place I'd stood in earlier. Dylan and Shannon were right. I could sense the magic that had been used on us. It felt dark, evil beyond anything I could imagine. If I hadn't known for sure that Nora was dead, I would've suspected she was behind the attack. But looking at Ethan, practically crawling in his own skin, I knew that wasn't possible. The only part of Nora that was lingering here was now inside Ethan. For a split second, I jumped to an awful conclusion. What if Ethan had caused the spell? What if the darkness we were about to trace led us back to him? Then what?

But no. It couldn't. Ethan had been knocked unconscious. If he'd caused the burst of dark magic, it wouldn't have hurt him, too. Or would it? He didn't know how to use the magic. He'd just been tapping into it by accident. Could the magic manifest itself without Ethan even knowing? Could it have clashed with the spell we were doing and backfired on all of us, including Ethan?

Oh, God, I hated that I was questioning him like this. He was Ethan. Perfect and sweet. Only he wasn't just Ethan anymore. He was a witch, a cursed witch. I had no idea what that part of him was capable of.

"Everyone ready?" Dylan asked.

Ever since Ethan's magic had changed, gone all screwy, Shannon had taken over leading the group spells. Dylan had stepped back, probably because what was happening to Ethan felt all too familiar to him. But this time Dylan was back in the leadership role. I wondered what had changed. Did he want to find Mirabella that badly?

Ethan and Shannon were nodding in reply. I followed along.

"Good. Be ready. We have no idea what's on the other side of this spell. If anything bad starts to happen, break the circle. Everyone understand that?" His eyes shifted to each of us. I'd never seen him look so serious, and considering Dylan wasn't much of a joker these days, that was saying a lot.

Apparently our attention wasn't a good enough answer because he repeated the question. We all said yes.

"Good. Now everyone follow my lead." He closed his eyes, so we did the same. "Through air and space, this magic we trace. Reveal the one from whom the spell was done."

We all repeated the lines, and like last time, I felt our combined powers flow between us. Every so often, I felt a tugging sensation in my stomach, like something was pulling me toward the center of the circle. Even though closing my eyes helped me stay focused, I felt the need to look at the invisible force pulling on me. I opened my eyes and saw an image. Afraid to speak and break the spell, I tugged on Dylan and Ethan's hands, hoping they'd open their eyes to see what was wrong. They did. I motioned to the image. Ethan tugged on Shannon's hand, and she opened her eyes, too.

None of us spoke. We just watched. It was a house in the woods. It looked secluded, but it was hard to tell. A light went on in the lower left window. Someone was there. A burst of green energy seeped under the window and snaked through the trees. It wiggled closer, coming straight at…us! Dylan's warning screamed in my head, and I broke the circle. I let go of Dylan's hand, still clutching Ethan's tightly, and jumped off the merry-go-round. Ethan came with me, leaving Dylan and Shannon staring where the image used to be. It was gone.

"Whoever it was tried to hurt us again," Shannon said.

Dylan nodded and jumped down from the merry-go-round. "And they were definitely using dark magic. That thing was green with dark power."

"But did it tell us anything? We still don't know who it is or where they are, and now they can trace our magic here, to us." I was seriously panicking. I hated snakes, and big, green, magical snakes were about a thousand times worse.

"We can trace it." Dylan walked to the car with Shannon right behind him. Ethan and I watched, not sure what they were doing. We were still pretty new to this stuff. Dylan turned the key in the ignition while Shannon mumbled a spell, holding her hands over the hood of the car. If anyone saw this—anyone who wasn't a witch—it would look like Shannon was talking to the engine. She put her arms down, and Dylan shouted, "Get in and buckle up." The engine revved, and I noticed Dylan didn't have his foot on the pedal.

"Is the car doing that on its own?" I asked, skeptical to get in a car that seemed to be possessed by magic.

"Yes, and if you don't hurry up and get in, it's going to leave without you."

Dylan's words slammed into me. Ethan and I ran for the back seat. We barely had the doors closed when the car peeled out of the playground. Shannon laughed. She was riding shotgun, and she'd managed to get her seat belt on before the Mazda turned into a psycho driving machine. Ethan and I weren't so lucky. We slid across the black leather seats. Ethan reached his hand around my head just seconds before I smacked into the window.

"Thanks." I grabbed my seat belt and clicked it into place. Ethan did the same. We were safe. For now, at least. "Where are we going?"

"Not a clue," Dylan said, his hands resting in his lap.

"You better put your hands on the wheel and at least pretend you're driving. People are going to be very suspicious of a car that looks like it's driving itself."

"It *is* driving itself." Dylan wasn't used to being around people all the time. Before he met Ethan and me, he hadn't even attended school. He was getting better at acting normal around non-witches, but every once in a while we had to remind him of things other people would think were weird. Like a car that drove itself.

"She's right, Dylan." Shannon put her feet up on the dashboard. "Put your hands on the wheel."

He huffed, but he listened.

"Do you mind?" Ethan asked Shannon. "The dashboard isn't a footrest."

Shannon groaned as she lowered her feet. "I was trying to get comfortable. Who knows how long of a drive we're in for?"

Which brought up the question, what would we do if we ran out of gas? "This thing is really going to take us to that house in the woods? How is that possible?"

"I told it to follow the trail of magic." Shannon twisted in her seat so she could see me sitting behind her.

"But we saw the snake thing in the image, not around us."

"We saw where it was coming from, not the entire path it traveled." She twisted her hair in her fingers like she didn't have a care in the world. I had a hard time understanding how she and Dylan were so nonchalant about all this.

"Have you guys done this spell before? You're a little too calm right now, when I think you should be freaking out like Ethan and I are."

Shannon laughed. "I bewitch my car all the time. It's like having your own personal chauffeur." Why was I not surprised?

Ethan rested his hand on mine. "We should call Gloria and Jackson. There's no way we'll be back in time for work."

We were missing a lot of work these past two days. "I hate leaving them hanging again. What if we lose our jobs over this? It's not like we can tell them the truth. I mean, imagine Gloria's face if I tell her, 'Sorry, we can't come to work today because our car is driving us to the source of this evil magic that tried to kill us.' She'd fire us on the spot for lying to her. Only we wouldn't be lying."

"We could do a spell to make her think you have the day off," Shannon suggested.

I shook my head. "Spells aren't the answer for everything."

She shrugged. "I can't say I agree. I haven't found a situation a spell couldn't fix."

How about this one with Ethan? But I couldn't say that. "I'm not doing a spell on Gloria. End of story."

"Fine." Shannon let out a long sigh. "Tell her Ethan's still sick and you had a relapse."

That wasn't bad, but we were on the highway now and even with the windows up, the noise outside would give us away. Gloria would never believe we were home sick. "She's going to hear the other cars out there."

Shannon smiled and wagged her eyebrows. "Not if we cast a silencing spell around the car. See, magic cures all." She turned around, no doubt feeling happy for winning the debate. As much as I didn't want to admit magic was the answer, this time it really seemed to be.

"Go ahead and do it," I said. It was easier to let Shannon cast the spell since she already knew it.

"Happy to." Her voice was so sweet I think it gave me a cavity. I waited for her to say the spell was cast before I took out my cell and dialed Gloria.

"Do you want me to do it?" Ethan asked. "I know you hate to lie."

True, but I'd had plenty of practice lately. "It's okay. Besides, she thought you were worse off than I was anyway. It makes more sense for me to call." The diner phone rang six times before Gloria picked up. Not a good sign. It meant they were busy.

"Pocono Diner, this is Gloria speaking. What can I do for you?"

"Gloria, it's Sam."

Shannon turned around and glared at me. Oh, right. I was supposed to sound sick. I coughed a few times.

"Samantha, you don't sound good. Don't tell me that boy got you sick again."

"I think I'm having a relapse. I thought I was feeling better yesterday when I stopped by the diner, but I might have overdone it."

"I'd say so, with the way you were running around doing everything around here. I've never seen anyone move that fast."

"Yeah, the fever made me act really weird. That's why I'm calling. I wanted to make sure you and Jackson are feeling okay. I'd feel terrible if I got either of you sick."

"Sugar, we're fine. Don't you worry about us. How's Ethan doing today? Any better?"

"No. Worse, actually. I don't think either of us will be able to come to work."

"Now, don't you even think of doing anything like that. You stay home and get some rest. I'll send Jackson by the next time we have a lull in the crowd. He'll bring you both some soup."

"No! Really, that's not necessary. Ethan's mom made enough soup for both of us. She sent some over a few minutes ago." Gloria and Jackson had no idea Ethan and I lived together. When Gloria hired us, I told her I didn't have all my identification or even a bank account since we'd just moved. She agreed to pay us both in cash for the time being, and she'd continued to do so ever since. Ethan and I hadn't filled out a single form, which meant Gloria didn't even have the fake PO address I used for school.

"Okay, then. If you're sure you have everything you need, we'll leave you be. But if you need anything, you call me, okay? Ethan, too."

"Thanks, Gloria. You're the best." I coughed again, realizing I hadn't in a while.

"Take care, Samantha." Gloria hung up. My chest tightened. She was so good to us, and we were lying to her. I hated it.

Ethan rubbed my shoulder. "You did the right thing."

"Then why do I feel like the worst person on the planet?"

He kissed my cheek, and I felt a little better. I was doing this for Ethan, and lying to Gloria was better for her, too. She didn't need to be wrapped up in all this magic.

We drove for hours. Dylan kept watching the gas gauge. Luckily, Ethan had filled the tank earlier in the week. Otherwise we would've been running on fumes by now. The car showed no signs of slowing down. None of us felt up to small talk. What did you say when you knew you were on your way to face some evil that had already tried to kill you twice?

Ethan rested his head on the back of the seat and wrapped his arm around me. I tugged on my seat belt, loosening it enough to snuggle into Ethan's side. If I closed my eyes, I could almost pretend things were back to normal. Almost. I must have relaxed at some point because, before I knew it, I was asleep.

Someone shook me lightly. I opened my eyes to see Dylan. "You snore. Just in case you were wondering."

"Great. Thanks." I didn't know what else to say to that. "We stopped."

"Yeah. I got the car to pull over."

"Why? How? What's wrong?" I sat up, and my movement woke Ethan.

"Are we here?" He had his sexy I-just-woke-up voice.

"No. Dylan stopped the car."

"Why?" He was fully awake now.

"Would you two chill? We've been driving for hours, and Shannon and I got hungry. She went into the mini-mart to get some sandwiches."

"How will the car pick up on the trail again?" I couldn't believe they'd stopped for food. Sure, Ethan and I had fallen asleep, but we hadn't messed with the spell.

"We only paused the spell. We're still on the trail. The mini-mart is on the way." He cocked his head to the side. "Would you trust me? It's no different than hitting pause on your DVR."

That didn't make me feel better, but I let it go. What was done was done. Shannon came back to the car holding a bag and a tray with four coffees. Bless her! I really needed a caffeine jolt right now.

"Oh, thank God you two are awake." She slid into her seat, handing the bag to Dylan. "You guys are perfect for each other. You both snore loud enough to wake the dead."

Ethan and I couldn't help smiling at each other. Neither of us knew the other snored. Apparently because we did it together.

"Who wants Italian and who wants roast beef?" Dylan asked, holding out two subs.

"Roast beef," Ethan and I both said.

"Sickening," Shannon mumbled. "It's like you two share a brain."

Ethan squeezed my leg before taking the sandwiches from Dylan.

"Everyone get strapped in before we get the spell going again," Dylan said.

Shannon buckled up and passed our coffees back to us. Luckily, the back doors had cup holders. There wasn't much this car didn't have. Thank God Ethan had kept it when we ran away. It was the one luxury we had left.

With everything secured, Shannon resumed the spell, and the car shot out of the parking lot.

"Couldn't you have told the car to observe the speed limits on the way?" I asked. "If a cop tries to pull us over, it's going to be hard to explain that it was speeding on its own."

"Ha-ha." Shannon took a big bite of her Italian hero. It amazed me how relaxed she was around us. In school she always tried to act so perfect all the time. I knew it was probably left over from her brief reign as the popular bitch of the school, but I liked her a lot better this way. I could even tolerate her sarcasm better.

Sirens blared behind us. We were going to find out how a cop reacted to this spell after all.

22

"**D**AMN it!" Dylan smacked the steering wheel, which he'd been forgetting to hold. I could only imagine what the cop thought of us as he pulled up in the lane to our left. Dylan had both hands on his hoagie. Just great. It probably looked like he was eating and steering with his knees on top of speeding. We were so getting a ticket. Maybe two.

"Drop the spell," I said, lightly kicking the back of Shannon's seat. She mumbled, hiding her face behind her sandwich so the cop didn't think she was cursing him out on top of the number of other offenses we'd already tallied up. The car began to slow and Dylan grabbed the wheel, pulling over to the side of the road.

"Switch seats with me," Shannon said, undoing her seat belt and tugging on Dylan's arm.

"What? Why?"

"Just do it!" She undid his seat belt. Dylan grunted and struggled to get over the middle console at the same time Shannon was trying to. If we weren't totally about to get busted, it would've been funny. Shannon was clicking her seat belt when the cop tapped on her window. She hit the window button and even though I couldn't see her face, I knew she was flashing her smile at Officer Going-to-Bust-Our-Asses.

"License and registration."

"Officer, did I do something wrong?" Shannon's innocent school-girl act was over the top.

He leaned down, shining the flashlight into the car. "You weren't driving a minute ago."

"Yes, I was." Her voice was serious now.

"No, I saw *him*." He pointed the flashlight at Dylan.

"I'm sorry, Officer, but you must be mistaken." Shannon's voice was scaring me now. What was she doing? "This is my car, and I've been driving very safely, obeying every traffic law. You pulled me over because you think I'm pretty and want to ask for my phone number."

Oh, good Lord! She was going to get us arrested! I squeezed Ethan's hand and prayed for a miracle, like Shannon shutting her mouth for once.

The cop bent down so his face was level with Shannon's. "I just wanted to say that I think you're very pretty and I'd be honored if you'd give me your phone number so I could call you sometime."

Oh gross! The guy was like forty. Ethan nudged me and pointed to the cop's face. He had a dazed expression, which could only mean one thing—Shannon had cast a spell on him.

"I'd love to give you my phone number, but unfortunately, I'm a minor. I wouldn't want a handsome police officer like yourself to get in trouble because of me." She ran her finger down the side of his face.

I gagged. Her magic wasn't the most powerful thing about Shannon. Apparently her stomach was made of steel because I was ready to spew my roast beef.

"I understand. Here's my card. You give me a call when you turn eighteen."

"I'll do that." Shannon put the window up. The cop stood there dazed for another minute before he finally turned and walked back to his car.

"Are you crazy?" I sat forward and smacked her arm.

"I saved our asses. You're welcome." She turned away and added, "And once again, magic solves everything."

"Just put the spell back up," Dylan said. "And this time, add a line about obeying traffic laws."

I wanted to throw it in her face that I was right, but I really didn't want a war with Shannon, so I kept my mouth shut.

We didn't talk for a while after we got going again. The spell was much more under control. No more dangerous speeds or almost running off the road. I knew Ethan was doing his best to stay calm, but it felt like every mile we got closer to finding the source of the dark magic that attacked us made him jumpier. I took advantage of any break in his tension, no matter how small.

"Don't worry about me," he whispered, kissing my ear. "I'm fine."

"You've been okay for a while now, you know that? I think you're getting a better handle on the magic. It's not controlling you anymore." I wasn't sure if I was trying to convince him or me.

"Yeah. I think I can handle this. At least until we find this Mirabella and she gets the dark magic out of me for good."

If she was willing to help us. I couldn't help feeling like it was her magic that had attacked us. It had certainly felt dark, and it looked an awful lot like the green magic that had snaked out of Ethan when he tapped into the curse Nora had placed on him. Dylan had said he'd been like Ethan. It would make sense that the dark magic Mirabella took from Dylan looked exactly like Ethan's. That didn't comfort me because what would we do if the one witch who could help us wanted us dead?

"Whoa." Shannon gripped the steering wheel like she was trying to fight the spell on the car. "I know this place." Her voice was full of panic.

"What's wrong? Where are we?" It was too hard to see. The streetlights had disappeared about two miles back, and the moon wasn't bright enough to light up the area. How in the world did Shannon recognize anything in this darkness?

"I've been here, or I've at least seen it." She shook her head. "I'm not sure which, but I have a really bad feeling."

"We've all seen this," Dylan said, his nose pressed against the window. "Part of it, at least. These are the woods we saw in the image at the merry-go-round."

Dylan was right. We'd made it. I wasn't sure how I felt about that. Relieved? Terrified? Shannon was obviously terrified by it, and that didn't sit well with me. Ethan squeezed my hand. "Hopefully, this will all be over soon."

I forced a smile and nodded, hoping the car was too dark for him to see the fear in my eyes. Shannon's panic wasn't helping either.

"Knock it off!" Dylan grabbed her wrists, pulling her hands from the steering wheel. The car turned off the road and onto the grass. We all screamed and bounced around in our seats. Ethan's Mazda wasn't exactly an off-road vehicle, and if this spell totaled the car, Ethan was going to total Shannon.

"Undo the spell! Undo the spell!" Ethan was gripping the seat, probably more out of fear for the car than for all of us. We came dangerously close to hitting a huge tree.

"Shannon!" I didn't know what else to do to snap her out of her shock or whatever it was she was going through. She wasn't listening. Dylan started mumbling a spell, and my heart raced, willing him to hurry up and finish it. The car must've hit a big rock or a tree root because we were actually airborne for a moment. Dylan's head slammed into the passenger door. He slumped sideways in his seat. "Dylan!" I reached for him, but there was blood dripping down his face. He wasn't going to be finishing the spell. Shannon was screaming hysterically in the front seat, still wrestling the steering wheel. Little Miss Spells-Work-for-Everything was doing everything *but* using magic.

I gripped Ethan's hand. "Follow my lead." I had no clue how to undo another witch's spell. It was completely foreign territory for me. So instead, I focused on stopping the car. That was it. Not ending the spell. We'd deal with that later. My mind raced, and I swear my brain was being jostled around with every bump we hit. The words weren't coming to me. Of all times to choke and freeze up, I had to pick now.

Ethan squeezed my hand. "Say what you want the car to do. The spell doesn't have to be pretty to be effective."

He was right. I'd done some really awful spells before, as far as wording goes, and they'd still worked. I took a deep breath, got jostled again, and started the spell. The first thing that popped into my head was a spell from *Harry Potter*, but I was no Dumbledore, not even close. I took Ethan's advice and went with my own words, not caring that they were nowhere near as cool as the headmaster's.

"Stop the car. Go no far." Totally craptastic.

Ethan picked up with the spell. It sounded better coming from him, and at least we'd be making fools of ourselves together. We chanted, letting our magic build and surround the car. The brakes squeaked, which I knew broke Ethan's heart. But brakes could be fixed. If the spell totaled the car, Ethan wouldn't be able to afford a new one, not even an old clunker.

A tree was directly in front of us. I pushed my feet and right hand against Dylan's seat. This was the point in Driver's Ed where the instructor stomps on his brake from the passenger seat. I didn't have a brake, but my foot didn't seem to understand that. I chanted louder, as if that was going to make the spell work any faster. I felt my magic growing in strength and threw all of that force behind my words. The car swerved slightly and came to rest only inches from the tree.

"Oh my God. Oh my God." Shannon was panting, and her knuckles were white from her death grip on the steering wheel.

"Is everyone okay?" I asked, knowing we weren't. Dylan was bleeding and out cold in the front seat. Shannon was a wreck who apparently could only mutter one phrase, and Ethan... His eyes were locked in front of us. "Ethan?" A chill went through me, starting at my hand, which was still in Ethan's. No. He wasn't using his dark magic. I was imagining things. He was shocked and relieved that we hadn't hit the tree. That was all. It had to be.

Shannon stopped saying "Oh my God" and turned toward us. Her eyes fell on Ethan. "Sam." Her face lost the little color it had left. "Get out of the car. Now!"

"Shannon, relax. It's okay. He's stunned. That's all."

"Don't be an idiot. He tapped into it again. Look at him."

I stared at Ethan's face, which was emotionless. "Ethan, look at me. Please. Focus. Fight this." I touched his cheek. He felt clammy. I was about to say his name again when something moved across the back of my hand. A greenish glow wound around Ethan's and my hands, tying us together.

"What is he doing to you?" Shannon's eyes were huge, and she had her seat belt off, ready to bolt. I knew she was thinking about the green snake that had attacked her in the clearing.

"I don't know. I'm okay, though. It doesn't hurt."

"Get your hand out of his before that thing attacks you." Shannon's voice squeaked.

I didn't want to let go of Ethan. I felt so disconnected from him already. I summoned my own magic instead. I focused on sending calming waves of energy at Ethan. I had to calm him down, get him to block the darkness within him.

"Sam." Shannon's squeak was worse, but I ignored her, continuing to concentrate on helping Ethan. This had to work. I wasn't losing him to this magic. "Damn it, Sam!"

What was her problem? Couldn't she see I was in the middle of a spell to save Ethan?

Creaking and the sound of wood splitting made me jerk my eyes open. The enormous tree in front of us was shaking. Literally shaking, despite its monstrous size. "What's happening?"

"Ask your boyfriend. I have a feeling he's behind this. Look at him." Shannon unclicked her seat belt and started her own spell.

She was right about Ethan. He was focused on the tree. His stone-cold face was nearly unrecognizable. How was this happening? He was going to bring the tree down right on us!

"Ethan!"

"That's not going to work." Shannon reached across Dylan and pushed his door open. He sat up in his seat.

"Dylan, are you okay?"

"He's under a zombie spell. He can't answer you. I ordered him to get out of the freakin' car. Now, you do the same."

"What about Ethan? I'm not leaving him to get crushed."

Shannon was out the door already, but she paused and looked at me. "I'll try a zombie spell on him, but there's no guarantee it will work. He's doing a hell of a spell of his own right now. I may not be able to break through."

"Try it." I pried my hand from his. His grip was so strong, but Shannon's spell was weakening him slightly. The tree continued to creak and sway. Some of the limbs came crashing down around us. I jumped with each thump and shake of the ground.

"It's not working," Shannon said, her face twisted in pain. "I'm giving this every ounce of strength I have."

"Go. Get out of here." I couldn't let her die. Ethan was my responsibility. I grabbed him and tugged him toward the door. He barely moved and stayed focused on the tree. My thoughts swirled with stupid idea after stupid idea. Nothing was going to move him. He was determined to crush this car with him inside. It made no sense. "This isn't happening!" I pulled myself onto his lap, putting my face in his and blocking his view of the tree. "Ethan! Look at me! Look at me!"

"Sam, get out! The tree is coming down!" Shannon ran, but her eyes stayed locked on me.

I turned in time to see the tree falling on the car and hear the crunch of metal.

23

MY hands flew up like I was going to catch the tree that was about to bash my skull in. A whoosh of energy burst out of me in a golden light, and then everything got still. Time seemed to stop. The tree was on the car, but it wasn't crushing us. I was actually holding it up, not with muscle, with magic.

"Holy crap!" Shannon rushed to the back door and yanked it open. "How are you doing that?" It wasn't so much the fact that my magic could support the tree. It was the fact that I'd been able to react and summon my magic in time, while still panicking. I had no clue how I'd done it.

"Can you help me? The spell is slipping, and I still need to get Ethan out of here." I couldn't look back to check on him. If I did, the spell would break. I was using all my magical strength to maintain the spell and keep us alive.

"Okay." Shannon raised her hands and mumbled under her breath. Hearing her made me realize I'd cast a spell without saying a word. I'd never cast a spell of this size without speaking the words aloud. This was huge. My powers were really coming around. "I've got it," Shannon yelled. "Get out."

Even though Shannon had her own spell going on, I was afraid to drop my hands. I tested it out, slowly lowering just one, making sure the tree didn't come down on the car any more. It held. I lowered the other hand. Still good. Ethan's head was resting on the back of the seat. His eyes were shut like he was sleeping. What had happened to him? "Ethan." I cupped his cheek.

"Um, we kind of don't have time to coddle him right now. This tree is massively heavy." Shannon's voice was strained. The weight of the spell was wearing her out. She didn't have the power of two witches inside her like I did.

I grabbed Ethan's arm, wrapping it around my neck. I wedged myself into his side and tried to lift him up. He slumped forward, nearly crushing me.

"Use a spell!" Shannon was in serious trouble, which meant I was in even worse trouble—dead trouble.

I concentrated my magic on lifting Ethan. He wasn't using any spells now, so his magic didn't fight me. He moved—well, like a zombie. Like Dylan had. Where was Dylan? I couldn't think about that. I had to keep going. The second Ethan and I were out of the car, Shannon dropped to her knees. I pushed Ethan forward so he wouldn't get hit by any branches. He slumped onto the grass. Shannon groaned as she lost control of her spell. The tree finished its fall with a squeal of bending metal. The remaining branches lashed out, hitting Shannon and me on the back and shoulders.

I went down hard, so hard my head bounced. My nose smacked into the ground on the second bounce. My eyes shut, and I drifted off. Not to sleep. To some weird semiconscious state. I knew I was hurt. I felt the pain in my back and nose. Yet I was somewhat detached from what was happening. I felt more like I was remembering an injury, rather than experiencing it. Like it was days or weeks old. Warmth spread throughout my body, making my face and back tingle. My magic was healing me. I didn't remember telling it to. It sort of did it on its own.

"Sam?" Ethan's voice sounded strained, filled with pain. Was I imagining him? I saw him fall down. He was unconscious, like Dylan. Maybe I was dead. Maybe we all were. "Sam." Hands gently lifted my head. "Can you hear me? Can you open your eyes?"

My eyelids fluttered. Ethan stared down at me. He sighed, and his entire body shivered. His eyes were bloodshot and filled with tears. "I thought you were dead." The words were a whisper on his lips, like he wasn't really intending for me to hear them.

"Is she…?" Shannon rushed over. "Oh, thank God." She had this look like she wanted to reach out and hug me.

I tried to sit up, but my body wasn't ready yet. My back was still healing. My magic was strong, and it was working as quickly as it could to fix me. That could only mean my injuries were pretty bad. I had no doubt I'd be paralyzed if I didn't have this magic inside me. My spine certainly felt shattered.

"Take it easy. Don't try to move yet." Ethan's bottom lip quivered. He was trying to act normal, but he knew this incident had happened because of the darkness within him. He used his shirt to wipe the blood from my nose.

"Do I look like I just went four rounds in the ring with…?" I couldn't think of a single boxer's name. My mind wouldn't function properly, probably because it was focused on the magic healing me.

"You look like you. You'll be fine. Shannon and Dylan will heal you."

"We don't need to," Shannon said. "She's doing it herself."

"It sort of happened on its own. Weird, right?"

Shannon shook her head, still looking like she wanted to wrap her arms around me. God, I must have looked awful for her to be that concerned. "It's not doing it on its own. Your subconscious told the magic to heal you."

"Huh. Well, that's good to know." I was trying to lighten the mood, but Ethan and Shannon were not having it. "Where's Dylan? Is he okay?"

"He's still unconscious. I was going to heal him, but after I healed my shoulder, I wanted to check on you."

"Go help him. I'll be fine."

She swallowed hard and nodded, but her face gave her away. She wasn't sure if I was going to be able to heal myself.

"Ethan, how bad is it? Really."

He brushed his hand against my cheek. "I'm never doing magic again. Never. I hurt you, Sam. God, I hurt *you*, of all people. I brought that tree down on us. And the worst part was that there I was, sitting in my body as if it didn't even belong to me. I was watching in horror, screaming on the inside, but my body wouldn't listen to me. The magic wouldn't listen to me." His breathing was shaky. He took a minute to calm down. "When the tree fell and you stopped it—I'd never felt so relieved. I thought it was over. I saw you holding the tree up and then I blacked out. When I woke up on the grass, you were…"

"I was what?"

"You were pinned under the branch." Pinned? I'd thought the branch had just hit me. But it had trapped me.

"I got it off you."

"How?" He must have used magic. There was no other explanation for how he could've moved the branch.

"It was the last spell I'll ever do."

"Don't say that. We'll fix this." My back pinched—no, it was more like someone was jamming my spine back together. "Ahh!" My body went completely rigid. Not that I would've tried to move. I was afraid to even breathe. The pain was so intense I couldn't see straight. Ethan was a blur, though I knew him well enough to know his face was contorted in panic.

"What is it? What happened?"

"Her body is healing itself." The sound of Dylan's voice made me relax a little. At least he was okay. We were all alive. I was the worst one, but after my spine was back to normal, I'd be okay, too. "I'm guessing her spine took a beating." He could say that again.

Ethan hugged me tighter, which brought on another scream. My body was already pushing and pulling on itself. I couldn't handle him doing it, too.

"Leave her alone," Dylan said. "Try not to move her. This has to be painful enough for her. We have to wait until it's over."

"Don't do anything? Can't you and Shannon do a spell to stop her from feeling the pain?"

"No. Pain is the way the body senses what's wrong. If she can't feel it, her body can't heal itself." Dylan was right. As much as I wanted to beg for a spell to ease this torture, I had to let my magic and body work together until I was back to normal again. My nose tingled for a split second, and I knew what was coming. It was broken and my magic was about to set it back in place. I squeezed my fists and clenched my teeth, but still the sickening crunch of bone and cartilage churned my stomach. I resisted the urge to throw up. I couldn't even roll onto my side. If I threw up while lying on my broken back like this, I'd probably choke to death on my own vomit.

"I can't sit here and watch her go through this!" Ethan yelled. "There has to be something we can do. I did this. I have to fix it." His words tore my heart to shreds. I hated that he felt responsible. It wasn't his fault. It was Nora's. All of this was her fault. I hated her even more for making Ethan feel this way. I wanted to tell him that, but the pain was blinding. I couldn't form words.

"I'm going to knock her out," Dylan said.

"What?" Ethan tightened his grip on me, and my back screamed in protest. "I'm not letting you touch her."

"Not like that. Her body started healing itself while she was unconscious. It's ten times more painful now that she's awake. If I knock her out again, she'll continue to heal, but she won't feel the pain as strongly." That made sense. That feeling of the pain being days old. Yes, that had been so much better than this.

"Do it," I managed to say.

Ethan's tears dripped onto my cheek. He nodded. Dylan knelt down next to me, holding his hands above my head. He muttered something, but I couldn't focus on the words because my head was only registering pain. Dylan's hands lowered to my eyes, which shut in response.

I drifted back to that state of in-between. Not conscious, not really unconscious, either. Dull. Everything felt dull. I could handle dull. I don't know how long I was like that, but I felt almost every vertebra in my back being repaired. After the final one clicked into place, I felt well enough to pull myself out of this state.

I opened my eyes. Ethan was still cradling my head in his lap. "Hey." My voice was hoarse. I sounded exhausted, probably because my body *was* exhausted. I'd spent all my energy healing myself.

"Hey." Ethan had that look again. Like he didn't want to be touching me. Like he wanted to put the distance of the Earth between us. Now that he knew I was okay, he was dying to get away from me for my own good. Only I didn't see it that way.

Dylan stood up and looked around. "We need to get her some-where where she can lie down and get some rest."

"How?" Shannon asked. "We don't exactly have a car anymore, and we're in the middle of the woods."

"Is the spell still on the car?" I propped myself up on my elbows, testing out my newly healed back. So far so good. "The spell I used was only supposed to stop the car, not end the spell."

"Then it should still be working, but that doesn't really matter. The car is totaled. It has a tree sticking out of it. Or into it." Shannon shook her head. "Either way, it's not going anywhere."

I sat up, still moving slowly. "Come on. Shannon Queen of Spells doesn't think we can use a little magic to lift the tree and free the car?"

She thought about it and looked at Dylan. "What do you think?"

He walked over to the hood of the car. "Most of the damage is to the roof and trunk. The hood looks okay. I'm guessing the engine is okay, too."

"I guess it's worth a try, then." Shannon held her hand out to me. I took it and let her pull me to my feet. I still felt a little woozy from all the magic I'd used. I was really hoping I could sit this one out. Now that Dylan was conscious, I didn't see why I couldn't.

Dylan waved Shannon to the car. "I'll raise the tree. You get the spell on the car working again. Everyone be ready to jump in."

Jump? I wasn't sure I could walk. I reached for Ethan for support. He looked scared of my hand, like he thought he'd melt me with his touch. "I'm still kind of shaky. I really need your help." Maybe playing the injured card wasn't the best idea considering how guilty he felt, but I didn't really have another option. I needed rest. Big time. I wasn't going to get it without his help.

He nodded and supported my weight. He half-carried me to the car and opened the door. We waited while Dylan worked the spell to lift the tree. I practically crawled into the back seat. Shannon jumped in the driver's seat and began working her spell. The passenger-side door was still open, so Dylan continued his spell as he walked toward it and got in the car. The car didn't sound great at all, but considering it looked like it had been through the compactor at the dump, it was doing just fine. Shannon helped the spell by steering to the left around the tree Dylan was still supporting. As soon as we were clear of the tree, Dylan let it fall. The ground shook, making the car shake and rattle, but we were on our way again.

Once we were out of danger, I fell asleep immediately. My body was too tired to keep going any longer. My head rested on Ethan's shoulder. I didn't even dream. I was completely dead to the world. When I woke up, the sun was coming up. The car was parked in the woods, but I could see a cottage up ahead. In so many ways, it reminded me of our cottage. It stood alone, with peeling paint, and rotting wood on the front steps. The windows were either broken or boarded up. I couldn't believe anyone would actually live here.

Ethan stirred and opened his eyes. "Hey, you okay?"

"Much better. When did we stop?"

"We found the cottage about twenty minutes after you passed out. We were all beat and wanted to rest up before we faced whatever's waiting for us, so we got some sleep."

"What if whoever's inside sees us?"

"Invisibility spell. No one will see us."

Shannon and Dylan stretched and turned around in their seats. Their eyes fell on me. I raised my hand. "Don't even ask. I'm fine. But where are we? This isn't the place we saw in the image at the merry-go-round."

"I know," Shannon said, lowering her eyes. "I think the spell messed up somehow."

"Great. What do we do now? Another locator spell?"

Dylan sighed. "I think we should go inside. We can call a cab or something."

"We're in a car." I wondered how bad his head injury had been, even if Shannon had healed it for him. "Besides, I don't think cabs come out into the woods like this."

"We're almost out of gas. We'd never make it out of here."

Of course. Just when I thought things couldn't get any worse. Silly me. "Maybe there's a gas tank around here somewhere. It doesn't look like anyone lives here, so it can't hurt to check."

Everyone nodded and got out of the car. Seeing it in daylight made it so much worse. Ethan's gorgeous red Mazda 6 looked like a crushed tin can. It broke my heart. So many good memories had happened in this car. All the long drives with Ethan holding my hand. Those were the highlight of my last few months before the cancer had taken over. I'd felt free driving in this car. And now it was gone.

We headed to the small shed first. No gas can. Really there was nothing but a dead raccoon and a couple of rusty gardening tools. We moved on to the house. We were here, so we might as well check everything. I swore the front steps were going to crumble under our feet, but they were surprisingly strong. I did a double take when I stepped on a hole and didn't fall through.

"Hey, check this out." Everyone watched while I did it again. "How is that possible?"

The front door opened. A beautiful woman with long auburn hair, a lot like Shannon's, stood before us. "It's possible because there's a spell on this house."

Dylan and Shannon's eyes bulged. "Mirabella?"

24

THIS was Mirabella? This forty-year-old woman who looked like she was a former supermodel? I'd been expecting a hideous witch, complete with warts. She stared at us, her eyes passing from Dylan to Shannon to me and, finally, resting on Ethan. "Well, isn't that interesting?"

"What?" I grabbed Ethan's arm, feeling very protective of him.

"The magic in this one is at odds with itself." She shook her head and *tsk*ed. "You all better come inside."

Dylan held his hand up. "Wait a minute. Why aren't you unhappy to see us?"

"Yeah," Shannon said. "We were kind of expecting you to curse at us or at the very least tell us to leave you alone. We never thought you'd invite us into your…" Shannon looked around at the peeling paint, broken windows, and rotting front door.

Mirabella smiled. "Like I said, it's under a spell. I don't want people to know I'm out here." She stepped aside, motioning for us to go inside. "Come in and you'll see what my home really looks like."

I looked at Shannon and Dylan. This was their call. They knew Mirabella better than I did. All I knew was she had taken the dark magic from Dylan. That had to make her somewhat evil, didn't it? I mean, look what it was doing to Ethan. Or had she learned how to manage it? How to suppress it?

Shannon shrugged. Dylan silently communicated a "keep your eyes open and be ready" before he stepped into the house first.

"How nice," Mirabella said. "You're all so in tune with each other. That's important for a coven." Of course she knew that was what we were. Ms. Matthews had said witches should be able to recognize other witches. Mirabella had seen the darkness in Ethan right away. It only made sense she'd pick up on the link that made us all a coven.

I followed Dylan inside, still holding on to Ethan. I wasn't letting go of him. Shannon walked in behind us. We were sticking together… just in case. The inside of the house was nothing like the outside. The furniture looked more expensive than Ethan's Mazda—before it got totaled by the tree. Even the carpet looked too expensive to walk on. I wondered if we should take off our shoes. I bet the plush silver carpeting would feel amazing on my feet, but it would also be harder to make a run for it with bare feet, so I let it go. Candles lit up the room. It must have been a witch thing because the lighting in here was incredible. Elaborate lamps and crystal light fixtures hung everywhere. This fit the image of the house we saw at the merry-go-round much better. The spell must have made us see the real house, not the dilapidated-cottage facade Mirabella was casting with her magic to keep out intruders.

"Whoa!" Shannon was in heaven. "Did you do all this with magic?"

"Not all of it, though it does take a lot of upkeep to make the outside of a house this grand look so—"

"Awful?" Shannon smiled at Mirabella. "Can you teach me how to cast spells like this? My room could totally use a makeover."

Dylan glared at her before turning to Mirabella. "What happened to you? Why are you being so nice to us? Last time we saw you, you said you never wanted to see us again. You practically spit in our faces after your spell backfired."

Mirabella laced her fingers in front of her and nodded. "Yes, I was angry. The darkness I took from you made me feel dirty. Like I was losing myself. I didn't know how to handle it at first." She started pacing the room. "But then I came here. I studied magic, specifically how to overcome dark magic. It was difficult, but over time, I managed to find myself again. And I found a way to put that darkness to use—turn it into something good."

Was that possible? How did you make something so evil become good? "Mirabella, you recognized the dark magic in Ethan as soon as you saw him, so I'm guessing you know why we're here."

"Of course she knows. She sensed our locator spell and attacked us." Dylan obviously wasn't giving in to the new-and-improved Mirabella.

She cocked her head to the side. "Attacked you? Why do you think I attacked you?"

"Don't play dumb. We were in the park, and you blasted us with dark magic. We saw your cottage."

"No, we didn't," Shannon said. "The cottage we saw didn't look anything like this one. It wasn't falling apart. The spell must have gone wrong."

"But then how did the spell you put on the car lead us here?" I asked.

Mirabella stepped toward us. "It sounds like someone is messing with the four of you. Another witch. The spell found me, but it was also tampered with." She narrowed her eyes, focusing on me. "Is there anyone who means you harm?"

I shook my head, but inside all I could think was Ms. Matthews. She knew we ran out of school. She knew we were trying to help Ethan. She and her coven had been following the traces of our spells for over a month. It had to be them. I looked at Ethan and the others. They were thinking the same thing. But did we tell Mirabella? We barely knew her.

Mirabella put her hands up. "I understand. You don't need to tell me anything. As long as you all know who it was, that's good enough." She walked to the couch and sat down. "Now, tell me what it is you'd like from me."

I rubbed Ethan's arm. "We want you to help Ethan, the way you helped Dylan."

Mirabella nodded. "I see." She stood up and walked to the bookshelf on the back wall of the living room. "What you're asking will require time. I already have dark magic inside me. I work very hard to suppress it. If I take Ethan's dark magic, there's a very good chance it will consume me. That there will be no trace of me left." She took a book from the shelf and faced us. "But there may be a way for me to help Ethan get better control over the darkness."

"No." That wasn't good enough. We had to get rid of it. Completely. "Mirabella, he's new at being a witch. This is too much for him." I stopped, regretting the words instantly. I didn't mean he was weak. Just that he shouldn't have to deal with this on top of figuring out how to use his magic. "Look, I'm guessing you had been practicing magic all your life before Dylan's dark magic transferred to you."

"That is correct. For over a hundred years, actually."

My jaw dropped. "I'm sorry, but did you say over a hundred years?" That was impossible. This woman couldn't have been a day over forty.

"I look good, don't I?" She laughed. "When you've been using magic for as long as I have, you learn a few tricks." She laughed again at her joke. "The aging process is a funny thing. It turns out the spell I used on this cottage works almost in reverse on people. I can make myself appear any age I want. I chose this age because it was the age my mother was when she died. I look like her."

"I'm sorry for your loss," I said. Somehow her story made her more human—even though she was a witch.

She waved it off. "That was lifetimes ago, and ironically enough, she died from dark magic. She dabbled in it. She pulled off some impressive spells, until one day when she tried one that was way out of her league. She wasn't ready for that kind of power, or the backlash that came from it. The green energy consumed her, leaving nothing but smoke and bones."

I let go of Ethan and stepped toward Mirabella. "That's why I don't want this dark magic inside Ethan. I can't lose him. He's everything to me." With tear-filled eyes, I turned back to him. He looked at me with such love, and for the first time, I understood how he'd felt at my bedside, watching the cancer consume me. I understood how hard it had been on him to stand by, knowing he could do nothing to stop it. But I had magic. I could do something to help him.

Mirabella hugged the book to her chest and sighed. "What's your name, dear?"

"Sam."

"Sam, I wish I could simply take the dark magic and cure Ethan for you. I can tell you deeply love each other. But that would be suicide for me. I'm sure you can understand why I don't want to go that course."

I nodded. I did understand. I hated it, but I understood.

"I do think I can help, though. With one of the spells in this book, I can control the darkness inside Ethan. I can help him bury it."

"But what if it resurfaces?"

She took a deep breath. "I won't lie to you. That is a possibility."

"Then it's not good enough." I wasn't taking a maybe. Maybe it would work. Maybe Ethan would recover. No. It had to be definite.

"Sam." Ethan walked over to me and wrapped his arms around me. "I can handle this. I have to. After the thing with the tree and the car… I can't ever let that happen again. I hurt you."

"The tree hurt me."

"Because of me. It was my spell that brought the tree down. I was trying to crush us all."

"No, the dark magic was. You even said you were powerless to stop it."

He squeezed me tighter. "That's why I have to do this. If there's a way for me to get control over the dark magic, I have to try it. I won't hurt you again. This is the only option."

The only option. Why was there always only one option? I never got a choice in anything. When I'd had cancer, dying was my only option. When Nora brought me back to life, killing had been my only option. And now watching Ethan battle dark magic, hoping he could learn to control it was my only option. "One option isn't an option at all. It's being backed into a corner."

He pushed me back by my shoulders so we were looking each other in the eyes. "I know. I've been there with you before." He was talking about watching me die. He kissed my forehead. "Please, Sam. Let me prove I can handle this. Let me try to be as strong as you are."

I wasn't strong. I was falling apart. I reached up on my toes and kissed his lips. I knew I had to let him do this. It was his call. "Okay."

Mirabella walked past us and waved for us to follow. "Good. I think we should start right away." She took us to the basement, the nicest basement I'd ever seen. The floors were hardwood. There were plush couches in a circle, and in the middle stood a fountain. An actual fountain.

"Oh my God! You have to teach me how you do this!" Shannon rushed to the fountain, staring at it like it granted wishes. Maybe it did.

Mirabella laughed. "Yes, that one took an awful lot of magic to conjure up."

"Will you teach me? Can you?" Shannon never looked so eager.

"Perhaps I could teach you a few things after I've helped Ethan." Mirabella turned to Ethan. Her eyes seemed to stare through him. It was unnerving, but I assumed she was trying to sense the dark magic inside him.

"Eeep!" Shannon squealed. "Oh, Mirabella, you are seriously the most awesome witch I've ever met."

I was still up in the air on that one. Sure the cottage was impressive, and she *had* cured Dylan. But I wasn't making any decisions about her until I saw what she could do for Ethan.

Mirabella waved us away. "Okay, I think the rest of you should go upstairs, make yourselves some tea, and relax. Ethan will need total concentration for this spell, and even then it will take multiple sessions for it to be complete."

"How many sessions?" I wanted this over with now—no, yesterday.

Mirabella shook her head. "I can't be sure yet. I should know more after we try this a few times."

After a few tries? That meant we were going to be here for a while. No school. No working at the diner. It was going to take some mega-sized spells to alter the memories of everyone at school again so they didn't think we'd skipped for days in a row. At least tomorrow was Saturday. We had two days without school. But that didn't help with the diner. I hated the thought of doing magic on Gloria and Jackson, but how else could we explain why we took off when Ethan and I were supposedly so sick? If I pretended we were still sick, Gloria and Jackson would insist on coming to check on us. That wouldn't work. "What are we going to tell everyone back home? We need some excuse for taking off."

Shannon groaned. "Ugh, you're right. Now that Tristan is dating Beth, I can't lie my way out of this. Normally, I wouldn't even have to say a word to Tristan. He'd assume I was off with friends. But now that Beth's around, he questions my every move."

I'd forgotten about Beth. This was getting worse by the second. "Ethan and I don't have family to report to, but we do have Gloria and Jackson."

"For once, I'm glad I have no one." But Dylan didn't sound glad at all. He'd lost so much, and I knew every ounce of him was wishing he had the problems we did right now.

"It can't be anything school-related," Shannon said. "Beth would figure that out."

"And we have to make sure we tell everyone the same excuse. If we tell Gloria and Jackson it's a school trip, she might say something to Beth and Tristan if they go to the diner."

We were stumped.

"You could do a spell to make everyone *think* you were still around," Mirabella said.

"How would that work? I wouldn't be able to wait tables, and Ethan wouldn't be able to cook. Gloria and Jackson would notice for sure."

Shannon rolled her eyes. "Beth, too."

"We could transform some deer into clones of you all. They'd walk, talk, and do everything you can do." Mirabella said it like it was so easy and totally obvious.

Shannon's face lit up. "You are seriously awesome! Let's do it!"

Dylan, Ethan, and I weren't quite as enthusiastic. Mirabella said she had her dark magic under control, but this spell felt completely dark to me.

25

I DIDN'T like this one bit, but once again, I had no idea what else to do. The idea of a deer parading as my clone seemed more than a little bizarre.

"So, what do you say?" Mirabella tucked her spell book under her arm. "Shall we go outside and find your new twins?"

Shannon was already opening the sliding-glass door. "Relax, guys. It will be fine, not to mention totally awesome!"

"How will they get back home?" We couldn't jump into this without thinking it through. "We don't even know where we are."

"You're in the northernmost part of New Jersey," Mirabella said. "Way up in the mountains."

So about an hour and a half from home. "I don't think the Mazda is in good enough shape to survive a trip that far."

"I bet Mirabella could fix the car in no time." Shannon beamed at Mirabella, who nodded in response.

I wasn't winning this battle. "All right. I guess it's worth a shot." A thought hit me. "Wait, if we're only an hour and a half from home, why did it take so long to get here? We drove for hours."

Mirabella sighed and shook her head. "Sounds like whoever is messing with the four of you is doing a pretty good job of it." She was right, which meant having deer clones was probably a good way to get the other coven off our backs for a while.

We headed outside and into the woods. I had no clue how to

catch a deer. All I knew was that they snorted when they felt threatened and they liked to eat leaves. I grabbed a branch with big green leaves and shook it. I was tempted to call "here, little deer" but I felt way too stupid already.

Mirabella laughed. "Wait until you've been at this as long as I have."

"You've made clones from deer before?" Why did that thought send shivers down my spine?

"I meant being a witch." She raised her hands in the air, and even though she wasn't saying a word, I knew she was casting a spell. She lowered her hands, folding them in front of her.

"Well?" I asked.

"Now, we wait. Shouldn't be long."

Rustling in the woods got my attention. A family of four deer headed toward us. The smallest one stopped to eat some leaves from the branch I was holding. It was hard not to smile. I'd never been this close to a deer before.

"This is amazing," Shannon said, walking over and patting the deer on the head.

Mirabella waved us over. "Come over here. I need each of you to stand facing a deer. I'm going to tell the deer to mirror your images."

I put the branch down and walked back into the yard. I wasn't exactly eager to do this. The little deer followed me, like it knew what to do. More like it was being told what to do by Mirabella.

"Good. Now hold very still. I don't want you to move until I tell you to." Mirabella closed her eyes and held her hands up.

I barely breathed while she performed the spell. But then again, breathing was hard to do, considering the deer in front of me rose on two legs and began transforming before my eyes. Its legs took human form first. The magic worked its way up until I was looking at my own face. Creepy. Truly creepy.

"Perfect," Mirabella said. "Now, if you will all raise your arms."

I wasn't sure why she wanted us to do that, but I listened. The deer-me raised its arms, too. Freaky.

"Good!" Mirabella clapped her hands. "Feel free to move about any way you'd like now."

I was having trouble doing anything in my state of shock, but

Shannon started dancing. And her deer look-alike danced, too. "Looking good, deer-me!" She laughed and continued like this was the best thing ever.

Ethan looked at me and shrugged. "At least we know she's powerful. That's good, right? It means she should be able to help me."

He was right. As weirded out as I was, I had to focus on the positive. Mirabella had the power to help Ethan.

"Let's get that car running and send these guys on their way." Mirabella headed into the trees where our car was.

"Wait!" I ran after her. "What about our thoughts and memories? These deer versions of us can totally screw things up without them."

"I cloned everything. They share every thought and emotion you do, but they can't do magic." Mirabella gently squeezed my arm. "Nothing to worry about, Sam."

Then why did I feel so scared? Mirabella had the car fixed as good as new in a matter of minutes. No doubt about it, the witch was powerful. She motioned for our clones to get in the car. The Ethan-deer went right for the driver's seat. It apparently *did* know the car belonged to him—or Ethan. Still, I wanted to be sure. I walked over to...well, myself. "Hang on." I grabbed the door before I—she—could shut it. "What's your real last name?"

"Thompson." Hearing my own voice answer was unnerving.

"And your fake last name?"

"Smith."

"Where do you work and who do you work for?"

"The Pocono Diner, and I work for Gloria and Jackson."

Ethan reached for my hand, and I saw deer-Ethan do the same with deer-me. My head spun. This was surreal. "It will be fine."

Mirabella put her arm around me. "You can trust me, Sam."

Trust was a hard thing for me. I was still learning to trust Shannon and Dylan, and they'd helped save my life.

With our clones on their way back home to live our lives for us, we headed back to the basement. I was eager for Ethan to start working with Mirabella. She'd proven she was strong enough to help him. Now, I had to work on the trusting-her part. I refused to leave the room. Dylan and Shannon stayed behind with me, even though I could tell they both wanted something to eat and drink.

Mirabella placed her spell book, which she hadn't let go of since she took it from her bookshelf, on the couch as she stood with Ethan in front of the fountain. She reached for his hands. "Now, I want you to clear your mind. I'm going to speak to you through your thoughts once we start. I don't want you to try to answer aloud. Simply think your responses when they are required. I'll hear you through our connection."

"Wait." I didn't like that idea. I'd be totally lost as far as what was happening. "Can't you talk out loud? I'd like to hear this."

Mirabella shook her head. "I'm sorry, Sam, but this spell requires a connection between Ethan and me. I'm afraid that connection makes it so our minds are joined. All our energy will be focused on the spell. Neither of us will be able to speak aloud. If Ethan tries to, it will weaken the spell, possibly breaking it all together."

I sighed. "I still want to stay. I want to be close in case—"

"Sam." Ethan's eyes pleaded with me. I knew I was babying him again, but I couldn't help it.

"You'd be the same way if it were me," I told him. He couldn't argue with that.

"I know. I'm asking a lot, but please trust me."

That *was* asking a lot. I'd watched him try to end his own life twice since this all started. But I nodded. He'd be so into the spell, he wouldn't notice my hovering. "Go ahead."

He smiled and turned back to Mirabella.

"Good. Now, Ethan, close your eyes and listen for the sound of my voice." She stopped talking out loud, but I knew she was still speaking—in his mind.

My foot tapped impatiently as I waited to see what would happen. Minutes ticked by with no movement or any sign of magic from Mirabella or Ethan. I wanted to ask Mirabella what was happening—if anything *was* happening—but I didn't want to interrupt if this was somehow helping Ethan.

Shannon tugged on my arm. "Come on. I'm starving, and you must be, too. You're stomach is making all sorts of noise."

I didn't want to leave, but I was hungry. "Okay. A quick snack, and then I'm coming back down here. I don't want to leave Ethan for too long. We have no idea what this is doing to him."

"Doesn't look like it's doing anything at all," Dylan said.

I had to agree. "I'm guessing the spell is more about what's inside Ethan. That's why we can't see it."

Dylan nodded. "I think you're right. Come on. Let's get something to eat."

We headed upstairs and raided the cabinets. Mirabella had everything. I wondered how she shopped out here, all alone and with no car.

"Think she conjured the food?" Shannon asked, sniffing some cheese in the fridge. "Oh, this is heavenly!" She brought it to the table and searched the drawers until she found a knife.

"She must have used magic for all this stuff." I couldn't imagine living like this, cut off from the entire world.

"It must be tough on her," Dylan said. His voice was full of sorrow, and I knew he felt guilty, responsible for the way Mirabella lived. I hadn't thought about it, but he was right.

Shannon sat down and began slicing the cheese. "I think she's amazing. She can do so many things. She can make animals look like people and talk to her if she wanted. I don't think she gets bored or lonely at all."

"Maybe, but is conjuring friends the same as having real people to talk to?" I doubted it, and apparently I'd made my point because Shannon didn't respond.

We filled up on crackers of every variety—herb and garlic, roasted red pepper, honey wheat. And the cheese *did* taste better than any I'd ever had. But as much as I was enjoying the food and the fact that my stomach wasn't rumbling anymore, I couldn't get something out of my head. "I don't get it."

"What?" Shannon said, crumbs falling out of her mouth. "How this tastes so good? Because I'm totally baffled by it, too."

"No. This spell Mirabella's doing with Ethan."

"What about it?" Dylan asked, taking a sip of iced tea. "She said she was going to help Ethan bury the dark magic, so it can't take over anymore."

"Yeah, I get that, but why do they need a connection to do the spell? If she's not taking his dark magic, then why do they need to be connected?"

"Relax. It's not like she's going to steal your boyfriend, if that's what you're worried about." Shannon shoved another cracker with cheese into her mouth. "She might look like a cougar, but she's over a hundred years old."

Ew! "I'm not worried about her stealing Ethan. I'm worried because we don't really know her, and she's doing this humongous spell without us seeing or hearing any of it."

Shannon held her hands out. "Look around, Sam. Mirabella knows what she's doing. She's been doing stuff like this forever."

Maybe. But none of this—the cottage, the food, the deer clones—had to do with actual living, breathing people. And this wasn't just anyone she was doing a spell on. It was Ethan. Why had I agreed to come up here? I should've been with Ethan, making sure he was okay. I put down my cracker and rushed back downstairs. Shannon and Dylan stayed behind. They didn't share my concern. That, or they didn't want to stop feeding their faces.

As I reached the bottom step, I saw a faint greenish glow around Ethan and Mirabella. The green snake thing that had attacked us. Ethan's dark magic. It had to be. "Ethan!" I rushed for him, but the snake turned on me and hissed. I stumbled back in shock. It really *was* a snake. I'd never seen it have a head like this. I'd only referred to it as a snake because of the way it moved, slithered.

I reached my hand up and pushed the snake back with my own golden energy. The snake recoiled, but it came back at me. Mirabella's eyes opened and landed on me. The snake turned to her and slowly began to wind back up into itself. It hissed one last time before disappearing like smoke.

Ethan let go of Mirabella's hands. "That was—" He collapsed on the hardwood floor.

26

I RUSHED to Ethan, sliding on the floor next to him. "Ethan!" I tapped his cheeks, trying to get him to open his eyes, respond in some way. Nothing. "What did you do to him? What was that?"

Shannon and Dylan were downstairs before Mirabella could answer. My screaming had apparently brought them running. "What's going on?" Dylan asked, his eyes falling on Ethan. They both rushed over, bending down beside him.

"Ask Mirabella. I came down here and that green snake thing was surrounding both of them. It tried to attack me. And when Mirabella saw me down here, she made it disappear. When Ethan came out of the spell, he collapsed. She did this to him!" My magic was surging inside me, wanting to get out. For the first time ever, I wanted to use my magic to hurt someone. To hurt Mirabella. I wanted her to pay for what she'd done to Ethan.

"Sam." Mirabella put her hands up. "I didn't do anything to him. The spell was working just fine, but then you interrupted. That's what made Ethan collapse. He came out of the spell before he was meant to."

"No! It wasn't working fine. That snake thing wouldn't have been here if you were burying the dark magic inside Ethan. You brought it to the surface. That's the opposite of what you said you were going to do!"

"Sam, relax," Dylan said. "Let's hear her out, okay? We don't know anything about this spell or how it works. This might be normal."

Normal? What was he talking about? "You're only taking her side because you feel guilty. She's here because she saved you, and that guilt is clouding your judgment."

Mirabella walked over to me and placed her hand on my shoulder. "Samantha—"

"Don't call me that!" No one called me that, except for Gloria. "And don't touch me, either. Stay away from all of us." I shook Ethan, trying to wake him again.

"He needs rest. He's weak from the spell. It took a lot of energy. The best thing to do is bring him upstairs and let him sleep. I have two spare bedrooms up there. Take your pick."

"Thank you." Dylan's words cut me like a knife. He was still taking her word for it. Ethan was unconscious, and yet Dylan was listening to Mirabella. "Sam, focus on Ethan. Let's get him upstairs so we can take care of him." He was playing dirty. He knew I'd do anything for Ethan, even put aside thoughts of ripping out Mirabella's hair.

"Fine. We'll take care of Ethan." I glared at Mirabella. "But you aren't coming near him again. Once he's awake, we're getting out of here."

Mirabella nodded. "You're upset. I understand that. But before you leave, I'd like to speak with you, explain the spell a bit more. I should've done that in the first place. I apologize for that. I was just eager to get started."

"Sounds good," Shannon said, pulling me away from Ethan. I stared at her in disbelief.

Dylan used a levitation spell to pick up Ethan. Seeing Ethan's unconscious form floating in the air brought tears to my eyes. When we got here and Mirabella had opened the door and appeared normal, I thought things were finally going to get better. But she hadn't agreed to taking his dark magic. And then that spell she did… I wanted to rip her face off and reveal the true monster—old and hideous—she really was. But Dylan and Shannon were on her side. Did that mean I was being paranoid? Was I seeing things? Imagining evil because it was my biggest fear? No, it had been real. I was sure of it.

I glared at Mirabella as I followed the others up the stairs. She stood by the fountain, clutching her spell book in her arms again. She was so attached to that thing. I had to get my hands on it. It was the only way to know for sure what she was doing. Only, without her saying the spell out loud, there was no way for me to pinpoint which spell she'd used even if I did get the book away from her. I was going to have to trace her spell, something I'd never done on my own before. But that didn't mean I couldn't.

Dylan brought Ethan upstairs to the second floor. To the right of the stairs were two guest rooms. Dylan brought Ethan to the bigger of the two, the one with a bathroom attached to it. Once Ethan was resting comfortably on the bed, I shut the door, locking Shannon and Dylan inside with me. I was getting answers. Now.

Shannon put her hands on her hips. "Sam, let us out. This isn't a game."

I crossed my arms, standing my ground. "No, it's Ethan's life at stake, and you two are willing to trust someone who, last time she saw you, wanted nothing to do with you. What changed? You were sure it would be a struggle to even get her to talk to us, and here you are now, all buddy-buddy."

"I thought you'd be happy Mirabella's willing to help us," Dylan said. "This is what you wanted."

"I would be happy about it, but I just witnessed that green snake thing again, and it tried to attack me. If Mirabella is burying the dark magic in Ethan, what was that snake doing slithering around the two of them?"

"I don't know." Dylan shook his head. "Mirabella is a hell of a lot older than us. She's more experienced. You think Shannon and I are powerful because we know more spells than you do. Well, Mirabella makes us look like amateurs."

"I'm not arguing there." It was a low blow, but I was angry and worried about Ethan and neither of them seemed to care. "What I'm saying is you're blindly trusting her. We weren't down there with her and Ethan. She could've done anything to him."

Shannon shrugged. "Why would she? Think about it, Sam. She said taking his dark magic would kill her. She can't handle any more than she already has. She's not stupid. She wouldn't put herself in danger. That's why she refused to use the spell she used on Dylan."

Dylan looked away. "I owe it to her to trust her right now."

"Owe it to her? You had no idea what that spell was going to do to her. You said it yourself; she's more knowledgeable, more powerful than you are. She should've known what she was getting into." It wasn't that I thought Mirabella deserved what had happened to her, and I wouldn't wish that on anyone, but there was a part of me that thought she'd had an idea of what might happen, and she'd done the spell anyway.

Dylan looked at me like I was a complete stranger. "You don't get it."

"No, I don't. All I know is Ethan was hurt by that spell. He's unconscious because of Mirabella."

"She said Ethan collapsed because you broke the spell," Shannon said.

I whipped my head around at her. "You think this is *my* fault? Are you serious?"

"Sam, I didn't mean it like that."

"Let me ask you this, Shannon. What would you have done if you walked downstairs and saw that green snake wrapped around Ethan?"

"I-I don't know." She turned and looked at Ethan lying on the bed.

"What about you, Dylan?" My eyes bored into his.

"I get that you freaked out. I probably would've done the same thing. But…" Was he kidding? How was there a *but*? "I think we should give Mirabella a chance to explain the spell to us." I turned away from him, but he grabbed my hand. How many times now had my hand ended up in his? I jerked away from him. "If there's a possibility that she really can help Ethan, are you willing to walk away from it?"

Not fair. Not fair at all. "Fine. She can explain the spell, but I want to see her spell book. The way she's guarding it is more than a little suspicious."

"That's because you're new to this stuff. Witches who've been around for a while create spell books. They get very protective of them."

No. That didn't make sense. "If she wrote the book, why would she need it for the spell? She was using it like a cookbook, like she was reading a recipe. She didn't know what she was doing on her own."

"Okay, maybe she didn't write it." Dylan shrugged. "That doesn't mean anything."

"Maybe it was her mom's," Shannon said.

Her mom's. That would make sense. "But didn't she say her mom died from dabbling in dark magic? If that's true, the book could be filled with the stuff. It would explain the green snake." I was more suspicious and angrier than ever.

"Don't jump to conclusions, okay?" Shannon squeezed my forearm. "We don't know anything for sure, and all this speculating is only making it worse. You're continuing to think the worst of her, yet you have nothing to go on."

"I wouldn't call that green snake *nothing*."

"Fine. I'll give you that one. But like Dylan said, let's hear Mirabella's side of the story before we go burning anybody at the stake, okay?"

I sighed. She made sense. Damn her. "Let's do this now, before Ethan wakes up. That way, if we decide Mirabella can't be trusted, we can get the hell out of here as soon as he's up and moving again."

"I think that's the best we're going to get out of her," Shannon said, giving Dylan a half-smile.

He reached around me and unlocked the door. "Then let's go."

I walked over to Ethan and kissed his forehead. "I won't let her hurt you again," I whispered. I motioned for Dylan and Shannon to lead the way.

Mirabella was in the kitchen making tea. It smelled great, but I wasn't going near anything she brewed, spell or beverage. "Oh, good." She smiled at us. "I'm glad you're here. Sit. I've made enough for everyone." I sat down, but I didn't relax. And I still wasn't drinking that tea. Shannon and Dylan didn't seem concerned at all. Was this all in my head? Were my feelings for Ethan making me act crazy?

Mirabella sat across from me. She poured the tea and set the pot in the center of the table. "Now, tell me what you'd like to know."

She knew what I wanted to know. "What was the spell you did?"

"Jump right in it is, then." But instead of jumping in, she sipped her tea. My impatience grew stronger, making my legs shake under the table.

"Ow, Sam." Shannon shot me a look. Apparently it wasn't the table leg I was kicking.

"The spell I used today was to locate the dark magic in Ethan."

"But you said you sensed it in him immediately. Why would you need to locate it, then?"

"Would you let her talk?" Shannon rolled her eyes at me. "Go on, Mirabella."

"It's quite all right. Saman—I mean Sam—loves Ethan. It's only natural that she'd be protective of him." She sipped her tea again. "I find tea to be very calming. You should try it." She held her cup up, motioning for me to drink the tea sitting in front of me. I didn't move. "I had to locate the exact source of the dark magic. Knowing it's inside Ethan doesn't help me. I have to know where it is."

"Are you saying it's all in one place, like his hand or something like that?" I'd always felt my magic surging through my body. It had never been concentrated to one spot unless I was trying to heal an injury.

"Something like that. It can travel, but it centers in one location."

"Where is it on Ethan?" I was afraid of the answer, but I had to know.

"Behind his eyes." Mirabella ran her finger along the rim of her teacup. "It's highly unusual, but it's almost like the dark magic is using his eyes to see what's going on around him."

I swallowed hard, thinking of the times Ethan had stared off into space. The way his eyes had focused on that tree. It made sense. Did that mean Mirabella was telling the truth about her spell? "What does this mean? Will it be harder to bury the magic inside him if it's centering behind his eyes?"

"Yes." She said it like it was obvious. "I'm sorry. I forgot you're new to this."

"How did you know that?" I'd never mentioned that I'd only recently become a witch. I hadn't even told her where Ethan got his dark magic from.

"I can tell. Feel it, really. Your magic is borrowed, but it's strong. Doubly strong, if I'm correct."

"She has the magic of two witches inside her," Dylan said. "Ben's and Rebecca's."

"Oh." Mirabella's eyes widened. "How did you get their magic?"

No way. I wasn't telling her what had happened.

Shannon put her tea down. "Sam died. Nora brought her back, but as a killing machine, and then Nora sent Sam after our coven. Sam killed Ben and Rebecca and absorbed their magic."

"Shannon!" She'd blurted out my secrets like she was rattling off a shopping list.

"Huh? Oh, sorry." She put her hand to her mouth. "It sort of slipped out."

Mirabella cocked her head to the side. "Well, this is interesting. Here you are questioning me and my methods with Ethan, and *you* are a known witch killer." She stood up and raised her hands like she was about to attack.

I jumped to my feet, ready to summon my magic and protect myself from whatever spell she was about to throw at me.

27

"**W**HOA!" Dylan knocked over the table, pushing it toward Mirabella. Finally, he was siding with me. "Everyone relax. There's no need for magic. Sam isn't a witch killer anymore, and it wasn't her fault to begin with."

Mirabella glared at him for a moment. "After all you've done to me, you're going to stop me from making sure of this for myself?"

"What do you mean *making sure?*" Shannon asked, still sitting in her chair, but looking like she was in shock.

"I have a simple spell to see if Sam means me harm. I think I'm more than justified in wanting to use it right now." Mirabella looked back and forth between Shannon and Dylan. To my surprise, they both nodded.

"What? Like hell she's doing a spell on me!" I ran out of the room and up the stairs, slamming the bedroom door behind me. I locked it and slumped down against the door. This was all unraveling so fast. First Ethan got hurt, and now Shannon and Dylan were willing to let some witch with dark magic do a spell to see if I was evil? I sobbed, pulling my knees to my face and resting my forehead on them. How did everything get so messed up?

"Sam?"

I jerked my head up at the sound of Ethan's voice. "Ethan!" I jumped up and rushed to him. "You're okay?" He was sitting up in bed. I held his shoulders, looking him over. "Do you hurt anywhere? What did she do to you?"

He wrapped his arms around me. "I'm fine. Relax. I think the spell worked, or it's starting to work. I know Mirabella said it would take a few sessions before I was fixed, but I feel good. Stronger almost. More like me."

I squeezed him, breathing in his scent. "You're really okay?"

He pulled me back, staring into my eyes. He didn't say anything. Instead he let his lips do the talking. He kissed my forehead, my cheeks, my nose, and rested on my lips. I melted into him. It felt so good to be close to him like this again. He pulled me closer until I was in his lap. My hands were all over him, his hair, his face, his chest. I wanted to touch every part of him and make sure he was still my Ethan, that Mirabella hadn't harmed him in any way.

We stayed in each other's arms for the rest of the day. I didn't care about Dylan or Shannon or Mirabella. For one day, it was just me and Ethan. He didn't protest, though as the sun set Ethan's stomach grumbled in hunger. He laughed. "Guess I'm hungry. I'm going to go downstairs and get something to eat."

I grabbed his shirt, tugging him back to me. "No. You stay here. You need rest. I'll get you some food."

"Are you sure? I'm really okay. I feel fine."

That was because I hadn't told him about the green snake making an appearance during the spell. I wanted to enjoy this time without Mirabella getting in the way. "I'm positive. I'll be right back." I tried to get up, but he pulled me in for one last kiss.

"Hurry back." He flashed me a devilish grin. Yeah, he was feeling better, all right.

"I will." I smiled at him as I left the room. I hoped everyone else was asleep, but I knew it was still too early to get that wish.

"Hey," Shannon said, getting up from the living room couch. "How is he?"

Mirabella was sitting in the chair across from Shannon. She looked at me, waiting for an answer. I walked by them and headed for the kitchen. This time I found Dylan making sandwiches. "Want one?"

"Two, actually." I wasn't really happy with him or Shannon, but he already had one sandwich made, so letting him finish the second would save me time and get me back to Ethan sooner.

"He's awake?"

"Yup." I went to the refrigerator and grabbed two bottles of water, checking the seals to make sure Mirabella hadn't tampered with them.

"Is he okay?" Dylan put the knife down and stared at me.

"Do you care?"

Dylan's fist collided with the counter. "What the hell, Sam? Of course I care."

"Really? So it's just me you're willing to throw to the wolves?" I slammed the refrigerator door.

"I didn't throw you to the wolves. I just understand why, after hearing you've killed witches, Mirabella wanted to confirm you don't do that anymore. It wasn't unreasonable. You would've insisted on the same thing in her place."

"Maybe, but the difference is I'm part of your coven. You're supposed to stick up for me."

"I did. I knocked over the table when I thought she might hurt you. I wouldn't have let her."

"How do you know she wasn't pretending she wanted to use a simple spell to see if I was going to hurt her? She could've said that so you'd step aside and let her kill me."

"I wouldn't have let her. I won't let you die again. I'll protect you with my life if necessary."

Whoa. I wasn't expecting that. "Is that proper coven protocol? If one of us is attacked, the others would lay down their own lives to protect them?"

He looked away. "Something like that." He put the sandwiches on a plate and shoved them at me. "Here. Go eat. Take care of Ethan." He walked out of the kitchen without making a sandwich for himself.

My heart and mind raced as I tried to figure out what had just happened. Dylan was such a mystery to me. He went from angry with me to... I took the sandwiches upstairs, not looking at anyone as I walked past the living room. Ethan was lying with his hands behind his head.

"That was quick, but I still missed you." He definitely sounded like himself again. If only things were back to normal. If only we were back in our cottage together.

I sat on the bed, placing the plate between us. "Let's play 'Where would you rather be?'"

"Okay." He moved the plate onto the nightstand and pulled me into his arms. "Right about…" His lips brushed mine. "Here."

"Good answer." I gently pushed off his chest.

"Well, you obviously have a different answer, so spill." He grabbed his sandwich and took a big bite.

For once I didn't pick Myrtle Beach with Ethan. "Do you remember when we stayed up all night watching old horror movies and eating popcorn with Gummy Bears in it?"

He laughed, covering his mouth since it was full. "We were laughing so hard because the special effects were ridiculously awful."

"And then we watched episodes of the original *Dark Shadows* series, and Barnabas's fangs fell out." I laughed until my sides hurt, remembering how much fun we had making fun of the low-budget show. But we loved it. We'd watched every episode about five times.

"That was a good night."

"Yeah, I even forgot that I had my first chemo treatment the next day. You were always able to make me forget anything bad."

"You do the same for me, Sam. Right now, all I can think about is you and how perfect you are. I'm not worried about what's going on inside me."

"Yeah, but talking about it means you're still thinking about it. I'm not doing a very good job distracting you."

"I know how we can change that." He raised an eyebrow, and I was expecting him to put his sandwich aside and pull me in for another make-out session. But instead, he reached for the television remote. He flipped through the guide until he found the horror channel. And there was *Dark Shadows*. Not the originals. The remake. "What do you think? We've never watched these."

"Hmm. The originals are classics, but why not?" I snuggled into him, and we watched what turned out to be a *Dark Shadows* marathon. There was still plenty to make fun of, and we compared the actors to the original cast. We pretty much dissected every part of the series. Even though the show was different, being together was very much the same.

It was late into the morning when I woke up in Ethan's arms. The clock on the nightstand read 11:56. I'd slept for hours, even though I'd stayed up half the night.

Ethan rolled onto his side. "Morning."

"Hey, you." I snuggled into him, as if I hadn't spent the entire night in his arms. "How are you feeling today?"

"Good. Really good. I got through the entire night without feeling like the dark magic was trying to creep to the surface. I really think that spell Mirabella did is working."

"That's great." I wanted to believe that was true. Nothing would've made me happier, but I was on edge where Mirabella was concerned.

"I should jump in the shower and get something to eat. Then Mirabella and I can get in another session. Maybe we'll even get to work on it more than once today. I'm so eager to get this over with. I want to be able to hold you like this forever and not worry about anything bad happening."

"Ethan." I raised my eyes to his. "I know you're excited because you're feeling good, but…" How did I tell him this? It was going to break his heart.

He raised my chin with his finger. "What is it? What's bothering you?"

"You know you collapsed after the spell yesterday, right?"

"Yeah. I figured it took a lot of my energy to fight this magic in me. Passing out is probably totally normal. You shouldn't worry about it. I'll even ask Mirabella if it will make you feel better."

"No. That's not it. At least not all of it." I kissed him before going on. I had to get that kiss in before he either got upset that Mirabella had tricked us or angry with me like the others. It could go either way.

"Sam, you're kind of freaking me out now. What's going on?"

"I wish I knew how to say this without upsetting you. I don't want you to be mad at me like everyone else is."

"Why would they be mad at you? What happened while I was passed out?" Worry lines creased his forehead as he stared at me.

"A lot, but it actually started before you passed out. Right before." I took a deep breath and let it out slowly. My hands shook, and my heart pounded. "Okay. Shannon and Dylan convinced me to go upstairs with them to get something to eat. Watching the spell was kind of boring because everything was happening inside you. We couldn't see or hear anything."

He nodded. "It must not have been fun for me either, because I can't remember it."

"None of it?" How was that possible? Ethan hadn't hit his head when he fell.

"No. Maybe I'm really wiped from it. I'm sure it will get easier. Go on. Tell me what happened."

"Well, we went upstairs, and I didn't feel right. Something about Mirabella was bothering me. We don't really know her, and she was doing a huge spell that none of us could be in on. I didn't like it, and I really didn't like that she insisted there had to be a connection between you two."

"Sam, that's what the spell called for. It's not like she's making this up or deliberately trying to keep you in the dark."

"Are you sure?" I paused, letting him think about it. I wanted his opinion. His unbiased opinion before we talked to Shannon and Dylan.

"What else? I can tell there's more."

"Tell me what you think first. I really want to know."

He shrugged. "I don't know everything yet, so I can't form a reasonable opinion."

That made sense. "Shannon and Dylan kept defending Mirabella. Dylan's feeling all guilty for making her live a life of solitude thanks to the dark magic she got from him. And Shannon," I scoffed, "she thinks Mirabella is the coolest witch ever."

"But you don't trust her and you…"

He knew me well enough to figure out I hadn't stayed in the kitchen. "I went back downstairs. I only wanted to keep an eye on you, but when I got there, that green snake thing was circling you and Mirabella."

"I did it again, didn't I?"

What? No! He felt responsible. "It's not your fault. It was her spell. And when she saw the snake, she wasn't the least bit concerned, even though it was totally trying to attack me."

"I attacked you?" He let go of me and leaned back on his pillow. His hands raked his hair.

"You didn't attack me. That thing did, and I don't think you conjured it. Mirabella was controlling the spell. It was her. The snake had a head and everything. The green magic that comes from you has never had an actual snakehead. It was different."

"Or the dark magic is getting worse instead of better." Ethan sprang to his feet.

"What are you doing?"

"This can't wait. I have to go find Mirabella and do the spell again. I have to get rid of this before something else happens. Before I hurt you."

"Ethan, no!" But he was out the door and running straight for the witch who probably wanted me dead.

28

I FLEW down the stairs after him. "Ethan, stop."

Mirabella was in the living room drinking tea. "Well, look who finally woke up." She smiled and stood up. "I guess that spell really wore you out. I think it's best that we start right away, since your recovery seems to require quite a bit of sleep."

"Ethan, we have more to talk about." I grabbed his hand and pulled him away from Mirabella.

His stared into my eyes, pleading with me to understand. "I have to do this. We can talk later."

I didn't know how to make him stay. He was as drawn to Mirabella as the others were. "Please." My voice shook.

"I really think it's better this way." He kissed my forehead and pulled away from me.

"Wonderful." Mirabella put her tea on the silver tray on the coffee table and walked over to Ethan, taking his arm. "Let's get started. Sam, you can help yourself to lunch in the kitchen."

"Ethan hasn't eaten yet, either. Why not wait until after lunch?" My attempt to stall was pathetic, but I was desperate.

"I'll see to it that he eats something. I can conjure food from anywhere." She laughed like she'd made a joke.

Ethan mouthed, "I'll be fine. Go eat." But I wasn't having it.

"Great, well, I'll come with you. You can conjure food for me, too." I took Ethan's other arm and walked with them. We didn't fit through the door to the basement, so I let them go first. I preferred to keep Mirabella where I could see her.

Ethan stood by the fountain again and waited for Mirabella. She was busy creating fruit and salad out of thin air. "Best to eat light when you're doing heavy-duty spells. I wouldn't want you to feel queasy." She placed the tray of food on the couch.

"I'm okay," Ethan said. "I'd really rather start the spell and eat later."

"But it took you so long to recover last time. It could be hours before you wake up and get some food in you. You shouldn't let your strength go down. I'm sure Mirabella would agree." I flashed her a phony smile.

"No need to rush, Ethan. Go right ahead and eat. I have to get my spell book anyway." She walked back upstairs.

"I'm surprised she lets that thing out of her sight," I mumbled, more to myself than Ethan.

"Why do you say that?" He was already digging into the food. So much for not wanting to eat.

"Yesterday, she held on to the book like it was her baby. It was weird, like she was hiding something."

"I don't know. She's a witch, an old one. I'm sure she's collected a lot of spells over the years. And now with us roaming around her house—especially me with this dark magic inside me—I'm sure she wants to make sure it doesn't fall into the wrong hands."

What if I thought the wrong hands were hers? I ate some strawberries while Ethan inhaled the rest of the food. He was definitely hungry.

"Here we go." Mirabella returned, holding the book in the air like a trophy. "All set, Ethan?"

"Yeah. I hope I didn't eat too much."

Mirabella eyed the plate. "I'm assuming Sam helped you with that."

Ethan shrugged and turned a little red. "She ate the strawberries."

Mirabella laughed. "Well, I guess it's good that Sam insisted you eat first. You obviously needed it." She turned to me. "Sam, I'd prefer it if you kept your distance while I do the spell with Ethan."

"Why? Afraid of what I'll see?"

"I don't want to bring up the ugly incident in my kitchen yesterday, but I don't like the idea of a witch killer hovering around when I'm in a vulnerable state."

"Wait a minute." Ethan put his arm around me. "Mirabella, Sam isn't going to hurt anyone. She's no more a witch killer than I am."

I'd forgotten to tell Mirabella how Ethan had gotten his power. I would've loved to throw it in her face now, but I wouldn't do that to Ethan.

"I understand you want to defend her, Ethan. That's perfectly normal."

"No, it's not just that. I mean, I'd do anything for her, yes, but I was talking about how I killed for my power, too."

Her eyes widened, and she stepped away from us. "Why didn't you tell me this before?" Her face turned stone-cold with anger. "I thought I was helping an innocent, and here you're no better than she is."

"It's not like that." Ethan stepped away from me and toward Mirabella. "I was dying. I didn't have a choice. And Nora…she was the reason I was—"

"Nora?" Mirabella cocked her head to the side. "Nora was the witch whose powers you stole?"

"Yes, but I didn't want to. She cursed Sam and me, and the only way to break the curse was to kill her. I was dying because of her. I didn't want to do it, but that thing she turned me into took over."

"So it's Nora's dark magic inside you. That means she's dead." Something about the way Mirabella looked—like she was almost happy—really made me shiver.

"I didn't think you really knew Nora."

"She was in Dylan's coven. She was the one who contacted me and asked me to cure Dylan."

"Then you *did* know her—before you met Dylan, I mean." That was certainly interesting. The fact that Mirabella knew Nora lost her even more points with me.

"We met briefly before that. It was at a meeting."

"What kind of meeting?" I wasn't letting her get off that easily.

"For witches. What else?"

"Why would Nora go to a meeting without the rest of her coven? That doesn't make sense."

"She told me she was looking to find a new coven with stronger witches."

"I bet you two hit it off." I was baiting her, hoping she'd walk into my trap.

"Not at all. I found her arrogant and power-crazed. All she wanted was information about dark magic. Of course she'd heard of my mother and sought me out at the meeting. She cornered me and started asking all these questions. I didn't like her one bit."

"Then why did you agree to help Dylan when she called you?" Ethan asked. Good. Maybe he was starting to see what I saw—something wasn't right about Mirabella.

"I wasn't going to help her at first." Mirabella hugged her spell book. "But then I realized I wouldn't be helping Nora. I'd be helping Dylan. I couldn't punish an innocent witch just because I didn't care for Nora."

Ethan nodded. Maybe it did make sense. I wasn't sure. I needed a crystal ball to predict the future for me. Even with all my witchy powers, I couldn't tell what was going to happen if Mirabella did another spell on Ethan, and that sucked.

"You're still going to help me, right?" Ethan asked. "I mean, now that you know it was Nora, you understand why I had to do what I did." He paused. "Don't you?"

Mirabella sighed. "Yes, Ethan. I understand. I know how Nora was. I know what she was capable of. I believe you had nothing to do with what happened to you. It was Nora's fault, not yours."

Ethan's shoulders relaxed.

"What about me?" I didn't really care if she liked me or believed me, but I wanted to hear her answer anyway.

"Same goes for you, Sam. Though I wish you'd extend me the same courtesy and show me a little trust in return."

Ethan reached for my hand. "She's right, you know."

Maybe she was. I still didn't know, and because it was Ethan's life on the line, I couldn't give in that easily. Although I could make her think I was. "Yes, you're right, Mirabella. I'm sorry. I love Ethan. I get sort of crazy when it comes to protecting him."

She nodded. "I understand completely."

"I'll stay by the stairs and promise not to interfere with the spell." I stood up, but Ethan stopped me.

"Thank you." He kissed me before taking his place in front of Mirabella.

I kept my word and walked over to the stairs. That much I could give her, but if anything went wrong, if any green snakes appeared, I was getting involved. "Oh, Mirabella, before you start, could you tell me why the green snake appeared during the last spell?"

"Certainly." She folded her hands. "The spell located the center of the dark magic, like I told you. After I found it, I had to shift it."

"Why?" Ethan asked.

"Because it was behind your eyes, keeping tabs on everything you saw and did. That's a very dangerous thing."

"Where did you move it?" I asked.

"It fought me at first. That's why you saw it, Sam. It fled from Ethan when it realized I wasn't going to let up."

"You're saying it got away?"

"Does that mean I'm cured?" Ethan sounded like a hopeful kid on Christmas morning. It made my insides ache.

"Unfortunately, no. The spell was broken, and the dark magic returned to you. I'll have to start all over and find out where it went."

"But what if it's already buried? You'd be finished, right?" A girl could hope.

"Believe me, the dark magic won't bury itself. It wants to take over."

Ethan put his hand up to stop her. "Wait. Back up a second. You said the spell was broken. How?"

Mirabella exhaled loudly. "Sam came into the room and apparently thought I was trying to harm you."

Ethan turned to me. "You broke the spell?"

"I thought you were in trouble, Ethan. What choice did I have?"

He nodded. He would've done the same thing for me, but that didn't stop him from being disappointed. In his mind, this all could've been over already. If I hadn't tried to help. The thought made me nauseous.

"Mirabella, can I have a minute alone with Sam?" Ethan said, walking toward me.

"Absolutely. I'll step outside." She opened the sliding-glass door and walked out.

"Ethan, please don't be mad. I know you think I ruined this for you, but I was scared. I saw that thing and all I could think about was stopping it from hurting us." I was careful not to say "you." Maybe if he thought I was scared for my own life too, he'd go easier on me.

"I get it. I know you didn't mean to mess things up, but—"

"But what?" I narrowed my eyes and shook my head at him. "Don't tell me you want me to leave you alone while Mirabella does this spell."

"What if it happens this time too, and you freak out again?"

"I won't. Now I know what the spell is supposed to do. I won't do anything." It pained me to promise that to Ethan. I knew I couldn't keep the promise if something bad happened. And he knew it, too.

"Sam, please don't make me say this." He looked away, avoiding my eyes.

"Say what? That you don't trust me? Is that it? You trust Mirabella—a woman you don't even know—enough to put your life in her hands, but me—the girl you've known for years and are in love with—you won't even let me be in the same room during the spell?"

"It's not that simple and you know it."

"No. What I know is you don't want me here. After all we've been through, you're telling me to walk away when I think you might be in danger. You're asking the impossible of me."

"Can you honestly say you won't interfere if things get bad?" Of course now he chose to look me in the eyes.

I didn't have an answer. Not one he'd accept, anyway.

"I'm asking you to trust me."

"No. You're asking me to trust *her*, and I can't."

"Then I need you to go." There, he'd said it. I turned and walked away before the tears fell from my eyes.

29

I WENT upstairs to my room—no, not *my* room, the room Ethan and I had slept in last night. I sat on the bed and let myself fall backward. Tears streaked my face, falling into my ears, and that pissed me off more. When was the universe going to stop screwing me over? When was it going to realize I needed a break?

"Knock, knock," Shannon called from the doorway. "Can I come in?"

"You're talking to me?"

"I never stopped." She sat on the bed next to me. "Look, I get that you and Ethan are like this 'so completely in love, practically married' couple, but I also think that's what's clouding your judgment on this one. You can't see all the good things about Mirabella. You saw something bad in the basement, and your mind jumped to all sorts of crazy, mean things. I get it. Really, I do."

I doubted that. I'd never seen Shannon date anyone for more than two weeks. She didn't have deep feelings for anyone but herself. As much as I liked her, I knew that was true.

"Dylan and I think we know what's going on here."

"If this is another theory about my jealousy, you can stop right there."

"No. It's about Ms. Matthews."

I sat up on my elbows to see her better. "What about her?"

"We think she and her coven are doing all these things. That they want to turn you away from Mirabella because they don't want Ethan to get help. Dylan's heard of witches who feed on dark magic. Like Mirabella's mom. We think Ms. Matthews is like that."

"I guess she could be. It makes sense. A lot of the bad things that have happened were after Ms. Matthews talked to me. She's got to be mad about us running off. Still…something doesn't seem right about it."

"Believe me, I don't want to think that sexy Mr. Ryan is evil. A bad boy, yes, but not evil."

"Oh, Shannon, yuck!" I reached for a pillow and smacked her with it.

"Come on! He's totally hot and you know it."

"No, I know you're sick."

Shannon grabbed the other pillow and fought back.

"Nice!" Dylan said. "I didn't think girls really did the whole pillow-fight thing. I always thought it was a made-up guy fantasy."

Shannon and I exchanged a look and attacked Dylan, hitting him over and over with our pillows. He laughed right along with us, and before we knew it, we were on the ground in a heap, out of breath and happy.

"I needed that."

"I think we all did," Shannon said, resting her arm on my stomach. I was too tired to care.

"Exactly how did the pillow fight start?" Dylan asked.

"Why?" My breathing was still heavy.

"I want to know for future reference. It was quite amusing to watch."

Shannon and I reached for the pillows and chucked them at Dylan's head. We scrambled to our feet before he could retaliate.

"Okay, okay. You guys win."

"You feeling a little better?" Shannon bumped my shoulder with hers.

"I guess. Ethan did seem better this morning, more in control. We had a really great night, too."

"We don't need details," Dylan said.

"I didn't mean it like that. We watched *Dark Shadows* and laughed until around five in the morning."

"Sure you did." Shannon wagged her eyebrows at me. If only she had a clue how deep my relationship with Ethan actually was.

"Anyway, Mirabella told me more about the spell and why the green snake was there. It makes sense. I still don't like any of this, but maybe I was overreacting and being a tad overprotective of Ethan."

"A tad?" Shannon laughed. "Whatever, I'm just glad you're smiling again."

"What do we do while Ethan is working with Mirabella?" Dylan asked.

"We could try some other spells together." Shannon's face lit up, and I knew exactly what spell she wanted to try.

"Why not?" I shrugged.

"Yes!"

"What?" Dylan asked.

Shannon and I each looped an arm through Dylan's and led him downstairs. We walked out the front door and to the shed. Dylan squirmed until we let go. "Seriously, what are we going to do? We've already been in the shed. There's nothing there but a dead animal and some rusty tools."

"Right now that's all there is." Shannon smiled, but Dylan still didn't get it.

"She wants to make it look beautiful like Mirabella did with the cottage." Even after I spelled it out for him, Dylan still looked confused.

Shannon threw her arms out. "Do you need me to draw you a picture?"

"No, I just don't get why you want to do this."

"Why not? Pretty things are nice, and I'm bored."

"Oh, well, if you're bored." Dylan rolled his eyes as if his sarcasm wasn't enough to get his point across.

Shannon waved her hand. "Whatever, Mr. I-Think-I'm-Better-Than-Everyone-Else."

"Okay, enough." I didn't need any more bickering. This was supposed to be fun. A way to pass the time and keep me from thinking about Ethan and what Mirabella might be doing to him. "Can we do this already?"

"Gladly." Shannon walked over to the wall of gardening tools and grabbed a rusty shovel. "Tea, anyone?" She waved her hand over the shovel and it turned into a golden teapot.

"Not bad." I had to admit I was impressed. "Did Mirabella teach you how to do that?"

"Yeah, last night. So cool, right?"

Except for the Mirabella part. I knew I had to relax. This was all in my head. It had to be. I was the only one who suspected anything fishy here, and Ethan really thought she was helping him. Until I saw otherwise, I was going to have to swallow my pride and go along with this. "Let me try." I needed something to distract me, keep my mind from racing. I picked up a rake. "What should I make?"

"How about a chair?" Shannon said. "We could use some seats."

"Why not? Tell me what to do."

Shannon held my hand over the rake and moved it in a circular motion. "Now think about what you want the rake to become. You don't have to say anything out loud. That's the coolest part about the spell. It seems like it would require words, but it doesn't. Just have a clear image of the chair and the spell will do the rest."

I thought of the elaborate wing-backed chair my mom had in her study. I'd loved it from the first moment I saw it. But before my magic could work its—well, magic—I thought of Ethan's ugly brown beanbag chair. The one we'd gotten from his cousin's storage facility. I really hated the chair, but seeing Ethan lounging in it was the cutest thing. I'd even snuggled up in it with him on more than a few nights. My magic coursed through me, and the rake began to change. First it changed colors, going from blue to brown. Then it widened and the handle shrunk down into a blob. I smiled as the rake became an exact duplicate of Ethan's beanbag chair.

"Um, ew." Shannon wrinkled her nose. "Of all the things you could create, you chose that disgusting thing? You couldn't have made it into a throne with velvet upholstery?"

"I like it." And I realized that was true. As ugly as it was, it reminded me of Ethan. Ethan before all this dark magic had started. The way I wanted him to be again. Distraction wasn't working. "I'm going back to the cottage. I can't get Ethan off my mind." I walked out of the shed, leaving Shannon to transform the beanbag chair into the throne she wanted.

Dylan followed me out. "That was Ethan's chair, wasn't it?"

Of course he knew that. He'd been inside my house numerous times. "He loves it."

"He's going to be okay, you know. I get that you don't trust Mirabella, but I'm proof she knows what she's doing."

"I know. I'm trying to get there. Really, I am. But trusting a witch I don't know isn't easy for me. The first encounter I'd had with a witch was the spell Nora put on me."

"And Mirabella hated Nora. That should tell you something."

It did. "It's just that after I found out about Ms. Matthews and Mr. Ryan… I can't get over Mr. Ryan. He seemed so nice. I thought he liked me—as a student, not the way Shannon likes him."

Dylan laughed. "She's such a hopeless case."

"Why do you two fight so much? Is it a schoolyard crush kind of thing? You pick on each other because you secretly like each other?"

"No." He shook his head. "I'm not Shannon's type at all, and she had a thing for Ben, so I'd never go there." No, he wouldn't after what had happened with Mindy.

"Okay, then what is it?"

"I don't know. I think it's that she was fine with following Ben when he was in charge. But after he…" He shook his head. "Well, I guess she wanted to take his place as leader. We're both kind of alpha personalities, so we clash."

"Oh, so it's a 'who has the bigger bite' kind of thing." That certainly did explain a number of their disagreements.

"Yeah. At least we both agree about Mirabella. It's kind of a miracle."

"You two will get past this, right? I mean, I'm still new to the coven, but I don't want either of you to leave. I like you both."

"I like you, too." His cheeks reddened, and he looked away. *Oh no, not this again.*

We walked inside, and I headed for the basement, but Ethan was already on his way up. "Hey, I was coming to find you."

"You're done already? And you're not tired?" He looked great. Refreshed, actually.

"Yup, all done, and I feel amazing. Seriously, it's like I'm the old me again."

I wrapped my arms around him. "Ethan, that's great. You have no idea how happy that makes me." As I squeezed him, Mirabella started up the stairs. She smiled at me. As much as I didn't trust her, I couldn't deny she was helping Ethan, and I had to make sure my feelings about her didn't interfere with that. I let go of Ethan and took a deep breath. "Could I have a minute with Mirabella? I'll meet you upstairs."

"Sure, but I'm headed to the kitchen. That spell made me famished."

I laughed. Yup, that was my Ethan. Always hungry. He kissed my cheek and walked away, leaving me on the top step with Mirabella two steps away. She stopped and faced me with her hands laced in front of her. I wondered where her spell book was. "Mirabella, I want to apologize. I jumped to conclusions about you. It wasn't fair. You're obviously helping Ethan, and I'm really grateful for that. So, I'm sorry, and thank you."

She stepped closer and pulled me into a hug. "My pleasure, Sam. Ethan deserves to be helped, and I'm glad I can do this for him. He's responding really well to the spells. I located the center of his dark magic. It had moved to his stomach, believe it or not. I think that's why he's so hungry now. I was able to bring it out of him a little bit. I don't want to take it all at once because it might have a negative effect on him *and* me."

"Wait." I pulled away so I could see her face. "Did you say you were able to remove some of the dark magic? Not bury it?"

"Yes. I didn't want to say anything earlier and get anyone's hopes up because I wasn't sure it would be possible, but I was able to remove part of it and send it elsewhere."

"Elsewhere?" Was there a safe place to send dark magic?

"Into a grave. My mother's grave."

"But wouldn't that, like, reanimate her corpse or something?" Oh, God, please don't tell me I just apologized to Mirabella after she'd brought her deadly witch of a mother back from the grave to come attack us all.

"No, no, no." She laughed. "You have quite the imagination, Sam. My mother is gone. She won't be coming back. The magic will lie with her for all eternity. No one will be harmed by it."

I exhaled, relief washing over me. "Good. So when can you work with Ethan again? He doesn't seem to need recovery time after this session."

"I'll monitor him, and if he's still good this evening, we'll do another session."

"That's great."

She patted my cheek and motioned for me to go with her to the kitchen. Ethan was pigging out on chicken wings and cold French fries. Yuck! "Hey, join me."

I sat down across from him. I didn't feel like eating. I wanted to watch him. Even sucking on chicken bones didn't bother me because he really did look like my Ethan again. Things were finally starting to turn around.

But my stomach lurched when I realized that, even though Mirabella might be on our side, we still had a coven of witches trying to find us. Trying to hurt Ethan.

30

"MIRABELLA?" I looked up at her as she made another pot of tea. I wondered if it was the tea that helped her maintain her youthful appearance. She certainly drank enough of it.

"Yes?"

"I was thinking. We have sort of a problem, and you should know about it since we're in your house."

"Oh?" She sat down with her teacup.

"We have a coven of witches after us. They traced the spell we used to find you, which means they can probably trace us here." That must have been what they did. They caused that green snake on the merry-go-round because they'd been using dark magic to find us.

"I see." Her lips pressed tightly together. "And given that you arrived yesterday morning, I'd say they probably already know you're here."

"We kind of took a few detours on the way." Stopped for food, got pulled over, almost got flattened by a tree. "And the spell we used was on Ethan's car, the one you sent back to the Poconos with our deer clones."

"Well, that's a plus. It means this coven might trace the car back to where you're from." She stood up. "Still, I should put a protection spell on the house. Keep it hidden from people who are searching for you."

"That's what I was thinking." I stood up. "I'd like to help, if that's all right with you."

She smiled. "I'd like that." Ethan smiled too, obviously happy I was getting along with Mirabella. I still wasn't sold on her, but between the change in Ethan and having another coven after us, I was willing to play nice. For now.

"Do you have a spell in your spell book? I could get it for you." I couldn't get the book off my mind. I had a feeling I'd learn all I needed to know about Mirabella if I could see what was in that book.

"That won't be necessary." She tapped the side of her head. "I have the spell we need right here."

Ethan and I followed her outside. Dylan was coming back downstairs. I'd somehow missed when he'd gone up there. Probably while I was busy checking on Ethan. "Where are you all off to?"

"We're going to do a protection spell so Ms. Matthews and her coven can't locate us here."

"Can you use another hand?" he asked.

Mirabella nodded. "The more magic, the more powerful the spell."

Shannon was walking toward the house as we stepped off the front porch. "Check out this crystal ball I made. I know it's a little hokey since they aren't real, but it's so pretty, and I even made pink smoke swirl around inside it." We all stared at her as she rambled on. "What? Did I miss something?"

I looped my arm through hers. "You're just in time for a little magic."

She smiled, always up for a spell.

Mirabella walked around the house, waving her arms in the air. She told us to picture the people in Ms. Matthews's coven and focus on blocking them while she put the spell on the house.

"So the spell you're doing masks the house, and what we're doing is adding extra protection specifically against Ms. Matthews's coven?" I asked.

"Exactly right," she said, immediately picking back up with the spell. We circled the house twice for double the protection. "That should do it." Mirabella sighed. "Who's up for making a really big dinner, magic style?"

"You know I am," Ethan said.

"How are you doing now that you've used your magic?" I worried that tapping into the source of his magic would bring on the darkness still lurking there.

"I'm totally fine." He kissed my forehead. "Still hungry, though."

We all headed into the house for dinner, which turned out to be really nice. Everyone talked, and for a little while, we forgot about all the things that were working against us.

Around seven, Ethan and Mirabella went back to the basement for another spell session. For the first time, my heart didn't race with worry. He was getting better. I could see that now. I gave him a kiss and sent him to continue his treatment, which was how I was viewing this.

"So." Shannon slumped onto the couch. "I'm too stuffed to do anything but watch TV. Is that okay with you guys?"

"Yeah." Dylan sat in the recliner. "I need to put my feet up and let all that food digest."

We'd practically made a seven-course meal. We had everything from salad, to potatoes, to steak, to fish, to you name it, and we'd tried all of it. Magical food tasted even better than the real stuff, and I wasn't sure if she'd been joking or not, but Mirabella had said the magic food was calorie-free *and* guilt-free. For the time being, I was choosing to believe that was true.

Shannon turned on the TV—using magic, because the remote was way on the other side of the coffee table. I could've gotten it for her, but I had my head on the edge of the couch and my legs draped over the back. Before I'd gotten cancer, my dad used to ask how this position could possibly be comfortable. I couldn't explain it. It just was. And I was too comfortable now to even think about reaching for the remote.

Shannon sat up slightly and nudged me with her elbow. "Hey, want to see if we can do a spell to make whatever show we want come on TV right now?"

I shrugged. Why not?

"How about a movie, then?" Dylan asked. "I'm always up for *Star Wars*."

Shannon rolled her eyes. "Ugh, I should've known you were a Trekkie."

"No, I said *Star* Wars, not *Star* Trek."

"Oh. Whatever. They're basically the same."

"Let's pick something we all can agree on." I didn't want to listen to them argue anymore. "*Transformers*? One and two were both awesome." Ethan loved the movies, and while I had my suspicions that it might have had more to do with Megan Fox than the Transformers, I didn't complain. The movies were actually really fun to watch.

"I'm good with that," Dylan said.

"Me too." Shannon waved her hand at the TV and the first *Transformers* movie started playing. "Look at that. I even skipped the previews and FBI warning. That's some great spell work right there."

We all fell asleep about twenty minutes into the movie. I saw Shannon's eyes close, and Dylan was snoring softly in his chair. My eyes closed shortly after. I woke up and looked at the clock on the wall. I squinted, thinking I couldn't be seeing correctly. It was two-thirty in the morning. Shannon and Dylan were still asleep, so I crept from the room and went upstairs. The door to the room Ethan and I were sharing was shut. I opened it slowly, trying not to make a sound. Ethan was asleep on the bed. He was still in the same clothes. The spell must have taken a lot out of him again, like the first time. Maybe doing more than one session in a day was pushing it too much. I'd have to talk to Mirabella about it in the morning.

I slipped into bed, snuggling against Ethan. He felt cold, so I pulled the blanket up and tucked it around him. He moved a little bit but didn't wake. I watched him, looking for other signs that he was worn out from the second spell today, but he looked okay. I wasn't sure how I was still tired, considering I'd fallen asleep by seven-thirty, but sleep overtook me in a matter of minutes.

When I opened my eyes, the clock on the nightstand read 2:10. I bolted up in bed and grabbed the clock. "That can't be right!"

"What?" Ethan stirred and rubbed his eyes. "Go back to sleep."

"We've slept away most of the day. Look." I shoved the clock in his face.

He pushed it away, but his eyes widened. "That can't be right."

"I already said that, but I think it is. The sun is out, and I don't know—it just feels like afternoon."

"I'm so tired, though."

"I get why you're tired. Those spells take a lot out of you."

"The one before it didn't. I felt fine."

"Yeah, well, this was the first time you did more than one in a day. It's too much on you. Stay here while I shower. Rest up, okay?"

"Rest up for what?" Even though he was exhausted, there was a devilish tone to his comment.

"Easy, Romeo. I really don't think your body could handle that right now." I kissed him lightly on the lips, but he was already asleep again.

I rushed through my shower, wanting to get downstairs and find out why no one had bothered to wake me, or Ethan for that matter. I had to drag him out of bed and physically put him in the shower. I made the water a little colder than usual to keep him awake. It worked. He jumped and reached for the faucet. Before long the entire bathroom was steamy.

"I'll meet you downstairs," I yelled to him before leaving. I turned toward the living room and nearly fainted. Shannon and Dylan were still asleep in the exact same positions I'd left them in last night. I rushed over to Shannon and shook her. "Shannon, wake up."

She smacked my arm away. "Leave me alone."

I tried Dylan next, but he was no better.

"Sam?" Mirabella called. "What's going on?"

I turned to face her. She was in her pajamas at the bottom of the stairs. "Mirabella, what happened? We all feel asleep really early last night, and then none of us woke up this morning."

Mirabella rushed to her bookshelf and started grabbing book after book. "It can't be."

"Can't be what? Do you know what's going on?" I picked up one of the books she'd dropped, since her arms were overloaded.

"Spread these out on the table." She dumped her armful on the coffee table and began searching through them.

"What are we looking for?" She ignored me and continued to page through the books. "Mirabella." I grabbed her arm. "I can't help you if you don't tell me what you're looking for."

"Sorry. I just can't believe they'd do this."

"Who?"

She stopped searching and looked into my eyes. "Who do you think would use a spell on us like this? One that would put us all into a deep sleep so they could sneak up on us?"

Ms. Matthews and her coven. "But we cast the spell on the cottage. They shouldn't have been able to find us."

"Apparently, they are a lot stronger than we gave them credit for. They're definitely using dark magic if they broke through our spell." She started flipping through the books again.

"How did they do it? Wouldn't we have felt at least some trace of the spell?"

"Looking back, I think I did, but I attributed it to the spell I'd done with Ethan. I thought I was tired from using all that energy. He was tired, too. He went straight to bed."

"Didn't you two see us sleeping in the living room when you came up from the basement?" They had to walk right by this room.

She shook her head, trying to remember. "I was so tired. I don't think I paid much attention. I'm sorry, Sam. I don't remember. It must be the effects of the spell. Judging by those two," she motioned to Shannon and Dylan, "we aren't supposed to be awake right now. Somehow we broke through the spell."

"I woke Ethan. He's showering."

"Good. At least he's okay, too. As soon as we find what I'm looking for, we can reverse the spell on Shannon and Dylan."

"What are we looking for? What kind of spell would undo this?" I wished I could be of more help, but I was still too new at this.

"I'm not completely sure. It would be easier if I knew how they did this to us. What kind of spell they used."

I thought back to last night. "We were watching *Transformers*. That's all I remember. And I didn't see much at all. Sam—the Sam in the movie, not me—hadn't even gotten Bumblebee yet."

"He got a bumblebee?" Mirabella shook her head. "Never mind. I don't need to know. I have to focus on finding a spell."

What else had happened? Had I felt strange? I'd been full. Really full. And tired. "That's it. It has to be."

"What?" Mirabella searched my face for an answer.

"The food. We were all so full, and it made us tired. We fell asleep almost as soon as we got comfortable. Ms. Matthews and her coven did something to the food. They drugged us so we'd fall into a deep sleep."

"Sam." Mirabella's voice shook. "If they tampered with the food we created, they could interfere with any of our spells."

"Any? You mean, even the one you and Ethan are doing?"

She nodded.

Not only was this other coven drugging us, and most likely plotting to kill us, but they were messing with Ethan. And this spell proved they had some wicked power on their side. More power than we could handle. We weren't safe here anymore.

31

Now that Mirabella knew what kind of spell the coven had used on us, she was able to find a way to reverse it. She told me to watch over the others while she used her magic on the food. I didn't like the idea of eating more of the food that had sent us all into this twisted version of *Sleeping Beauty*, but Mirabella said it was the only way. *Only way*—I was really getting tired of those words.

Ethan came downstairs, looking like he was ready to pass out again. He sat on the couch next to Shannon and even slumped over onto her a few times.

I reached for him, making him look me in the eyes. "You have to stay awake, Ethan. If we give in to this, we'll be sitting ducks. They could rush in here at any moment and kill us all."

He shook his head and slapped his cheeks. "I'm good."

I paced the room, waiting for Mirabella. I was anxious to reverse the spell, but I was also trying to keep myself moving so I didn't crash like the others.

Mirabella came back with a tray of food. She placed it on the table. "Dig in. Everyone needs to eat enough to counteract the previous spell."

"You mean we need to pig out like we did last night?" My stomach was still full from all I'd eaten.

"I'm afraid so. It's the only way to make sure you get the harmful spell out of your systems." Mirabella returned to the kitchen, no doubt for tea. When this was all over, I decided, I'd ask her what her obsession with tea was all about.

Ethan was already digging into the food. "It doesn't taste as good as it did last night."

"Probably because you're still stuffed," I said.

"Nah." He patted his perfect abs. "There's still room in there."

"You're like a bottomless pit." I sat next to him, reaching for his abs. "A really hot bottomless pit."

"I'd kiss you, but…" He held up the forkful of steak he was eating.

"I'll take a rain check." I ate a few potatoes and a little salad. It was the best I could do. I was seriously about to explode. My stomach twisted and turned like I was going to be sick. I leaned back on the couch. "Whoa."

Ethan was on his second baked potato, but he stopped eating and looked at me. "You okay?"

"I feel sick."

"That's the spells working against each other." Mirabella sat in the chair across from us, and, sure enough, she had a cup of tea in her hand. "It will pass."

"Why aren't you eating?" I asked her.

She held up her tea.

"Why can't we drink tea instead of eating?" That seemed so unfair. Gorge ourselves while she drank tea?

"I'll pour you a cup." She rose from her seat. "Try waking Shannon and Dylan. They need to get food in them, too."

I nodded. Ethan nudged Shannon since he was sitting next to her, and I went to Dylan, shaking him lightly. "Dylan, time to wake up. We need you to eat or drink tea, whichever. There's a spell on you."

At the word *spell*, his eyes opened. "What happened?"

"We were magically drugged."

He sat up straighter, still looking dazed. "By who?"

"Who do you think?" I wasn't about to tell him Mirabella had been the one to figure this out. Let him think it was me.

"We seriously need to transfer schools when this is over."

"Don't worry. I have a feeling it's going to come down to us or them. One coven won't be around to be at school." Until I'd said it, I hadn't realized it was true. We were going to have to face Ms.

Matthews, Mr. Ryan, and the rest of their coven. It still killed me to think about it. "Mr. Ryan seemed like such a nice guy. He's helped me out so many times."

"Ms. Matthews has been really nice to me," Ethan said. He had pretty much the same relationship with her that I had with Mr. Ryan.

Shannon finally sat up. "Yeah, well, Mr. Malinowsky has cut me more than a few breaks. It's like they targeted us, got close to us so we wouldn't suspect them of being evil witches who want to kill us."

Mr. Malinowsky cut Shannon breaks? I hadn't known that. "I don't get it, though. Why Mr. Mal? You're always flirting with Mr. Ryan. I'd think he'd get close to you."

"I think Mr. Ryan didn't want to get *that* close to her," Dylan said. "He could've lost his job with the way Shannon threw herself at him."

"Very funny." Shannon picked up a baked potato and chucked it at Dylan's head.

"Eat that," I told him. "Mirabella cast a spell on the food. That's how the coven got to us. They drugged our food last night, so Mirabella used a spell to counteract it."

Shannon grabbed her stomach. "Oh, yuck! I have to stuff myself again?"

"Mirabella is pouring us some tea that she cast a spell on, too. You can drink that instead if you want. That's what I'm doing."

"Oh, thank God."

"Whatever. I'm eating." Dylan put the potato down and dug into a steak. Boys and food. I was never going to understand it.

Mirabella returned with the tea. "Good, everyone's up." She put the tray with four cups in front of us. We each took one.

Drinking the tea was much easier than eating. I downed mine in two gulps. "What do we do now? How do we stop them from getting to us again? The spell on the cottage obviously isn't strong enough."

"No." Mirabella sighed. "We'll need to find a stronger spell. One that will make you all untraceable."

I set my teacup on the table. "But they've already traced us here. How would becoming invisible now help?"

"We'll have to make it seem like you've left. Like you figured out they put a spell on you and you ran." Mirabella got up and walked to her bookshelf. "I must have a strong enough spell in here somewhere." She stopped looking and shook her head.

I walked over to her. "I'm sorry we put you in the middle of this. I didn't mean for you to be in danger. We thought the deer clones would get the coven off our backs."

"It's okay." She looked at me, and her eyes filled with tears. "It's just that I'm afraid the spell we need will tap into magic I'm afraid to use. The more power and the darker the spell... I'm still trying very hard to keep the dark magic I took from Dylan buried inside me. I can't remove it from myself."

I put my hand on her shoulder. "Once we're safe from the other coven, we'll try to help you the way you're helping Ethan. We'll try to get that dark magic out of you. I promise." Maybe it was traces of that dark magic that made me keep questioning her even after all she was doing to help us. "What about the spell book you're using for Ethan? There must be a spell in there, right?"

She inhaled sharply at the suggestion. "There are only a select number of spells in that book. It won't help us with this." She pulled a book off the shelf and dusted the cover with the palm of her hand. "This one should do. Give me some time to work through the logistics. You all eat and drink up. I'll be back soon." She walked out of the room, leaving me to wonder if she could handle this. It was the first time I'd seen her falter. She was always so confident, almost to the point of cocky. Now, she was practically cowering at the thought of using magic.

"That was strange," Shannon said.

"Good. I'm not the only one who noticed that." I was starting to question my perception of everything lately. But this time, I wasn't imagining things. She really was acting strange.

"Give her a break," Dylan said. "Taking that dark magic from me really screwed her up. She's doing great, and she doesn't want to revert back to whatever the magic originally changed her into."

My thoughts raced. "What did it change her into?"

Everyone turned in my direction. "What do you mean?" Ethan asked, finally putting down his fork.

"Well, the dark magic had to do something to her, right?"

Dylan nodded. "Trust me, it screwed me up big-time. I killed someone I loved." He turned away.

"Yeah, your brother's girlfriend." Ethan's jaw clenched. I knew exactly what he was thinking. If Dylan would go after his own brother's girlfriend, he'd go after anyone's girlfriend, if he liked her. And he'd done enough to make us all think he liked me. This wasn't going to end well.

"You don't understand." Dylan turned to me instead of Ethan, which only made things worse. Ethan stood up and walked over to me, wrapping his arm around my waist. I was getting really tired of the territorial guy stuff lately, but I didn't want Dylan to have any misconceptions about me. I wasn't available.

"I just want to make sure *you* understand," Ethan said.

Dylan huffed. "You think I went after my brother's girl, right?"

"That's the way it sounds." Ethan's tone was getting more unfriendly by the second.

"Yeah, well, you know what they say about people who assume things." Dylan's comment made me bite my lip. He was only making things worse. Insulting Ethan was the last thing he should've been doing.

"And you know what they say about guys who go after another guy's girlfriend." Ethan let go of me and stepped toward Dylan. His fists were clenched and ready to throw the first punch.

"Stop!" I stepped between them. "No one is going after anyone else." I reached for Ethan and pulled his face to mine. I lightly kissed his lips and smiled at him. I'd never leave him. It wasn't even an option. He relaxed and kissed me again. I couldn't help wondering if the kiss was for Dylan's benefit, but I didn't care. I never objected to a kiss from Ethan.

"*She* came after *me*," Dylan said, after Ethan and I pulled apart. "She liked the thrill of dating brothers."

Shannon pulled her knees to her chest so she was sitting almost in a ball on the couch. "That's really sick."

"Believe me, I know." Dylan broke a dinner roll into tiny pieces. His frustration was clearly getting the better of him. "I resisted her for a while. Ben could be a jerk, but he took care of me. I didn't want to hurt him like that. But Mindy was persistent."

Shannon rolled her eyes. "And you're a guy."

"Not all guys give in like that," Ethan said. "I'd never date another guy's girlfriend. And Mr. Ryan didn't give in to you, Shannon."

She flashed him a dirty look. "Thanks for pointing that out."

"Yeah, well, most guys aren't fighting dark magic inside them that fueled those emotions."

"Dylan, where did your dark magic come from?" I didn't know why I'd never thought to ask.

"Nora. Where else?"

"What?" My eyes could've popped out of my head. "Nora? But you said Ben took you away. Brought you here."

"Right, but I'd met Nora online. She turned me on to some spells. I didn't know they were tapping into dark magic at the time. She'd neglected to tell me that."

"She tricked you." I wasn't surprised. Everything Nora had done to me had been trick after trick after trick.

"Yup. I think she wanted to create a coven of dark witches. When she convinced Shannon to use the popularity spell, she thought that meant she'd get her way. But when I insisted on seeing Mirabella…"

"Wait. You said Nora introduced you to Mirabella."

"She did."

"But why? If she wanted you to become dark like she was, why would she point you to the one witch who could help you get rid of the dark magic?" Nora must have had a plan. She always had a plan. But what had it been?

Dylan stood up. "You're right. Do you think she was trying to turn Mirabella?"

I hated to get back on the Mirabella-is-evil train, but I couldn't help thinking it. "What if she succeeded?"

32

"DON'T start that again." Shannon stood up and went to the window, leaning her back against it. "You're wearing me out with the way you keep changing your mind about her, Sam."

"I'm sorry, but there's so much we don't know."

"Then let's ask her," Ethan said.

Shannon laughed. "What, come out and say, 'Hey, Mirabella, we were wondering if you're really evil?' Good luck with that."

"Besides," Dylan said, "she already told us she didn't like Nora."

"Fine, but what if Nora was trying to harm Mirabella?" I said. "Trying to pawn your dark magic off on her. If you were Mirabella, wouldn't you want to know if that had been Nora's plan?"

Shannon crossed her arms in front of her. "Are you blaming Nora or Mirabella? Because I'm confused."

I didn't really know, but I didn't want to start the whole debate over Mirabella again, so I went with the lesser evil—well, actually the *bigger* evil. "Nora. I'm blaming Nora."

"It does make sense," Ethan said. "Nora was setting us all up."

Shannon nodded. "No argument there."

I turned to Dylan. "What do you think? Should we tell Mirabella our theory about Nora?"

He shrugged. "Why? She's obviously still battling the dark magic, and trying to help Ethan is probably making it harder on her."

"Why would you say that?" I asked.

"Because." He walked past me to the bookshelf. "She's working with the dark magic inside Ethan. She's got to be terrified that it might transfer to her, like it did when she helped me."

"She told me she's sending it to her mother's grave, burying it there forever."

Dylan stopped scanning the book titles and looked at me. "Yeah, and what if she messes up? What if she loses control over the dark magic and it doesn't make it to her mother's grave? What if it decides to settle in her instead?"

"You're talking about the magic like it's a living, breathing thing that can make decisions for itself."

"Because it basically can."

"No." I might be new to this whole witch thing, but I knew the magic was useless without a witch to tap into it. "It can't do anything on its own. It has to be controlled."

He glared at me. "Get some dark magic inside you and then tell me if you can control it, or if it's controlling you."

His words burned into me. I'd had dark magic inside me. Nora had put it there when she brought me back, and I'd been powerless against it. I'd killed because of it.

Ethan squeezed my hand, reading my mind. "He's right, Sam. You remember what it was like. This magic lingering inside me is a lot like that. I lose control. It takes over, and I do what it wants me to. It might require a host, but that's all we are to it—a shell. It becomes the brain."

"I see what you're saying, but isn't this all the more reason to tell Mirabella what we think Nora tried to do to her?"

"What she *did* do to her," Dylan said. "She's already lived it, Sam. We don't need to spell it out for her. I'm sure she's guessed on her own."

"Okay, I think I've got it." Mirabella walked into the living room, and we all went silent. She looked up at us with the book open in her hands. "Did I miss something? Or have I interrupted something?"

"No," I said. "We were just waiting for you."

"Oh. Okay then. I found a spell that should work."

"Does it require dark magic?" I asked.

"No. There's a stronger one that does, but we'll try this one first."

Her fingers clutched the book tighter. She didn't want to have to use the stronger spell. Neither did I.

I forced a hopeful smile. "Great. Tell us what to do."

She brought us down to the basement. Apparently that was where she liked to cast big spells. I wondered if the fountain had anything to do with that. If it was magical—aside from having been conjured from thin air.

Mirabella made a circle in the air with her index finger. "Stand in a circle around the fountain, please. We'll need water to seal the spell."

"We're tapping into the elements?" I'd never used a spell that required the elements. The thought made me excited and scared.

"Only one. It will be fine." She inhaled, and her shoulders shook. That didn't reassure me at all.

We formed a circle. Ethan and Shannon were on each side of me. Both looked as nervous as I felt.

Mirabella filled in the circle between Dylan and Ethan. After the almost-fight in the living room, I was glad they were separated. "Good. Now, I want you to focus your magic on concealing yourself from everyone who is not present in this room. No one should be able to see you or locate you, no matter what the spell. Understand?"

We all nodded. This didn't seem too bad. A lot like the invisible spell we'd used when we'd changed Dylan's schedule to match Ethan's. But I knew it was so much more, or it would be when Mirabella did her part.

Mirabella closed her eyes and raised her hands in front of her, her fingertips brushing the water in the fountain. "Follow my lead. Do as I do."

I reached forward, letting the water brush my fingers. Instantly, it heated up. How strange.

"To all who seek to find, do make these four now blind." I didn't like that line at all. It sounded like she was making *us* blind, not the witches coming after us. "Become right now unseen, as water washes clean. Erase them from space. Leave behind no trace." Mirabella opened her eyes and smiled. "It is done."

Oh crap! I'd forgotten to focus on concealing myself. I'd been so thrown by Mirabella's words that I hadn't held up my end of the spell. Everyone was looking relieved, and I felt like a complete idiot. How did I tell them I'd screwed up?

"More tea, anyone?" Mirabella asked. "I'm going to make another pot, and then Ethan and I should get back to work."

Ethan nodded, looking more than ready to get the dark magic out of him once and for all.

"You feeling okay?" I knew using any magic at all made him nervous. It was risky with all that dark magic trying to break through. I just had to check with him again.

He rubbed my arms. "Yeah, I'm good. I could use some Sam time, though."

"We're out of here," Shannon said, tugging Dylan toward the stairs.

I wrapped my arms around Ethan's waist and pulled myself into him. "How's this?"

"A good start." He leaned down, finding my lips with his. "This is better," he managed to say between kisses. Somehow we ended up on the couch. I hadn't even felt our feet moving, but I was on Ethan's lap with his hands on my face. I was starved for his touch. The dark magic inside him made it difficult to get close like this. He was always so afraid of losing control and hurting me, but this time he wasn't holding back. He deepened the kiss, and his hands drifted under my shirt.

"Ahem."

I jumped off Ethan and into the seat next to him. Mirabella gave me a harsh look. "That is not a good idea until all the dark magic is out of Ethan. Believe it or not, Sam, you are the worst thing for Ethan right now."

Worst thing? That felt like a sucker punch. How could that be possible? Ethan and I had always been the best thing for each other.

"Don't ever say that, Mirabella." Ethan wrapped his arm around me. "I'm nothing without Sam."

Every time I thought I couldn't love the boy any more, he proved me wrong. I kissed his nose. "Have a good session, and come back to me without dark magic." I leaned toward his ear. "I'll miss you."

"You have no idea," he said, squeezing my hand. He looked like he wanted to kiss me again, but I didn't want another lecture from Mirabella, so I stood up. Ethan sighed and let go of my hand. "I'll see you soon."

"Love you." I kept my eyes on Ethan as I walked upstairs. Shannon and Dylan were in the living room, drinking more tea. "Seriously? How do you guys drink so much of that stuff?" It tasted like stale cardboard.

"I like it," Shannon said.

"Yeah, it sort of grows on you." Dylan took another big gulp.

"If you say so. I'm sticking to bottled water, though." I went to the kitchen and grabbed a bottle out of the fridge.

"That was a cool spell, huh?" Shannon said, following me and sitting down at the kitchen table.

"Yeah." I hadn't told anyone that I'd screwed it up. I wasn't as invisible as the rest of them were. I hoped Mirabella's spell had been enough to conceal me. "Hey, why aren't you in the living room with Dylan?"

"I need a break from that boy. You're lucky you have Ethan."

I sat down across from her. "What did Dylan do?"

"He made some stupid comment." She shrugged a shoulder like it wasn't a big deal, but I could tell it was really bugging her.

"It wasn't a stupid comment," Dylan said, leaning on the doorframe.

"Whatever. Go drink your tea and leave me alone." Shannon waved him out of the room, but he stayed put.

"You just can't handle the truth."

"Oh, yeah and you're the expert on my feelings, right?" She stood up, her chair screeching against the floor.

"I know you're jealous of Sam and Ethan's relationship."

She was? Shannon didn't seem like the relationship type, but maybe that was all an act. Maybe she did want what Ethan and I had. I couldn't blame her.

"Whatever." She turned to me. "This is why guys and girls shouldn't be in covens together."

"Why don't you go join an all-girl coven? You could curse the entire male population the next time you're all pissed off and PMSing together."

"Screw you, Dylan!"

I stood up. "Seriously, enough. I'm so tired of playing referee. Our coven is falling apart, and right now we need each other more than ever. Ethan isn't better yet. We have another coven coming after us and trying to kill us. *And* we keep finding out more ways that Nora has screwed us all over. The last thing we need to be doing is fighting, so get over it."

Shannon crossed her arms. "He started it."

I glared at her. "You're not five." Dylan laughed, drawing my attention to him. "And you can be an insensitive prick sometimes. You push her buttons on purpose."

"That's because she—"

I held up my hand. "I don't care. We're family. Got that? We help each other, not make life more difficult."

Shannon sat down again. I looked at Dylan until he sat, too. "I'm not apologizing," Shannon said.

"Me either."

"Good enough for me." I slumped into a chair and drank my water, enjoying the silence. "What started your fight anyway?" I could never figure out what set either one of them off.

Shannon shrugged. "I was trying to enjoy my tea when he got on my case about how I'm jealous of you and Ethan."

"I was only trying to say that you pretend you don't want a relationship when you obviously do. You wanted one with my brother, too."

"Don't bring Ben into this, okay?"

I silently seconded that. It was still hard for me to talk about anyone I'd killed during my monster days.

"You were in love with him," Dylan pressed.

"And you were in love with his girlfriend." Shannon took another sip of her tea. I hadn't even noticed she'd brought it in here. "You were jealous of Ben and wanted everything he had. That's why you gave in to Mindy so easily. You can say you tried to fight her off, but you didn't. You broke down like two days after she started flirting with you."

"Thanks, Shannon." Dylan slammed his fist on the table. "At least

I'm not like you. I actually loved Mindy. You sleep with anything that has a car."

"I do not!"

"Trevor? Tell me what else there was to see in that guy?"

Great. Let's bring up another one of my victims. "Guys, you have to stop this." I practically yelled, but they ignored me. They were screaming at each other. Spilling secrets that I'm sure neither wanted me to know. Shannon flailed her arm, and her tea fell to the floor, the cup breaking into pieces.

"Look what you made me do!" Shannon pointed to the tea, which had begun to fizz.

"What is that?" I bent down to get a better look. Green swirls mixed with the black tea, making little bubbles.

Shannon knelt down next to me. "Is that—?"

"Dark magic." I'd recognize it anywhere. The tea was laced with dark magic.

33

"WE need to get Mirabella," Shannon said. "She needs to see this."

I grabbed her arm. "No. Wait." I couldn't help thinking this was my fault. I'd screwed up the spell downstairs, and now the tea Shannon and Dylan were drinking was laced with dark magic. My first thought was that Mirabella was responsible, but she drank the tea all the time, so that didn't make sense. Had the coven done this? They'd already drugged our food. Why not the tea this time? "Guys, I have to tell you something." I stood up, afraid to get too close to the dark magic creeping across the floor in the spreading tea. Shannon and Dylan backed away too, but their eyes remained locked on me. "Downstairs, I kind of messed up my end of that spell."

"What do you mean?" Dylan asked.

"I was so caught up in what Mirabella was saying that I forgot to do my part. I never made myself invisible."

"Why didn't you say something?" Shannon asked.

"Because I felt stupid and I kind of thought maybe the spell would be okay anyway because Mirabella's words were working to mask us, too."

"Yeah, well obviously, that's not what happened." Dylan pointed to the swirling, green magic. "The coven obviously found you, and they cast a spell on the tea this time."

"Only you didn't drink it. Dylan and I did." Shannon shivered. "Does this mean I have dark magic in me now?"

Dylan sighed. "It *does* explain why you and I were at each other's throats." He shook his head. "I really didn't mean all that stuff. At least, not the way it came out."

Shannon nodded. "I know. Me too."

Well, they were getting along again—that was something. Who knew dark magic could have a positive effect on them?

"What do we do?" I asked.

"We have to tell Mirabella," Dylan said. "She might need to help us get rid of the dark magic inside us."

"Hang on." I bent down by the dark magic again. "Why is it still here? I mean, if we were right earlier and the stuff has a mind of its own, then why didn't it *all* go inside you when you took your first sips?"

"I don't know," Shannon said.

I looked at Dylan. "Did you finish your tea?" He nodded, looking green at the thought. I realized the irony. Green with sickness and green with dark magic. Great. Now I was the only member of the coven who didn't have dark magic inside them. "You're right. We need to go to Mirabella."

"What if she isn't finished with Ethan?" Dylan asked. "You remember what happened to him when you interrupted the first session."

Yeah, I didn't want him to go through that again. "Okay. We won't interrupt, but we need to dump that tea down the drain before anyone else drinks it."

"I'll do it." Shannon walked out of the room.

"I'll clean up the floor," Dylan said.

"Look for some latex gloves under the sink or in the closet. Don't come into contact with the tea. I'm going to sit quietly on the stairs and wait for Mirabella and Ethan to finish their spell. I'll bring them up as soon as they're done."

Dylan nodded.

I headed downstairs, careful not to make a sound. If I made either of them lose concentration, Ethan would pay the price. Mirabella was hovering about three inches off the ground. I'd never seen anyone levitate before, so it was more than a little weird. How was she managing to do that and perform the spell with Ethan? Unless levitation was a side effect of the spell. I sat down on the bottom step and continued to watch in silence. Ethan's eyes were closed like Mirabella's, but he looked like he was sleeping. Mirabella's eyes twitched under their lids, and her forehead wrinkled in concentration.

After a few minutes of nothing happening, I got bored. My eyes scanned the room. Mirabella's spell book was open on the couch next to her. Curiosity had never been my friend, but it consumed me now. I'd wanted to see that book since the moment Mirabella had clutched it to her chest and protected it like her baby. I stood up, careful not to make a sound, and crept over to the couch. Mirabella's hands were holding Ethan's—more like clutching Ethan's. She was keeping their connection secure, no doubt about it. Her mouth moved in a silent spell that she was probably saying over and over in her mind. I remembered she'd said she and Ethan would be able to speak in each other's minds while they were connected. I'd hated the idea, but at least he could hear the spell.

Since I couldn't, and my need to know what was involved in the spell was growing by the second, I tiptoed to the book and scanned the pages. Most of the words were written in a really slanted script that was as difficult to read as my brother Jacob's chicken scratch. I tilted my head, thinking that might help. It did a little. I was able to make out a few words here and there. *Darkness. Transfer. Host.* It seemed like more of an explanation than a spell. Maybe it was on the wrong page. Sometimes spells created wind. The page could have turned. I reached for the corner and turned the page back, careful not to let the paper crinkle or make the slightest sound.

This page wasn't about the same spell. It had something to do with time and slowing the aging process. That explained Mirabella's appearance. She'd gotten the spell to make her look younger from this book. Part of me wanted to read more. A spell like this could definitely come in handy in the future, but I had to find out more about the spell Mirabella was using on Ethan. I made sure they were still deep in their session before I turned the page back to the previous spell I'd read.

I scanned the handwriting, starting to get more used to the slanted script. *Dark magic can be transferred to a willing host, but the new host body must be strong enough to take it. The magic has to be severed from the previous host and pulled into the new one. It cannot be transferred by a third party. The new host must be the one pulling the magic into their own body.*

I whipped my head around and gaped at Mirabella. She wasn't sending the dark magic to her mother's grave. That would've made her a third party. The only way Mirabella could take the dark magic was if she put it into her own body. I had to show this to Shannon and Dylan, but if I took the book, Mirabella would be seriously pissed off, and she might stop helping Ethan. As much as I questioned Mirabella, she was still taking the dark magic from Ethan. Even if she was lying about how she was doing it, she was still curing Ethan. I couldn't do anything to jeopardize that.

Still, I couldn't let this go without showing the others. I needed proof. There had to be a spell that would help me get this information to them and allow me to read more of the book. I glanced at Mirabella and Ethan again. They were still oblivious to my presence in the room. The spell had them so deeply connected that they couldn't sense me. I picked up the book and closed it. Fanning through the pages as quietly as possible, I whispered, "Absorb the knowledge from within this book. Remember it all with the briefest look." As soon as I got to the last page, I flipped back to the spell Mirabella had opened and placed the book back on the couch exactly where I'd gotten it. I backed out of the room, making sure Mirabella didn't open her eyes and catch me. As soon as I reached the stairs, I ran up.

Dylan and Shannon were in their room. I still wasn't sure how they were sharing a room without killing each other, but at least now I knew their issues were being caused by spells the coven kept placing on our food and drinks. I knocked on the open door. "I have huge news." I rushed inside and shut the door behind me.

"What's up?" Shannon asked. "More green, swirling magic? Because I just finished cleaning up all the tea in the house. Mirabella had cups of the stuff everywhere. She must keep a pot around at all times. Ms. Matthews's coven picked the perfect thing in this house to spike with dark magic."

I sat down on the edge of her bed and tried to catch my breath. "It's not the tea. It's Mirabella's spell book."

Shannon sat up straight. "What happened to it? Did the coven somehow steal it?"

"No. It's downstairs on the couch where it always is during Ethan's sessions, but I read some of it."

Dylan *tsk*ed. "You snooped around in Mirabella's private spell book?"

"Yeah, that's like reading a witch's diary," Shannon said. "Big no-no."

"Well, I'm glad I read it. Something's up. Mirabella is taking the dark magic into her own body." I resisted the urge to say "I told you she was evil."

Dylan threw his feet over the side of the bed. "That's crazy, Sam. I think you need some rest. Your head is—"

"I know what I saw. That spell wasn't just to remove the dark magic from Ethan. It was to place it in a new host."

"She said she was sending it to her mother's grave." Shannon shook her head. "Honestly, Sam, why are we going through this again?"

"The new host has to be the one to remove the dark magic and pull it into herself. That's what the spell said."

"No one would willingly do that," Shannon said. "It's suicidal."

"Maybe not. Look at Nora. She was totally evil. She tried to tap into dark magic all the time. And so did Mirabella's mom. She took in so much of it, it killed her."

"Exactly," Dylan said. "So why would Mirabella try the exact same thing that killed her mother?"

"I don't know. I'm not saying I understand any of this. I'm just telling you what I read."

"Show us." Dylan crossed his arms.

"How? You want me to march up to Mirabella and demand she show us the book?"

"No. You used magic to access those pages, right?" Dylan stared at me so intently, like he was waiting for me to admit I'd made this all up. I nodded. "That means you can project the pages you saw into the air for Shannon and me to read."

I could do that? "How?"

"Picture the pages and say, 'From my mind, project the image I wish to find.' Then wave your hand in a counterclockwise motion, and we'll see the image."

Okay, that sounded simple enough, and then they'd have to believe me. I raised my right hand, holding it still until I said the spell. "From my mind, project the image I wish to find." I rotated my hand counterclockwise and watched as the air rippled and the pages appeared. "There. Read it." I stepped away, letting Shannon and Dylan get a better look.

Shannon ran her finger across the image as she read it. "This says in order for dark magic to leave its host, a new host must be ready to accept it. But it doesn't say the host has to be alive. Mirabella easily could have done a spell to make her mother's body accept the dark magic."

"What? Yes, it does. I saw it." I pushed them away and studied the image myself. Had I done the spell wrong? Were words missing from the image? I read the words, but I had to read them again and again. "They're not the same. This isn't what I read in the book."

"Sam, you did the spell. It projects what you saw. This is what the book said." Dylan put his hand on my shoulder, probably trying to be sympathetic, but the gesture sent me through the roof.

I shrugged Dylan's hand away. "No! Something went wrong. The spell didn't work right." These weren't the same words I read downstairs. Something was interfering with my spell. Someone didn't want me to share the true spell with Dylan and Shannon.

Shannon shrugged. "Are you sure you pictured the pages right in your mind first?"

This couldn't be happening. I hadn't imagined this. I wasn't crazy or delusional.

"Sam, we're all stressed. We're being hunted by other witches, and Ethan is struggling with the final sessions. It's a lot on you right now. We understand that you're not thinking clearly, but you can't go accusing—"

I pushed past Shannon before she could finish. If she didn't believe me, I had to go to Ethan. He was the only one who could hear the spell Mirabella was using. He must have had some idea of where the dark magic was going. And if he didn't remember, I'd have to use magic to get the memory out of him.

34

Eᴛʜᴀɴ and Mirabella were just finishing up when I came back downstairs. Ethan turned to me, looking rather groggy. "Perfect timing." He wobbled and had to grab the fountain to keep from falling over.

I rushed to him. "Are you okay?" I couldn't help looking at Mirabella, wondering what she'd done to him.

"Yeah, I'm good. A little lightheaded, I guess. I don't remember feeling this way after the other sessions. Not since I passed out the first time."

"I think you should rest," Mirabella said, her book clutched to her chest once again. "We are almost finished ridding you of the dark magic. Your body needs time to adjust."

"Shouldn't he be feeling better without the dark magic inside him?" I had to ask.

"He will soon. Trust me." She walked by us and up the stairs.

Trust her? Not likely. Not after what I'd read in that book. "Come on. I'll help you up to our room."

"Can we sit for a minute? I don't think I'm strong enough for stairs just yet." He sat on the couch and pressed his palm to his forehead.

"Headache?"

"Sort of. I'm dizzy and kind of spacey. I'm sure it will pass, like Mirabella said. My body's got to be happy to be almost rid of the dark magic."

"Yeah, about that." I lowered my voice even though we were the only two people in the basement. "I came down here during the spell, and I happened to see Mirabella's spell book." Ethan lowered his hand so he could look at me. Before he could give me a lecture on snooping, I continued. "I saw the spell she's using on you, and it's not exactly how she described it to us."

"What do you mean?"

"According to the spell, the person who removes the dark magic is the one who takes it into herself. Mirabella is getting your dark magic."

"You must've read it wrong." He shook his head, then cringed. "Ugh, that hurts."

"Ethan, do you remember the spell? Do you remember what she says during it?"

"No. I'm in sort of a trance. I can hear her talking, but I can't process what she says."

Wasn't that convenient for Mirabella? "Would you let me cast a spell to trigger your memory?"

His eyes widened. "You want to use magic on me? Now? While I'm like this?"

"I guess it can wait." I looked down at my knees. They shook with fear. Fear for Ethan. Fear for my coven. "I just don't want to be blindsided again. I trusted Nora. I thought she was trying to help me, and instead she used me in her own vicious game of kill the witch. I'm not going to sit around while Mirabella plans her own deception. If she's up to something, I want to beat her to the punch."

He took my hand. "You know I love you, right?"

"Of course." I leaned forward and kissed his forehead. I let some of my healing magic spread through my lips and to his head. "Feel any better?"

He smiled and pulled me closer to him. "Much." He kissed me, softly and passionately, like only Ethan could. Not that I'd dated much before him, but no other guy had ever kissed me like that, with so much love. He pulled back and sighed. "You really don't trust her?"

"I don't trust anyone with your life. I need to make sure she's not hurting you with this spell."

He took a deep breath. "Okay, do the spell. Try to get my mind to reveal what Mirabella said during the spell."

I really could've used Shannon and Dylan's help with this. I'd never tried to access someone's memory before, but they weren't exactly on my side with this issue. "Can you lean back and close your eyes?"

Ethan rested against the back of the couch, but as soon as he closed his eyes, he opened one again. "Is this some plan to catch me off-guard so you can have your way with me?" His mouth curved into a sly grin.

"I'm glad you're feeling better, but no. Now, close your eyes." I held my hands above his head and closed my eyes, too. I focused on seeing what Ethan had seen, but it didn't work. "Think about the spell. Anything you can remember would help."

"I'll try, but I don't remember much at all."

I concentrated again, and little images flickered in Ethan's mind's eye. Green energy snaking through him. Still, I didn't hear anything. I moved one hand above Ethan's right ear. Sound began to filter through, but it was muffled. I was about to give up when I heard the phrase, "Settle into me." That was enough for me. I opened my eyes and lowered my hands.

"Done already?" Ethan sat up. "That was fast."

"I heard all I needed to. She's definitely taking your dark magic. She told it to settle into her. But why? Why would she want it?"

"You should have waited for us," Dylan said.

Shannon stood next to him on the bottom stair, her hands on her hips. "You know I love spells that have to do with accessing people's minds. I can't believe you'd keep me out of it."

No sense denying it. They'd heard me. They knew what I'd done. "We have to get that book away from her. I need a better look at it. If we know what spell she's doing, we'll be able to fix this." I hoped.

Ethan stood up. "I don't think she's trying to hurt me, Sam. She's been really nice."

I stood up and took his hand. "Maybe she isn't trying to hurt you, but she isn't doing what she says, either. I know it, Ethan. Please, trust me."

He brought my hand to his lips, kissing each fingertip. "You know I trust you."

"Thank you." I could always count on Ethan.

"So, she's really taking the dark magic," Shannon said. "Do you think it gives her a power boost? Lets her do all of this?" She motioned to the room around us. Everything in it had been magically conjured.

"Maybe. I kind of think she figured out what her mom did wrong."

"What do you mean?" Dylan waved his hand, and I recognized the protective bubble he'd put around us to keep Mirabella from overhearing our conversation.

"She said her mom was mixed up in dark magic and died because of it. I think that spell book belonged to her mother. I think she's trying to master the spells and figure out what her mom did wrong."

"Makes sense," Ethan said. "But then, I might be right. She might not mean me any harm."

"I don't think she does," Dylan said. "She could've killed us all already. She's old and wickedly strong. She wouldn't keep helping Ethan if she wanted to hurt us."

"Why not?" I asked. "What if she's only keeping us around until she gets what she wants from Ethan? She said the spell is almost finished. If she doesn't have any use for us anymore, what's to stop her from using that dark magic on us?"

"Oh, come on." Shannon's shoulders slumped. "We finally find a cool old witch who knows just about every spell. Why does she have to be up to something? I wanted her to teach me all this stuff."

"We have to get that book," I said, ignoring Shannon's whining. "Tonight. I think we should plan to meet up while she's asleep."

Shannon stroked her hair. "I need my beauty sleep, you know."

Dylan shot her a look. "You'll live." He turned to me. "I'm not crazy about the idea of snooping through Mirabella's stuff."

"Look, I get that you feel a debt to her for saving you, but I don't think she did it with good intentions. She got something out of it. Just like she's getting something out of helping Ethan. We need to figure out what her endgame is before she turns on us."

"*If* she turns on us," Shannon said.

"Anyone down there?" Mirabella called from the top of the stairs.

I glared at Dylan. "Lower the spell before she senses it and questions why we put it up."

Dylan ended the spell with a swirl of his hand. "Yeah, we're down here checking on Ethan."

"Well, come upstairs. I made some tea."

None of us moved. We were fixed to the floor, questioning everything we'd come to learn about Mirabella. How much like her mother *was* she?

"We'll be right up," I yelled. "All right, get ready to act normal. We can't go through with our plan until nighttime."

Ethan held my hand as we walked upstairs and met Mirabella in the living room. I was scared of this woman. She had so much power, and it was a power I knew nothing about.

She sipped her tea. "I was wondering where you'd all run off to. I couldn't find you anywhere. It was like you'd disappeared."

I managed a smile and a nervous laugh. "I think that invisible spell we did earlier to throw off the other coven might have worked too well. I had trouble finding Shannon earlier."

"That's funny. It shouldn't have worked that way on us." Mirabella cocked her head to the side. "I hope you all did the spell correctly."

"Now that you mention it, I'm not sure I did." Okay, it wasn't a real confession, but it would do. "I was afraid to say anything earlier because I hate that I'm still so new to all this, and I guess I was embarrassed."

"I see." Mirabella nodded and smiled at me. "Well, we can redo the spell if need be. I wouldn't want anyone getting lost from our little group's sight." She laughed like she'd made a joke.

"We were hoping you could teach us a few spells," Shannon said, sitting on the couch. "You know, before we go back home. Sam and Ethan said you're almost finished getting the dark magic out of Ethan, so I'm guessing that means we'll be leaving soon."

"I have a lot I could teach you, but before we get to that, I'd like to know more about all of you." She motioned for Dylan, Ethan, and me to sit. We all chose the couch, keeping the coffee table between us and Mirabella—as if that would offer any protection from a witch laced with dark magic. "Please." She pointed to the cups of tea, which were already poured.

"You sure like tea, don't you?" I asked.

"What's not to like? It warms you and makes you more open to good conversation." Mirabella paused, waiting for us all to drink. I started to bring the cup to my lips, so that Mirabella wouldn't be suspicious, but then stopped, realizing this was the perfect time to test her, to see if she'd known about the dark magic. "Something wrong, Sam?"

"Yeah, we forgot to tell you something."

"Oh?" She sat forward in her chair.

"The tea we were drinking earlier...it tasted different. Was it a different kind?"

"Actually, it was. It was a variety of green tea with passion fruit and jasmine. It's a personal favorite of mine. I only bring it out for special company."

"Is this the same?" I held up my cup.

"Yes, it is. If you look closely, you can see hints of green."

I bet I could. Green, swirling dark magic. "You know, my mom used to drink green tea, except it was a light green color. This is much darker."

"The benefit of conjuring your own tea leaves is they come out darker. Richer too."

Darker as in full of dark magic. "You know, I'm kind of tired. I feel like this has been a really long day. I think I'll take my tea up to my room and rest."

"But it's almost dinnertime," Mirabella protested. "I thought we could conjure another meal together. As you said, our time together is running out."

"I'm not sure I'm up to a big meal," Ethan said. "I'm wiped out from that spell. I'll grab something from the fridge and head to my room, if you don't mind."

"I'll go with you." I stood up, with Ethan following my lead. "I can't help it. I like to make sure he's okay after his sessions."

Mirabella's mouth formed a tight grin. She wasn't happy about this. I looked to Shannon and Dylan, hoping they'd come up with excuses of their own. I could practically see Shannon's brain smoking.

She was out of ideas, so I bailed her out. "Oh, you guys, I totally forgot to tell you that the spell we did last night to try to alter the memories of the other coven must not have worked right. It did something to my memories instead. I think we should try it again, and I'd rather not wait. We have no idea when they're going to try to attack us again."

Mirabella's eyes narrowed at me. "You're doing magic on the other coven? That's extremely dangerous. We did the invisibility spell. You don't need to go casting other spells that the coven could trace back to you—back to me."

"We were really careful. We covered our tracks." I didn't even know if that was possible, but Mirabella didn't seem to want us having any contact with the other coven.

She jumped up, knocking her tea onto the floor. Swirls of green magic glistened in the spilled tea. She was drinking the same dark magic. "Promise me you won't try that spell again. I'm not letting you out of my sight until you do. You'll be leading them right to us, and I've worked too hard to let you destroy this life for me." Her hands clutched my wrist, squeezing tighter by the second. She was scared. And if she was scared of the other coven, what did that mean for us? I'd been so preoccupied with Mirabella, I'd almost forgotten she wasn't the only danger we had to worry about.

35

"OKAY, relax." I pulled my arm from her grasp, and Ethan immediately checked it for signs of bruising.

"You could've hurt her." I'd never heard him say an unfriendly thing to Mirabella, but he was protective of me.

"I'm sorry." She looked away. "It's just that I can't get involved with people like that again. People like Nora."

I didn't know if she was trying to throw us off with the Nora comment, or if she was legitimately scared and desperate to make us understand. I already knew she wasn't afraid of dark magic, and part of me wanted to confront her about it now. But if I did, she might not help Ethan anymore. That was the only thing stopping me.

"We won't let them find us," I said, rubbing my wrist. "But I do think we should all call it a night. I don't have an appetite at all anymore. I think we could use the extra rest. Get our heads on straight for tomorrow."

Mirabella didn't protest. She sat down in her chair without looking at us. I looked at Dylan and Shannon and nodded toward the stairs. They followed. I waited until we were in my room with the door locked before I said anything. "We have to move on this tonight. There's no way we can put it off."

"She's seriously freaked out about that other coven," Shannon said, sitting cross-legged in the desk chair.

Dylan paced the room. "She must think they want dark magic."

"And she has enough of it," I finished for him. If Ethan hadn't been holding my hand, I probably would've gone to Dylan, tried to make him feel somewhat better about being the one who'd given Mirabella dark magic in the first place. Maybe she hadn't asked for this. Maybe she hadn't known the spell she'd cast on Dylan would do this to her. It was possible the magic had turned her into what she was now—a black-magic-crazed witch. Dylan felt responsible. I got that. My eyes found his as he walked the length of the room. "No one blames you."

He stopped pacing and glared at me. "I bet Mirabella wouldn't agree." He gestured toward the door. "She's probably sitting down there right now cursing me for causing this mess."

"Don't say that." Shannon had never been one to defend Dylan, but even she was sympathizing with what he must have been feeling. "You didn't know what it would do to her."

"Oh, no? I knew what that crap did to *me*." He pounded his chest with his palms. "What more proof did I need?"

I broke free from Ethan and stepped closer to Dylan. "Okay, but you didn't know it would go into her when she cast the spell. You all thought she knew what she was doing, but she was in over her head, a lot like her mother had been." I reached for his shoulder, thinking it was the safest place to touch him without bringing out that weird crush of his that surfaced at all the wrong times—not that there was a *right* time for it. "Are you going to sit in this room and feel sorry for yourself, or are you going to do something about what's going on? Because last time I checked, you're a major part of this coven, and we need you to help us. Mirabella is up to something that might mean the end of all of us. I'll be damned if I allow you to sit around and let it happen."

Dylan looked each of us in the eye. "Where do we start? She never leaves that spell book out in the open. She guards it with her life." Good. He was jumping right in. We didn't have time to waste on a group hug anyway.

I dropped my hand from his shoulder. "I think she uses magic to conceal it."

"I agree," Ethan said. "Every time we finish our sessions, she leaves with the book. But at the start of each session, she conjures it from somewhere. Ever since she first pulled it from the bookshelf, anyway."

"So it's under a spell." I nodded. "That's good. Spells are traceable."

"Unless she made sure to cover her tracks." Shannon pulled her knees up under her chin and hugged them. "She's not stupid. If she doesn't want us to see that book, she'll make sure we don't."

"Except I *have* seen it." I'd gotten so close to it. Close enough to read it, to touch it. "Oh my God!" How hadn't I thought of this sooner? "She knows I read the spell!"

"How?" Ethan was at my side again.

"I tried to use magic to show Dylan and Shannon the pages I'd read. Only what was projected wasn't the same as what I'd seen. It had been tampered with. Don't you see? Mirabella realized I read the spell book and she made sure I couldn't replicate the pages with magic. She knew I'd go to you guys, so she made sure I'd look like I was making it all up." Damn, she was good at being evil!

"This is seriously creepy stuff." Shannon couldn't get into a smaller ball on that chair if she tried.

Dylan started pacing again. "We have to wait until we know she's asleep before we get the book. Otherwise, she'll catch us. She's way more powerful than I gave her credit for."

"We all underestimated her," Ethan said. "I've been with her more than you guys, and I had no idea about any of this."

I rubbed his arm. "You were in a trance. You didn't remember anything she said or did. It's not your fault."

"Maybe, but what else has she done? If she fooled me so easily—"

"She fooled all of us." I squeezed Ethan's arm. I didn't want him blaming himself. As I stared at him, another realization hit me. "I think she drugged the tea."

"What?" Shannon shook her head. "That's crazy. She was drinking the same tea. We've already figured out it was the coven that put the dark magic in it."

Ethan whipped his head back and forth between Shannon and me. "There's dark magic in the tea?"

I'd forgotten he wasn't around for that. "Yes, but it stayed in the cups. We're all fine." I met Shannon's gaze. "Maybe she didn't drug the tea, but she put a spell on it—before we found out about the dark magic. Kind of like the spell Ms. Matthews put on me that day in her classroom. I started talking and saying things I'd never meant to say."

Shannon narrowed her brows. "Maybe. I really didn't mean to tell her all that stuff about you in the kitchen. I never meant to tell anyone about what Nora did to you. It sort of slipped out."

"Because you'd finished your tea."

"We don't know that," Dylan said. "Shannon can be a blabbermouth sometimes. It's her 'tell it like it is' attitude."

"I don't think so. I think Mirabella used the tea to get information from us. I think she's still trying to use it that way. That's why she wanted us to drink tea just a little while ago. She's suspicious of us."

"What about the dark magic, though?" Ethan asked.

I shrugged. "I'm not sure. She might not know about it. It's most likely Ms. Matthews and Mr. Ryan's coven is trying to get to us again. Or Mirabella suspected we were on to her and the dark magic in the tea so she laced her own tea with it."

"Guys," Dylan said, "we need to get back to finding the spell book. All these other things can wait. It's not like we have answers to these questions anyway."

"No, we just keep getting more questions," Shannon said.

Sometimes I really missed Shannon's old cocky attitude. Ever since she'd removed the popularity spell, she wasn't the same person. I never thought I'd miss the old Shannon, but she had been pretty kickass, and we could've used that right now. "Magic is the answer to everything, right?" I smiled at her. "Let's bring back that theory and use our magic to find the spell book." I hoped the reminder would snap her out of her frightened state.

She stood up and walked over to me. "Remember the first day we met? You walked into class and Mr. Ryan was totally giving you all the attention?" Of course I remembered. All I'd wanted to do was hide, but instead he'd made me read aloud from *The Strange Case of Dr. Jekyll and Mr. Hyde*, which could've been my diary at the time. "I hated you. I hated that he paid attention to you for no reason, and he brushed me off like I was nothing but a pest."

I knew what she was doing. She was trying to make herself mad, because pissed-off Shannon didn't take crap from anyone, not even a truly scary witch like Mirabella. "Tristan told me all about you," I said. "How you were his twin sister, how you asked Mr. Ryan questions just to hear him say certain words that you'd later pretend he was saying because he was as into you as you were into him."

Shannon looked about ready to explode. "I'm good. Tell me what we're looking for exactly. What did the page say? We can find the words, and they'll lead us to the book."

Now we were in business. Shannon was taking charge, which of course made Dylan mad, but maybe it would fuel him the same way. "I'm not sure I remember the exact words."

"You have to, or the spell won't work." Dylan was by my side again, closing our circle. "Think."

My mind raced. I pulled together the magic inside me, using it to search my brain. It only took a moment to find what I was looking for. "Got it."

Shannon and Dylan had a swirling mist of golden energy glowing in the center of our circle. This was the magic that would search out the words I spoke. They nodded to me. I looked at Ethan, who mouthed, "You can do this."

I took a deep breath and began reading the words that were now floating around in my mind. "'Dark magic can be transferred to a willing host, but the new host body must be strong enough to take it. The magic has to be severed from the previous host and pulled into the new one. It cannot be transferred by a third party. The new host must be the one pulling the magic into their own body.'" When I finished, the golden magic thinned out and floated under the door.

"What do we do now?" Ethan asked.

Dylan looked at his watch. "We hope Mirabella doesn't see the golden energy on her way to bed."

We'd been up here talking for a while. Mirabella might have gone to bed, or she could've made a big meal for herself. There was no way to be sure without risking getting caught. "I'll go see where she is," I said.

"No." Dylan reached for my hand. His fingers grazed mine as I pulled away. "We're doing this together. No splitting up from this point on."

I nodded. Strength in numbers and all that. I opened the door and peeked down the hallway. Mirabella's door was closed. That didn't mean much, because she always kept it closed. Shannon waved us toward the door. She definitely had a spell in mind, and since my only plan was to sneak around and pray we didn't get caught, I was on board. Shannon raised her hand and ran it in a circular motion. "Form a window clear as glass," she whispered. "Let me see what now does pass." The door shimmered, and in seconds a circular window appeared. I stepped back when I saw Mirabella sitting on her bed. "She can't see you," Shannon said.

I crept closer, trying to figure out what was in Mirabella's hand. It was a little green snake of dark magic.

"That's all the proof I need," Ethan said. "She's using dark magic. Probably mine."

"But for what?" Shannon asked.

Mirabella opened her hand, and the green snake slithered through the air, coming straight for us. No doubt about it. Mirabella had cast that thing to spy on us—or maybe worse, to kill us. Either way, we were sitting targets. "Run!" I said in a loud whisper.

We headed downstairs. For some reason I was leading the group, and all I could think about was how I wasn't going to be the girl in the horror movie who trapped herself upstairs when the killer was chasing her. I wanted to get to the basement, where the exit was nearby and easily accessible.

"We can't keep running," Dylan said, closing the basement door behind us, not that it would even slow down the green snake. "We have to find the book."

"We need to stop that thing first." Shannon was already casting another spell.

I grabbed her hand. "No! Wait!"

"What?" She shook me off her. "Are you crazy? That thing is going to kill us."

"And Mirabella will do it herself if we destroy that thing. We have to get it to obey us." Everyone looked at me like I was green and full of dark magic. "Okay, maybe not obey us, but we can confuse it. We'll create images of ourselves and let it spy on those. Then it can report back to Mirabella or do whatever else it was supposed to."

The green snake slithered under the door. I pulled Ethan to the sliding glass door. "Now! Create a duplicate image of yourself!" I made my twin in seconds. Shannon and Dylan had theirs ready too, but Ethan was standing there looking confused.

"It's not working."

I created the image for him and pushed him outside, leaving the door cracked so we could hear our clones. Shannon and Dylan followed. We hid in the bushes, watching our images. Shannon controlled them like puppets. Making them talk about stupid things like missing school and what our deer-twins were doing in our places back home. It was pretty convincing. The green magic swirled above them for several minutes before it left the way it had come. We ended the spells, making our images disappear.

"What happened?" Ethan stared at his hands. "I couldn't get my magic to work at all. I felt it stir a little, but it was like it wasn't fully there."

Goosebumps ran up my arms and legs. I'd been right all along. Mirabella was taking Ethan's dark magic into herself. But what I hadn't realized was that she was taking *all* of his magic. When she was finished with the spell, Ethan wouldn't be a witch anymore.

36

DYLAN, Shannon, and I shared a look. Finally, they were catching on, figuring out Mirabella's plan. She was stealing more than just Ethan's dark magic. She was taking every ounce of magic in him. She was bleeding him dry. That was why his spell had failed. That was why he'd felt so lightheaded after the last session. The transfer of power was almost complete.

"I'm losing it all, aren't I?" Ethan's eyes met mine. He looked lost and helpless. "I won't be like you guys anymore. Can I even survive without magic after what's happened to me? I was a monster. A killer. What am I now?"

"You're Ethan." I wrapped my arms around him, hugging him to me. "You'll always be my Ethan. I don't care if you have power or not. It doesn't change anything."

"Yes, it does." He pulled back, but I took his face in my hands.

"Listen to me. You won't change. Even when you became a witch, you were still you."

"I won't be part of the coven anymore. I'll lose that connection to you." The pain on his face was unbearable. "You'll be closer to Shannon and…" he swallowed hard, "…and Dylan than you will be to me."

"No." I shook my head, but I knew in a way it was true. The bond within the coven was so strong. Even when we fought, we knew we'd risk our lives for each other. We were one. My relationship with

Ethan got even stronger after we'd bound our magic. If that tie was cut, things really wouldn't be the same.

"Magic is a tricky thing." We all spun around at the sound of Mirabella's voice. "It fools the senses. It makes something out of nothing. Like the image of me in my room."

She'd used the same spell we had, and we'd fallen for it. "That wasn't you. You tricked us."

"Much like you tried to trick me." She walked around us, forcing us to stay close to each other. "I saw the entire thing. Those images were quite convincing. You're all getting much better with your spells. All except Ethan, that is." She stopped to smile at him. "Such a shame—for you, I mean. It's all good for me."

I stepped between Mirabella and Ethan. "We already know you're taking his dark magic. That you want it for yourself. So why don't you fill in the blanks for us and tell us why?"

"Was it the dark magic you got from me?" Dylan asked. "Did it do this to you when the spell backfired?"

Mirabella laughed. "You stupid boy. My spell never backfired. It did exactly what I wanted it to. It gave me *more* dark magic."

I had to keep her talking while we figured out a way to get out of here. Stroking her ego was my best bet, even if it meant lying through my teeth. "Wow, and I thought Nora had been a good actress, but the performance you put on makes hers look like—"

"Child's play." Mirabella smiled. "That was the problem with Nora. She thought too small. She was like an annoying little mosquito. But no matter. She got me what I was after, and now I have almost all of Ethan's dark magic, too, which was technically hers. So in a way, I owe Nora a thank you." She looked down as if peering into Hell. "Thanks, sister."

"Sister?" They couldn't really be related.

"Just an expression. We *were* in the same coven, after all."

"What?" Dylan and Shannon said, giving each other confused looks.

Mirabella laughed again. "Oh yes, she did that stupid little spell to bind herself to your pathetic coven, too, but the binding ritual she and I had was much different. It required blood, and a huge sacrifice."

"What kind of sacrifice?" I asked, knowing someone must have died for their evil ways.

"Funny you should ask, Sam." Mirabella walked over and patted my cheek. I smacked her hand away, but she thought that was funny, too. "It's a shame when a young girl dies from such a tragic disease. Cancer is such a nasty thing, and to think your treatments didn't work. Not even a little. Did you ever wonder why? Did you think God had abandoned you?"

My blood felt like it was boiling in my veins. How did she know so much about my illness?

"Hmm," she said. "I do hope those doctors were giving you the right treatments. You know how careless medical professionals can get when they're understaffed and overworked."

"What are you saying, Mirabella?" Ethan said through clenched teeth.

"I'm saying the reason Sam was so unfortunate in her battle against cancer was because I had a better use for her body than she did."

"You needed a sacrifice, and you chose me." I swallowed hard, remembering all the times the doctors had been baffled by how unresponsive my body was to the treatments. "What did you do? Make the doctors think they'd administered the treatment? Make *me* think they'd administered the treatment?"

"Yes, and sometimes no." She smiled. "I had to make it look somewhat real. I simply made sure what they were giving you would make you sick the way chemotherapy would have. A little spell to induce vomiting at first, then some tainted medications. It was all quite simple, and I had my sacrifice."

I could've thrown up now. I might have gotten better. I might have lived a normal life, but Nora and Mirabella had made sure that hadn't happened. I wanted to rip her head off with my bare hands. I wished I was still the witch killer Nora had made me into. I had the perfect witch to drain right here.

Ethan lashed out, throwing his hands forward and knocking Mirabella with a blast of magic.

She hurtled into the wall and slumped on the floor, but she didn't stay down. "Now, now, Ethan. That's no way to treat your host."

We were all stunned Ethan's spell had actually worked. He didn't have much magic left. Our delayed reaction was all Mirabella needed. She threw strands of green energy at us, binding our magic and keeping us held in our own little prisons. It was a lot like the spell Nora had used on Shannon in the diner, the one I'd broken by pouring salt on the ring that held her. Only I was trapped now too, and there was no salt in the cottage. I struggled within the confines of the green snake coiled around me.

"Does it look familiar, Dylan?" Mirabella taunted. "It should. It's the dark magic I took from you." Dylan fought against the magic holding him, but it was obvious he was no match for it. Mirabella walked over to Ethan. "We have one last session to finish. I need that last bit of magic inside you." She raised her hands palms up, and Ethan floated to the fountain in the basement. "I was going to do this alone, but I think it will be more fun with you all watching. Especially you, Sam. Say good-bye to your magical boyfriend. He'll be an empty shell when I'm finished with him."

"Don't touch him!" I was filled with rage, and my magic swelled in response. Only it was powerless against the binding. My feet left the ground, and I floated through the door and back into the basement. Shannon and Dylan were right behind me. Mirabella shut the door and cast a spell to seal the house shut. She wasn't taking any chances of us getting away now.

"Enjoy the show, Sam." Mirabella smiled at me before taking Ethan's hands. His eyes met mine briefly before the spell pushed them shut. Tears streaked my cheeks. She was going to kill Ethan, and I couldn't do anything to stop it. What was the point of being a witch when I had no power to save the one person I loved? I sobbed uncontrollably, barely able to breathe. I knew the spell wouldn't take as long this time. Ethan was already almost drained from the previous session. I was folding in on myself when the house shook like it had been rammed by a herd of stampeding rhinos.

"What was that?" Shannon asked as the house was hit again.

I swallowed hard. "It has to be the other coven. They must have found us." Thanks to me. It wasn't enough that I was losing Ethan. I was going to get the rest of us killed, too.

"We have to do something. If they get in here, they'll kill us." Shannon's voice cracked with fear.

I didn't think my mind was capable of rational thoughts, but a plan started forming. "We're dead either way. But if they get in, there's a chance they'll go after Mirabella. She seems to think they're after dark magic—like she is. If they see she has it, they may focus on her and we could get free."

"How?" Shannon tugged on the binding spell. "We're trapped."

"We have to break free somehow." I looked at Dylan, but he turned away. That was it! "You've used dark magic before. You know how to control it. Dylan, it has to be you."

"No." He shook his head, looking like a terrified toddler. "If I try, it might consume me again."

"Then we'll bring you back. Dylan, look at me." He slowly raised his head. "I won't let you go. I won't let this magic take you. We're family. I promise we'll keep you safe."

"Please." Shannon's voice shook with tears. "Dylan, you're our only hope. We need you. You're our leader." After all their fights for dominance, I knew that last comment meant something to Dylan. I hoped it would be enough.

He didn't say a word for several seconds. The house kept being bombarded. Ethan and Mirabella were deep within the spell. I knew Mirabella wouldn't stop unless she was forced to, and the attack on the cottage was probably making her work even faster. Dylan looked like he'd given up, but then I saw the green energy around him loosen. He was pushing it away. He sank down and wiggled out of its grasp. As soon as he was free, his eyes met mine.

"Thank you," I said.

He moved toward me, his hands pulling the green magic away from me just enough that I could slip free like he had. He did the same for Shannon, and just in time, too. The house shook so hard we fell to the floor. This was it. We had to stop Mirabella and get ready to fight the other coven. Without Ethan, I didn't think we stood a chance, but I wasn't giving up.

"Can you get these green bindings around Mirabella?" I asked.

"Yeah, but if I could control them, then so can she. We'd be fueling her dark magic."

Bad idea. "Send them out of here. Get them far away where she can't use them."

He nodded. With a swipe of his hand, the magic swirled in circles, getting smaller with each turn until it burned itself out. Was that possible? Did he get rid of the magic for good? Without sending it anywhere? I almost smiled, but I didn't have time to because Ethan fell to the floor.

"Ethan!" I rushed to him, knowing the spell was complete. Mirabella had his magic. The only question was, had taking it killed Ethan? I cradled his head in my lap. "Dylan, help me."

"No, Dylan. Stay where you are." Mirabella waved her hand, creating an invisible barrier between Dylan and us. Shannon rushed toward Mirabella, but Mirabella cast another spell that froze her in place. With them taken care of for now, she smiled down at me. "You suspected me from the start, didn't you?"

"Is Ethan still alive?" I couldn't find a pulse on him.

"I asked you a question, Samantha. I expect an answer."

I sent a wave of magic to Ethan, telling it to cure whatever was harming him. It was all I could do for him, my best shot at saving his life. But if I didn't get rid of Mirabella, we'd all be dead. I stood up, gently placing Ethan's head on a couch cushion. "Listen, you psychotic bitch."

She laughed. "I think you mean *witch*, dear."

"No, I mean bitch. I *did* suspect you from the start. I saw right through your act. You think you're so great at fooling people, but you never fooled me. I didn't drink your tea."

"You should have. I laced it with dark magic to help you see things my way."

So it *had* been her. "I sort of thought you might be the one behind the dark magic in the tea, but why were you drinking it, too?"

"No harm in drinking the dark magic that had come from me. For all of you, on the other hand…"

Yeah, *bitch* had definitely been the right word. "So, now what? You kill us all? Because in case you haven't noticed…" I paused and closed my eyes. I had no clue if I was making things worse or giving us the only chance to get out of here alive, but I focused my magic on tearing down the barrier around the house. Everything got so quiet, we could actually hear the *click* of the lock on the sliding-glass door. I opened my eyes again. "We have company."

Mr. Ryan burst into the basement with the rest of his coven following behind him. I almost expected him to come straight at me and kill me on the spot. But instead, he glanced in my direction before blasting Mirabella with magic. She flew into the fountain, and the water gushed out of the fountain and swirled around her in a wet prison. "That won't hold her for long, and she has too much dark magic for us to defeat her on our own." It took me a minute to realize he was talking to me.

"What?" I said.

"Sam, we need you and your coven to join with us. Just temporarily, nothing permanent. Together, we can get rid of Mirabella for good." He was Mr. Ryan again. The same guy who'd stopped Shannon from ripping my hair out in the stairwell a few months ago.

"Is this a trick?" How could I trust him after everything? After he'd fooled me into believing he was only human? After he'd tracked me down?

"I know we're asking a lot of you, but we need you to trust us." He stepped closer and looked me in the eyes. "You know me, Sam. I may not have told you I'm a witch, but I'm asking you to see how alike we really are. I'm here to help you. We all are. We've been trying to do that from the start. You don't know what we've gone through to get past Mirabella's spells to get here. All that dark magic she used…"

Dylan and Shannon were free from the spells Mirabella had cast on them. That could've been part of the trick, too, but something inside me said it wasn't. Something in my gut said that Mr. Ryan's coven hadn't used any dark magic on us. Mirabella sensed we didn't trust them and she used that against us, lying and making them out to be the bad guys. I nodded at Mr. Ryan. "Let's do it."

We all formed a circle. Shannon, Dylan, and I mingled with the other coven, like we were part of them, which we soon would be if we succeeded before Mirabella broke free. Mr. Ryan led the spell to bind our powers. It was different than the one Dylan had used, and I realized this binding was more of a temporary partnership or joining of forces in a common goal. And that goal was to kill Mirabella.

We had just finished when we were all thrown into the wall. Mirabella was free.

37

I STUMBLED to my feet, but my body felt like it had been shattered. Mirabella was ridiculously strong. I had the power of two witches inside me, but she had more than that. Ethan had been at least the second witch whose magic she'd stolen, and I didn't doubt there had been more I didn't know about.

"Grab my hand," Mr. Ryan said. I took it without question. We all joined hands, which made Mirabella laugh.

"Touching," she said. "But even together, you are no match for my dark magic. You weaklings never understood that white magic isn't anywhere near as powerful."

I looked at Ethan lying motionless on the floor. "My magic isn't all white," I lied. "You thought Ethan was the powerful one, but you were wrong. I'm the one you should've targeted. I think maybe deep down you knew that. That's why you feared me and how suspicious I was of you. Isn't that right, Mirabella?" I squeezed Mr. Ryan's hand, and surprisingly I heard his voice in my head. *You lead. We'll follow.* We were all connected. One power. One witch killer. I'd never wanted to do this again, but I still knew how. One more for the money—or whatever that old expression was.

I stepped toward Mirabella, and instead of fighting, she stepped back. I'd stunned her with my lack of fear. "Do you want to know how I killed all those witches?" As I got closer, I noticed Ethan's hand twitch. He was alive. I could bring him in on this, let him take Mirabella's power and be a witch again, but then he'd be the one filled with dark magic. I couldn't let him go through that. I'd rather he not have any power at all.

"You think I'm just going to let you kill me?" Mirabella laughed, but her voice shook.

"I don't think you have a choice."

She lashed out, hitting us with a blast of magic. We stumbled but stayed on our feet. She tried again, but I raised my hand to block her spell. The rest of the group covered me as I got closer. I had her within reach when little green spots formed in the air around her. The dark magic Dylan had made disappear was back. He hadn't gotten rid of it, and now it was settling back into Mirabella, making her stronger. I grabbed her neck and pushed my palm to her chest. She fought me, but I pulled at her magic. It burned as I pulled it out of her.

Mr. Ryan and the others began mumbling a spell. I couldn't make it out because my entire body shook. Mirabella was in worse shape than I was, but not by much. We both cried out in pain—her from losing the magic and life inside her, me from fighting the darkness that now wanted to inhabit my body. Pain soared through me, squeezing my lungs and burning my throat. I choked, and my knees gave out. Mirabella's eyes rolled back into her head as we both collapsed to the ground.

***

Ethan's lips pressed against mine. I opened my eyes and wrapped my arms around him. "You're okay." I had no idea where I was or what was going on, but I didn't care. Ethan was alive.

"And so are you. Mirabella is gone. Dead. She burned up when the dark magic left her. You took her out, Sam." He smiled, and as odd as it was to have my boyfriend be proud of me for killing another person, that was exactly what it was. Because the person I'd killed was as evil as witches came. "The others made the dark magic bury itself in the fountain so it couldn't enter you. It wasn't easy, but they pulled it off. Then they sent the fountain to some tomb that's guarded by good witches or something like that."

Mr. Ryan laughed. "Something like that."

I looked around. We weren't in Mirabella's cottage anymore. We were outside, but I couldn't get a good view of where we were since everyone was hovering over me. "Where are we? How long was I out?"

"A day and a half," Ethan said. "You had me so worried."

A day and a half? "We're home, aren't we?"

He nodded. "The deer-clones are gone, and no one suspects a thing about either coven. Mrs. Melrose is a seriously powerful witch—in a good way."

I stood up, realizing we were in our clearing. I wasn't surprised. It was where we did most of our spells, and we were definitely here to do another. I didn't doubt it. "So, you guys weren't trying to hurt us. That was all Mirabella." I already knew this, but I wanted to hear him say it.

"Yes," Mr. Ryan said. "We got to you as quickly as we could, but she had some pretty heavy-duty spells protecting the cottage. We were only able to sense Sam in the end, but luckily that was enough."

Yeah, luckily, I'd screwed up Mirabella's protection spell. "What happens now?"

Mr. Ryan put his hands on his hips. "Well, after a lot of debate, we agreed that another spell was necessary. One to make Beth less suspicious of not only you and Ethan but the rest of us, too."

"You used magic on her?" That wasn't what I called setting a good example. I kind of expected more from teachers.

"I can assure you Beth was not harmed in any way," Mr. Snyder said. "We simply made it so that she doesn't take an interest in any of us anymore."

"But how…?" I waved my hand. "Never mind. It doesn't matter." Beth wasn't really my big concern right now. "What about Ethan? What happens to him now that Mirabella took his magic?"

Ms. Matthews smiled at me. "We can restore your coven. Make Ethan a witch again by transferring some of your power to him."

Of course! I didn't need the power of *two* witches inside me. My heart raced. This was what I wanted, but I couldn't make the choice for him. "Ethan, it's up to you. If you'd rather be human—normal—I understand." I looked down, trying to gather my strength for whatever decision he'd make. "But if you want to be a witch," I kept myself from saying "with me" even though my selfish side really wanted to throw that in there and guilt him into this, "I can give you some of my power." I looked at Dylan. "I could give you Ben's power. I think he'd be happy to know you were using it."

Ethan looked away, weighing his options. I was glad. As much as I wanted him to be part of the coven and to share this with me, I didn't want him rushing into the decision. This had to be what he really wanted.

Finally, he raised his head. He stepped closer so we were only about a foot apart. His hand cupped the side of my face. "Ever since the day I met you, all I've wanted was to be with you. To be worthy of your love. You're the strongest person I know. You fought cancer right to the very end."

Tears took over as the emotions of the past year flooded me. "I fought it because you gave me a reason to fight. I wanted more time with you. Out of all the things I knew I'd be missing out on by dying at seventeen, you were the one I couldn't come to terms with losing. I love you, Ethan." My body shook, but Ethan steadied me.

"I guess we're both the same, then." A nervous laugh escaped his lips. "I mean, I brought you back from the dead. I found a witch to bring you back. I gave up my life so you could live." I already knew all this, but hearing him say it made it that much more real. "And I'd do it all again. Even the dying. Even the dark magic. Every painful moment. Because you're worth all of it."

Shannon sobbed, and I was glad I wasn't the only one bawling like a baby. Once she lost it, the others broke down too. All of them. Ms. Matthews, Mrs. Melrose, even the guys, right down to Dylan, who turned away to avoid anyone who might see his watery eyes.

Ethan pressed his lips to mine, letting them linger in a soft kiss. "If you're a witch, Sam, then I want to be a witch right alongside you. We deserve this life together. A magical life with no more sickness or darkness of any kind. For us, the third time's a charm."

I couldn't hold back any longer. I reached for him, wrapping my arms around his waist and pulling him to me. Our lips crushed together in a kiss full of desperation, love, and hunger. Ethan was my air. He was my reason for living after I'd lost everything and everyone. And he was right. This was our time. Our fairy-tale ending.

By the time we pulled apart, everyone had turned away. They'd tried to give us privacy. That, or we'd made them so incredibly uncomfortable they couldn't bear to look at us anymore. Either way, it didn't matter.

"Anyone want to explain how I transfer my magic to Ethan?" At the sound of my voice, they all turned.

Mrs. Melrose walked over to me. "I can help you."

"Thank you, Mrs. Melrose."

"I suppose you should start calling me Eileen outside of school."

"I'm not sure I can do that." Calling teachers by their first names was weird. And while Mrs. Melrose wasn't a teacher, she still worked in the school. "Besides, are you planning to hang out with us a lot outside of school?" I was grateful to each and every one of them for helping Ethan, but again, they were teachers. The weird factor was still there.

Mr. Ryan laughed. "Relax, Sam. We don't plan on moving in on your coven or trying to play a parental role here. But we'd be happy to help you all learn more about your powers, if you're interested."

"More teaching?" Shannon rolled her eyes. "Lovely." At least she seemed to be over her crush on Mr. Ryan.

"So, what do I do?" I asked, trying to get everyone's focus back on transferring my power to Ethan.

"Wait." Dylan walked over to me. He turned to Ethan. "Do you mind?"

I had no idea what he was asking. Mind what? But Ethan nodded. After everything we'd been through, he trusted Dylan—or maybe it was just that Ethan trusted me.

He reached for my hand and held it in his. I felt my cheeks redden, not because I felt something for Dylan, but because I was afraid I was going to have to turn him down in front of a bunch of teachers and Ethan. "Dylan—" I tried to cut him off, but he shook his head.

"Please, let me say this. I should've said it a while ago."

Oh, no. Don't do this. He wouldn't ruin his relationship with Ethan now, would he?

"That vibe you were picking up on, the one that started in the bathroom…"

No! He was really going to say it.

"You weren't totally wrong. You did sense something. Only it's not what you were thinking."

I exhaled, letting out the breath I'd been holding since he'd touched my hand.

"You remind me of her. Mindy."

I remind him of the girl who cheated on her boyfriend? Who strung him along and tore his heart to shreds? Ouch.

"I didn't mean that as an insult." He seemed to be reading my mind. "She could be really sweet and protective. She had a side to her that was so strong and caring at the same time. But where she lacked loyalty and honesty, you make up for it. You're like a better version of her. The person I'd thought she could be." He let go of my hand and looked at the ground. "I'm sorry if my emotions have been up and down where you're concerned. But sometimes when I looked at you, I saw her." He met my eyes again. "Now, I see that wasn't fair to you. You're your own person, and I'm lucky to have you as a friend. At least, I hope we're friends."

I smiled. "We are friends, but we're more than that, too. We're family."

He nodded. "I can handle that."

"Can we get on with the spell and get our family back to the way it should be?" Shannon asked. "Ethan needs to be one of us again."

"Wait." Dylan held his hand up. Now what? "I think Ben would want you to keep his magic. If he'd gotten the chance to know you, he would've wanted it this way."

That was hard to hear. I wasn't sure the guy I'd killed would want me to have his magic, but I owed Dylan this much. Ben was his brother. Even in death, their bond remained. If Dylan wanted me to keep Ben's magic, I would. "I'd be honored to keep Ben's magic."

Shannon laughed—completely inappropriate and totally Shannon. "How funny is it that Sam's going to have a guy's magic and Ethan will have a girl's?" We all glared at her, including the teachers. She held her hands up. "Sorry, just trying to lighten the mood. Everyone's getting all mushy and emotional."

Mrs. Melrose stood behind me and placed her hands on my shoulders. "Ready, Sam?"

I looked at Ethan. "You sure about this? If you go through with this, you're pretty much stuck with me for good."

"Then in that case..." he paused, but then he reached for my hands. "I'm positive."

"Good," Mrs. Melrose said before I could respond. "Now, the rest of you, form a circle around Ethan and Sam."

I heard everyone shuffling around, but my eyes were locked on Ethan. He smiled and squeezed my hands. I wanted to kiss him so badly, but I didn't want to delay the spell any longer. There'd be plenty of time for kissing later.

"Now, everyone repeat after me," Mrs. Melrose said. "From one to another, grant this magic its new home. Tied forever, each fully in control."

As we all chanted, with the exception of Ethan, a golden glow surrounded the circle. It built up energy and closed in on Ethan and me. As it touched us, I felt a rush of magic leave through my hands and travel into Ethan. I saw Rebecca's face in my mind, and as the last drops of her magic left my body, her image disappeared.

Mrs. Melrose let go of my shoulders. "It is done."

Ethan didn't hesitate. He scooped me into his arms and kissed me like we were the only two people on Earth. Everywhere he touched me, I felt electrified. His magic was touching mine. The sensation was amazing. I felt lighter than air in his arms. And the best part was that I knew the magic between us was only going to get better.

I'd been through hell more than once, but the universe was finally giving me my magically ever after with Ethan.

Acknowledgements

As always, thank you to Kate Kaynak and the incredible Spencer Hill Press team. I couldn't be happier to work with you all. Trisha Wooldridge, I love you more with each book we work on together. I know I've said it before, but you just get me and the way my mind works. I can't tell you how amazing it is to read an editor's comments and have them resonate so much that revisions are fun. Thank you for all you do to make my books the best they can be. To my team of copy editors, Joselle Vanderhooft, Laura Ownbey, and Rich Storrs, your meticulous work on this book is what gives me the confidence to release it into the hands of readers. Thank you for making sure everything is in order and as perfect as possible. To my cover designer, Lisa Amowitz, I think this is my favorite cover you've designed for me. You captured Ethan so well and I thank you for that. To Jennifer Allis Provost and Brooke DelVecchio, my marketing gurus, I absolutely love working with you both. Thank you for getting word out about my books.

To my daughter and best bud ever, Ayla, I promise I will let you read these books I dedicate to you one day. Sorry Mommy has to write such dark books before you're old enough to read them. To my husband, Ryan, you continue to amaze me with your support. I doubt many writers have husbands who tell them not to worry about the bills and just write. It means the world to me. To my mother, Patricia Bradley, thank you for helping me get this book in shape before anyone else saw it. To my father Martin Bradley, you continue to be the best cheering squad I could ask for. Heather DeRobertis, my very talented sister, thank you for your support and for always being there to listen. To my friends and family, thank you for understanding how much writing means to me and for accepting that there are times when I dive into my writing bubble and don't emerge until a book is finished.

To my street team, Kelly's Coven, I don't even know how to express my gratitude. Your support means so much to me, and every day you all remind me why I write. Thank you for continuing to support me and my books. And to my readers and the awesome book bloggers, thank you a million times over for reading my books. I couldn't be an author without all of you.

Colophon

This book is typeset in Baskerville, a transitional serif typeface designed in 1757 by John Baskerville, Birmingham, England. It is positioned between the old style typefaces of William Caslon and the modern styles of Giambattista Bodoni and Firmin Didot. The Baskerville typeface is the result of John Baskerville's intent to improve upon the types of William Caslon. He increased the contrast between thick and thin strokes, making the serifs sharper and more tapered, and shifted the axes of rounded letters to a more vertical position. The curved strokes are more circular in shape, and the characters are more regular. These changes created a greater consistency in size and form.

About the author

Kelly Hashway grew up reading R.L. Stein's *Fear Street* novels and writing stories of her own, so it was no surprise to her family when she majored in English and later obtained a masters degree in English Secondary Education from East Stroudsburg University. After teaching middle school language arts for seven years, Hashway went back to school and focused specifically on writing. She is now the author of three young adult series, one middle grade series, and several picture books. She also writes contemporary romance under the pen name Ashelyn Drake. Hashway is represented by Sarah Negovetich of Corvisiero Literary Agency. When she isn't writing, Hashway works as a freelance editor for small presses as well as for her own list of clients. In her spare time, she enjoys running, traveling, and volunteering with the PTO. Hashway currently resides in Pennsylvania with her husband, daughter, and two pets.

www.kellyhashway.com

CPSIA information can be obtained at www.ICGtesting.com
Printed in the USA
LVOW04s0553250615

443794LV00004B/9/P